PULLED UNDER

ALSO BY MICHELLE DALTON

Fifteenth Summer

Sixteenth Summer

A Sixteenth Summer

PULLED UNDER

A Novel

MICHELLE DALTON

Simon Pulse

New York London Toronto Sydney New Delhi

SIMON PULSE
An imprint of Simon & Schuster Children's Publishing Division
1230 Avenue of the Americas, New York, NY 10020
This Simon Pulse edition May 2014
Text copyright © 2014 by Simon & Schuster, Inc.
Cover photograph copyright © 2014 by Corbis
All rights reserved, including the right of reproduction
in whole or in part in any form.
SIMON PULSE and colophon are registered trademarks of
Simon & Schuster, Inc.
For information about special discounts for bulk purchases,
please contact Simon & Schuster Special Sales at
1-866-506-1949 or business@simonandschuster.com.
The Simon & Schuster Speakers Bureau can bring authors to your live
event. For more information or to book an event contact the
Simon & Schuster Speakers Bureau at 1-866-248-3049 or visit
our website at www.simonspeakers.com.
Cover designed by Jessica Handelman
The text of this book was set in Berling.
Manufactured in the United States of America
2 4 6 8 10 9 7 5 3 1
Library of Congress Control Number 2013051004
ISBN 978-1-4814-0701-4 (hc)
ISBN 978-1-4814-0700-7 (pbk)
ISBN 978-1-4814-0702-1 (eBook)

For Carey and Terry,

who took me to the boardwalk

and taught me about the beach

PULLED UNDER

June

*D*ifficult questions come in all shapes and sizes. They can be big and philosophical, like "What's the meaning of life?" Or small and personal, like "How do you know if you're really in love?" They can even be evil (Yes, I'm talking about you, Mrs. Perkins), like "For the quadratic equation where the equation has only one solution, what's the value of C?" But of all the world's questions there is one that stands alone as the single most difficult to answer.

"Does this bathing suit make me look fat?"

If you've ever been asked, then you know what I'm talking about. It's not like you can just say, "No, but your butt kinda does." And it's not like you can say, "Oh no, it looks great. You should definitely wear that on the beach, where every guy you know will see you." Instead you have to find that delicate place between honesty and kindness.

I know this because I hear the question all the time. I work weekends and summers at Surf Sisters, a surf shop in Pearl Beach, Florida, where women asking you how they look in all varieties of swimwear kind of comes with the turf. (Or as my father would say, it "comes with the *surf*," because, you know, dads.)

It's been my experience that a great many of those who ask the question already know the answer. This group includes the girls with the hot bodies who only ask because they want to hear someone say how great they look. My response to them is usually just to shrug and answer, "It doesn't make you look fat, but it is kind of strange for your torso." The proximity of the words "strange" and "torso" in the same sentence usually keeps them from asking again.

Most girls, however, ask because while they know a swimsuit doesn't look right, they're not exactly sure why. That's the case with the girl who's asking me right now. All she wants is to look her best and to feel good about herself. Unfortunately, the bikini she's trying on is preventing that from happening. My first step is to help her get rid of *it* for reasons that have nothing to do with *her*.

"I think it looks good on you," I answer. "But I don't love what happens with that particular swimsuit when it gets wet. It loses its shape and it starts to look dingy."

"Really?" she says. "That's not good."

I sense that she's relieved to have an excuse to get rid of it, so I decide to wade deeper into the waters of truthfulness. "And, to be honest, it doesn't seem like you feel very comfortable in it."

She looks at me and then she looks at herself in the mirror and shakes her head. "No, I don't, do I? I'm no good at finding the right suit."

"Luckily, I can help you with that," I say. "But I need to know what you're looking for, and I need to know how you see yourself. Are you a shark or a dolphin?"

She cocks her head to the side. "What do you mean?"

"Sharks are sleek and deadly. They're man-eaters."

"And dolphins?"

"They're more . . . playful and intelligent."

She thinks it over for a moment and smiles. "Well, I probably wish I was more of a shark, but . . . I'm a total dolphin."

"So am I. You know, in the ocean, if a shark and a dolphin fight, the dolphin always wins."

"Maybe, but on land it usually goes the other way."

We both laugh, and I can tell that I like her.

"Let's see what we can do about that," I say. "I think we've got a couple styles that just might help a dolphin out."

Fifteen minutes later, when I'm ringing her up at the register, she is happy and confident. I know it sounds hokey, but this is what I love about Surf Sisters. Unlike most shops, where girls have to be bikini babes or they're out of luck, this one has always been owned and operated by women. And while we have plenty of male customers, we've always lived by the slogan, "Where the waves meet the curves."

At the moment it also happens to be where the waves meet the pouring rain. That's why, when my girl leaves with not one but two new and empowering swimsuits, the in-store population of employees outnumbers customers three to two. And, since both customers seem more interested in waiting out the storm than in buying anything, I'm free to turn my attention to the always entertaining *Nicole and Sophie Show.*

"You have no idea what you're talking about," Nicole says as they expertly fold and stack a new display of T-shirts. "Absolutely. No. Idea."

In addition to being my coworkers, Nicole and Sophie have been my best friends for as long as I can remember. At first glance they seem like polar opposites. Nicole is a blue-eyed blonde who stands six feet tall, most of which is arms and legs. This comes in handy as heck on the volleyball court but makes her self-conscious when it comes to boys. Sophie, meanwhile, is petite and fiery. She's half Italian, half Cuban, all confidence.

Judging by Nic's signature blend of outrage and indignation, Sophie must be offering unsolicited opinions in regard to her terminal crush on the oh-so-cute but always-out-of-reach Cody Bell.

"There was a time when it was an embarrassing but still technically acceptable infatuation," Sophie explains. "But that was back around ninth-grade band camp. It has since gone through various stages of awkward, and I'm afraid can now only be described as intervention-worthy stalking."

Although I've witnessed many versions of this exact conversation over the years, this is the first time I've seen it in a while. That's because Sophie just got back from her freshman year at college. Watching them now is like seeing the season premiere of a favorite television show. Except without the microwave popcorn.

"Stalking?" Nicole replies. "Do you know how absurd that sounds?"

"No, but I do know how absurd it *looks*," Sophie retorts. "You go wherever he goes, but you never talk to him. Or if you do talk to him, it's never about anything real, like the fact that you're into him."

"Where are you even getting your information?" Nicole demands. "You've been two hundred miles away. For all you know, Cody and I had a mad, passionate relationship while you were away at Florida State."

Sophie turns to me and rolls her eyes. "Izzy, were there any mad, passionate developments in the Nicole and Cody saga while I was in Tallahassee? Did they become a supercouple? Did the celebrity press start referring to them as 'Nicody'?"

I'm not about to lie and say that there were new developments, but I also won't throw Nicole under the bus and admit that the situation has actually gotten a little worse. Instead, I take the coward's way out.

"I'm Switzerland," I say. "Totally neutral and all about the chocolate."

"Your courage is inspiring," mocks Sophie before directing the question back at Nicole. "Then you tell me. Did you have a mad, passionate relationship with Cody this year?"

"No," Nicole admits after some hesitation. "I was just pointing out that you weren't here, so you have no way of knowing what did or did not happen."

"So you're saying you did not follow him around?"

"Cody and I have some similar interests and are therefore occasionally in the same general vicinity. But that doesn't mean that I follow him around or that it's developed into . . . whatever it was that you called it."

"Intervention-worthy stalking," I interject.

Nicole looks my way and asks, "How exactly do you define 'neutral'?"

I mimic locking my mouth shut with a key and flash a cheesy apology grin.

"So it's not because of Cody that you suddenly decided that you wanted to switch to the drum line?" Sophie asks.

"Even though you've been first-chair clarinet for your entire life?"

"You told her about drum line?" Nicole says, giving me another look.

"You're gonna be marching at football games in front of the entire town," I say incredulously. "It's not exactly top secret information."

"I changed instruments because I wanted to push myself musically," Nicole explains. "The fact that Cody is also on the drum line is pure coincidence."

"Just like it's coincidence that Cody is the president of Latin Club and you're the newly elected vice president?"

Another look at me. "Seriously?"

"I was proud of you," I say, trying to put a positive spin on it. "I was bragging."

"Yes, it's a coincidence," she says, turning back to Sophie. "By the way, there are plenty of girls in Latin Club and I don't see you accusing any of them of stalking."

"First of all, there aren't *plenty* of girls in Latin Club. I bet there are like *three* of them," Sophie counters. "And unlike you, I'm sure they actually take Latin. You take Spanish, which means that you should be in—what's it called again?—oh yeah, Spanish Club."

It's worth pointing out that despite her time away, Sophie is not the least bit rusty. She's bringing her A game, and while it might sound harsh to outsiders, trust me when I say this is all being done out of love.

"I had a scheduling conflict with Spanish Club," Nicole offers.

"Besides, I thought Latin Club would look good on my college applications."

It's obvious that no matter how many examples Sophie provides, Nicole is going to keep dodging the issue with lame excuse after lame excuse. So Sophie decides to go straight to the finish line. Unfortunately, I'm the finish line.

"Sorry, Switzerland," she says. "This one's on you. Who's right? Me or the Latin drummer girl?"

Before you jump to any conclusions, let me assure you that she's not asking because I'm some sort of expert when it comes to boys. In fact, both of them know that I have virtually zero firsthand experience. It's just that I'm working the register, and whenever there's a disagreement at the shop, whoever's working the register breaks the tie. This is a time-honored tradition, and at Surf Sisters we don't take traditions lightly.

"You're really taking it to the register?" I ask, wanting no part of this decision. "On your first day back?"

"I really am," Sophie answers, giving me no wiggle room.

"Okay," I say to her. "But in order for me to reach a verdict, you'll have to explain why it is that you've brought this up now. Except for Latin Club, all the stuff you're talking about is old news."

"First of all, I've been away and thought you were keeping an eye on her," she says. "And it's not old. While you were helping that girl find a swimsuit—awesome job, by the way . . ."

"Thank you."

". . . Nicole was telling me about last week when she spent two hours following Cody from just a few feet away. She followed him in and out of multiple buildings, walked when he walked, stopped when he stopped, and never said a single word to him. That's textbook stalking."

"Okay. Wow," I reply, a little surprised. "That does sound . . . really bad. Nicole?"

"It only sounds bad because she's leaving out the part about us being on a campus tour at the University of Florida," Nicole says with a spark of attitude. "And the part about there being fifteen people in the group, all of whom were stopping and walking together in and out of buildings. And the fact that we *couldn't* talk because we were listening to the tour guide, and nothing looks worse to an admissions counselor than hitting on someone when you're supposed to be paying attention."

I do my best judge impression as I point an angry finger at Sophie. "Counselor, I am tempted to declare a mistrial as I believe you have withheld key evidence."

"Those are minor details," she scoffs. "It's still stalking."

"Besides, you have your facts wrong," I continue. "It wasn't last week. Nicole visited UF over a month ago, which puts it outside the statute of limitations."

It's at this moment that I notice the slightest hint of a guilty expression on Nicole's face. It's only there for a second, but it's long enough for me to pause.

"I thought you said it was last week," Sophie says to her.

Nicole clears her throat for a moment and replies, "I don't see how it matters when it occurred."

"It matters," Sophie says.

"Besides," I add, also confused, "you told me all about that

48a Cottage Hill
Elm TI W13

visit and you never once mentioned that Cody was there."

"Maybe because, despite these ridiculous allegations, I am not obsessed with him. I was checking out a college, not checking out a guy."

"Oh! My! God!" says Sophie, figuring it out. "You went back for a second visit, didn't you? You took the tour last month. Then you went back and took it again last week because you knew that Cody was going to be there and it would give you a reason to follow him around."

Nicole looks at both of us and, rather than deny the charge, she goes back to folding shirts. "I believe a mistrial was declared in my favor."

"Izzy only said she was *tempted* to declare one," Sophie says. "Besides, she never rang the register."

"I distinctly heard the register," Nicole claims.

"No, you didn't," I say. "Is she right? Did you drive two and a half hours to Gainesville, take a two-hour tour you'd already taken a month ago, and drive back home for two and a half hours, just so you could follow Cody around the campus?"

She is silent for a moment and then nods slowly. "Pretty much."

"I'm sorry, but you are guilty as charged," I say as I ring the bell of the register.

"I really was planning on talking to him this time," she says, deflated. "I worked out a whole speech on the drive over, and then when the time came . . . I just froze."

Sophie thinks this over for a moment. "That should be your sentence."

"What do you mean?" asks Nicole.

"You have been found guilty and your sentence should be that you *have* to talk to him. No backing out. No freezing. And it has to be a real conversation. It can't be about band or Latin Club."

"What if he wants to talk about band or Latin Club? What if he brings it up? Am I just supposed to ignore him?"

"It's summer vacation and we live at the beach," Sophie says. "If he wants to talk about band or Latin, then I think it's time you found a new crush."

Nicole nods her acceptance, and I make it official. "Nicole Walker, you are hereby sentenced to have an actual conversation with Cody Bell sometime within the next . . . two weeks."

"Two weeks?" she protests. "I need at least a month so I can plan what I'm going to say and organize my—"

"Two weeks," I say, cutting her off.

She's about to make one more plea for leniency when the door flies open and a boy rushes in from the rain. He's tall, over six feet, has short-cropped hair, and judging by the embarrassed look on his face, made a much louder entrance than he intended.

"Sorry," he says to the three of us. There's an awkward pause for a moment before he asks, "Can I speak to whoever's in charge?"

Without missing a beat, Nicole and Sophie both point at me. I'm not really in charge, but they love putting me on the spot, and since it would be pointless to explain that they're insane, I just go with it.

"How can I help you?"

As he walks to the register I do a quick glance-over. The

fact that he's our age and I've never seen him before makes me think he's from out of town. So does the way he's dressed. His tucked-in shirt, coach's shorts, and white socks pulled all the way up complete a look that is totally lacking in beach vibe. (It will also generate a truly brutal farmer's tan once the rain stops.) But he's wearing a polo with a Pearl Beach Parks and Recreation logo on it, which suggests he's local.

I'm trying to reconcile this, and maybe I'm also trying to figure out exactly how tall he is, when I notice that he's looking at me with an expectant expression. It takes me a moment to realize that my glance-over might have slightly crossed the border into a stare-at, during which I was so distracted that I apparently missed the part when he asked me a question. This would be an appropriate time to add that despite the dorkiness factor in the above description, there's more than a little bit of dreamy about him.

"Well . . . ?" he asks expectantly.

I smile at him. He smiles at me. The air is ripe with awkwardness. This is when a girl hopes her BFFs might jump to her rescue and keep her from completely embarrassing herself. Unfortunately, one of mine just came back from college looking to tease her little high school friends, and the other thinks I was too tough on her during the sentencing phase of our just completed mock trial. I quickly realize that I am on my own.

"I'm sorry, could you repeat that?"

"Which part?" he asks, with a crooked smile that is also alarmingly distracting.

When it becomes apparent that I don't have an answer,

Sophie finally chimes in. "I think you should just call it a do-over and repeat the whole thing."

She stifles a laugh at my expense, but I ignore her so that I can focus on actually hearing him this go-round. I'm counting on the second time being the charm.

"Sure," he says. "I'm Ben with Parks and Recreation, and I'm going to businesses all over town to see if they'll put up this poster highlighting some of the events we have planned for summer."

He unzips his backpack and pulls out a poster that has a picture of the boardwalk above a calendar of events. "We've got a parade, fireworks for the Fourth of July, all kinds of cool stuff, and we want to get the word out."

This is the part when a noncrazy person would just take the poster, smile, and be done with it. But, apparently, I'm not a noncrazy person. So I look at him (again), wonder exactly how tall he is (again), and try to figure out who he is (again).

"I'm sorry, *who* are you?"

"Ben," he says slowly, and more than a little confused. "I've said that like three times now."

"No, I don't mean 'What's your name?' I mean 'Who are you?' Pearl Beach is not that big and I've lived here my whole life. How is it possible that you work at Parks and Rec and we've never met before?"

"Oh, that's easy," he says. "Today's my first day on the job. I'm visiting for the summer and staying with my uncle. I live in Madison, Wisconsin."

"Well," I hear Sophie whisper to Nicole, "that explains the socks."

Finally, I snap back to normalcy and smile. "It's nice to meet you, Ben from Wisconsin. My name's Izzy. Welcome to Pearl Beach."

Over the next few minutes, Ben and I make small talk while we hang the poster in the front window. I know hanging a poster might not seem like a two-person job, but this way one of us (Ben) can tape the poster up while the other (me) makes sure it's straight.

Unfortunately when I go outside to look in the window to check the poster, I see my own reflection and I'm mortified. The rain has caused my hair to frizz in directions I did not think were possible, and I have what appears to be a heart-shaped guacamole stain on my shirt. (Beware the dangers of eating takeout from Mama Tacos in a cramped storeroom.) I try to nonchalantly cover the stain, but when I do it just seems like I'm saying the Pledge of Allegiance.

"How's that look?" he asks when I go back in.

I'm still thinking about my shirt, so I start to say "awful," but then realize he's talking about the poster he just hung, so I try to turn it into "awesome." It comes out somewhere in the middle, as "Awfslome."

"What?"

"Awesome," I say. "The poster looks awesome."

"Perfect. By the way, I'm about to get some lunch and I was wondering . . ."

Some psychotic part of me actually thinks he's just going to ask me out to lunch. Like that's something that happens. To me. It isn't.

15

". . . where'd you get the Mexican food?"

"The what?"

That's when he points at the stain on my shirt. "The guacamole got me thinking that Mexican would be *muy bueno* for lunch."

For a moment I consider balling up in the fetal position, but I manage to respond. "Mama Tacos, two blocks down the beach."

"*Gracias!*" he says with a wink. He slings the backpack over his shoulder, waves good-bye to the girls, and disappears back into the rain. Meanwhile, I take the long, sad walk back toward the register wondering how much Nicole and Sophie overheard.

"I noticed that stain earlier and meant to point it out," Nicole says.

"Thanks," I respond. "That might have been helpful."

"Well, I don't know about you guys," Sophie says. "But I think Ben is 'awfslome'!"

So apparently they heard every word.

"And I think it's awfslome that our little Izzy is head over heels for him," she continues.

"I'm sorry," I respond. "What are you talking about?"

"What we're talking about," says Nicole, "is you full-on crushing for Ben from Wisconsin."

"Is Wisconsin the dairy one?" Sophie asks.

"Yes," says Nicole.

"Then I think we should call him Milky Ben," Sophie suggests.

"We are not calling him Milky Ben!" I exclaim.

"Cheesy Ben?" she asks.

"We're not calling him *anything* Ben."

"See what I mean?" Nicole says. "She's already so protective."

"You're certifiable. All I did was hang a poster with him. That qualifies as head over heels crushing?"

"Well, that's not all you did," she corrects. "In addition to the guacamole and the '*awfslome*,' there was the part when you were so dazzled by his appearance that you couldn't hear him talking to you. That was kind of horrifying, actually."

"I know, right?" says Sophie. "Like a slasher movie. Except instead of a chain saw, the slasher has really bright socks that blind you into submission."

"You guys are hilarious," I say, hoping to switch the topic of conversation.

"Are you denying it?" Nicole asks, incredulous.

"It's not even worthy of denial," I reply. "It's make-believe."

"Um . . . I'm going to have to challenge that," she says. "I think I'm going to have to go to the register."

"You can't go to the register," I say. "Besides, *I'm* on register."

"Really?" says Sophie. "'Cause it looks like I am."

It's only then that I notice that Sophie slipped behind the counter while I was helping Ben.

"Wait a minute," I protest. "This is a total conspiracy. I'm being set up."

Sophie doesn't even give me a chance to defend myself. She just goes straight to the verdict. "Izzy Lucas, you have been found guilty of crush at first sight."

"You should make her talk to him like she's making me talk to Cody," Nicole suggests, looking for some instant payback. "Karma's a bitch, isn't it?"

"No," I reply. "But I know two girls who might qualify."

"Really?" says Sophie. "You're going to call me names right before sentencing?"

"Oh," I say, realizing my mistake. "I didn't mean *you two girls*."

"Too late," Sophie laughs. "Isabel Lucas, sometime in the next two weeks you must . . . have a meal with whatever-embarrassing-nickname-we-ultimately-decide-to-call-him Ben."

"A meal? Are you drunk with power? Nicole stalked a guy across six counties and all she has to do is talk to him. Why is my sentence worse than hers?"

"Because she has a whole school year coming up with Cody," Sophie explains. "But Ben said he's only here for the summer. That doesn't leave you much time."

Before I can beg for mercy, she rings the register, making it official.

*P*earl Beach is a barrier island, eight and a half miles long and connected to the mainland by a causeway bridge. I've spent all sixteen years of my life as an islander, and when I think of home, I don't think of my house or my neighborhood. I think of the ocean.

That's why, despite the fact that it's summer vacation and I should be fast asleep, I'm awake at six thirty in the morning putting on my favorite spring suit—a wet suit with long sleeves and a shorty cut around the thighs. The combination of last night's storm, the rising tide, and a slight but steady wind should make for ideal surf conditions.

It's a two-block walk from my house to the beach, and when

I reach the stairs that lead down from the seawall, the view is spectacular. Purple and orange streak through the sky and the sun is barely peeking up from the water.

The only remnants of the storm are the tufts of foam that dance across the sand like tumbleweeds and the thin layer of crushed shells that were dredged up from the ocean floor and now crackle beneath my feet. The early morning water temperature shocks the last bit of sleep from my system, and as I paddle out on my board, there's not another living soul in sight. It is as if God has created all of this just for me.

I inherited my love of surfing from my dad. When I was little, he'd take me out on his longboard, and we'd ride in on gentle waves as he held me up by my hands so that I could stand. We still surf together a lot of the time, but this morning I slipped out of the house by myself so that I could be on my own and think.

It bothers me that I got so flustered the other day when I met Ben. I don't want to make a big deal out of it, but the truth is when it comes to guys, I'm not a shark or a dolphin. I'm a flounder. I just don't have the practice. I've never had a boyfriend or been on a date. I've never even been kissed. Part of this is because I'm introverted by nature, and part of it is because I've grown up on an island with all the same boys my whole life. Even if one's kind of cute now that we're in high school, it's hard to forget the middle school version of him that used to call me Izzy Mucus and tell fart jokes.

Ben is different. My only history with him was less than five minutes in the surf shop. And, while I wasn't about to admit it to Nicole and Sophie, during those five minutes I was definitely guilty of "crush at first sight." I don't know why exactly. It's not just that he's cute. I'm not even sure if most girls would classify him as cute. It's just that there was some sort of . . . I don't know what to call it . . . a connection, chemistry, temporary insanity. Whatever it was, it was a totally new sensation.

And now, because Sophie snuck onto the register when I wasn't looking, I have to try to convince him to share a meal with me. It's a total abuse of power on her part, but I meant what I said about us taking traditions seriously at Surf Sisters. The girls won't hold it against me if I'm not successful. But if I don't give it a real try, I'll never hear the end of it.

I sit up on my board with the nose pointed to the ocean and straddle it so that I can watch for waves. I see a set of three coming toward me and suddenly all thoughts of boys and crushes wash out of my mind. I lie out on my stomach and slowly start to paddle back in. I let the first two swells pass beneath me, and the moment I feel the third one begin to lift me, I paddle as fast as I can, trying to keep up.

Just before the wave starts to break, I feel it grab hold of the board and I pop up on my feet. This is the moment that takes my breath away. Every time. This is when it's magic. In one instant you're exerting every ounce of energy you have, and in the next it feels like you're floating through air as you glide along the face of the wave. You stop thinking. You stop worrying. You're just one with the wave, and everything else melts away.

The ride doesn't last long. No matter how well you catch it, the wave always crashes against the shore and snaps you back to reality. But those few moments, especially at times like this when I'm alone, those few moments are perfect.

If only boys were as predictable as waves; then I'd know just what to do.

*T*he Bermuda Triangle is a section of the Atlantic Ocean where ships and planes mysteriously vanish into thin air. It's totally bogus and based on some ridiculous alien conspiracy theory. But it inspired my dad to come up with The Izzy Triangle. He likes to say, "It's where daughters disappear for the summer."

Unlike the Bermuda Triangle, however, this one has some truth to it. If you're looking for me anytime from June through August, the odds are you're going to find me in one of three places: the beach (surfing), my room (reading), or Surf Sisters (hanging out or working). In fact, I'm not exactly sure when I officially started *working* at the shop. I was just there all the time, and I slowly started to chip in whenever they needed help.

That's where I'm heading now, even though it's my day off. I surfed this morning and finished my latest mystery novel, so I figure I should do something that involves other humans. (Introvert, push yourself!) Besides, both Sophie and Nicole are working, and once their shift's over, we're catching a movie.

The problem is that I know they'll be ready to pounce on me the second I walk through the door. It's been a few days since the Ben Incident (Sophie wants to call it the Bencident, but I refuse to let her), and they'll want to know if I've made any progress with him. If I say that I haven't, they'll give me a hard time and start talking about how I'm going to run out of time. That's why I decide to take a calculated risk and stop by the bandshell on my way to the shop.

The bandshell is our town's outdoor stage. It's at the north end of the boardwalk and where we have little concerts and annual events like Tuba Christmas and the Sand Castle Dance, which we all make fun of but secretly love. It's also where the Parks and Recreation office is located. I figure Ben probably spends most of his time *parking* and *recreating*, so the odds are pretty good that he won't be in the office. If I drop by, I can at least tell the girls that I tried to see him. Even if he happens to be there, I don't have to actually talk to him. I can act like I'm there for some other reason and tell the girls that I saw him, which would technically be true.

The office is in a plain cinder block building right behind the bandshell. Its only architectural flourish is a mural painted on one side that's meant to look like *The Birth of Venus*, except instead of Venus it has a pearl. Written above it is the slogan PEARL BEACH, GEM OF THE OCEAN. It's so tacky that I actually think it's kind of perfect.

When I open the door, I'm greeted by an arctic blast of air-conditioning. And when I look around the office and see that Ben's not there, I have a sinking feeling. I realize I was maybe secretly hoping he would be. This fact surprises me and is just another indication that all of this really is new for me.

Just as I'm about to turn and leave, I hear a voice call my name. "Izzy?"

I look over and see Ms. McCarthy behind a desk. She lives

down the street from us and is good friends with my mom. I totally forgot that she works here.

"Hi, Ms. Mac. How are you?"

"Good," she says. "What's brings you by?"

"I'm looking for . . ." I'm halfway through the sentence before I realize that I don't really have a good finish for it. I stammer for a second and say, "Well . . . there's a new boy who just started working here and . . ."

"Ben?" she asks, with that knowing smile that grown-ups give when they think they know what's up. "Are you looking for Ben?"

Mental warning bells sound as I realize that this information will get back to my mom within seconds of me leaving.

"Actually, I'm not looking for *him*. I'm looking for a *poster*. He dropped one off yesterday at the shop, and Mo, one of the two sisters who own the surf shop, wants me to pick up another one for us to hang up. You know . . . to help support the town . . . and all of its wonderful activities."

Ms. McCarthy gives me a slightly skeptical look. "Okay. If it's just a poster you want, there are some extras over there."

She points to a table, and I go over and see a stack of posters.

"Yep, this is it," I say, picking one up. "*This* is the reason that I came by. It's a nice poster. Attractive and informative. Thanks so much. Mo will be really happy about this."

I realize I'm overdoing it and decide my best course of action is to stop talking and nod good-bye.

As I head out the door, Ms. McCarthy says one more thing. "I know it's not why you came here, but if you had come to see

Ben, I would have told you that you just missed him and that he was headed down the boardwalk to get some lunch."

I find this information very interesting, but I don't want her—and therefore my mom—to know this, so I just make a confused expression and say, "Whatever." I maintain this "whatever" attitude up to the instant that I'm beyond her field of vision, at which point I sprint toward the boardwalk.

The boardwalk is the main tourist strip for Pearl Beach, and it stretches eight blocks from the bandshell at one end to the pier at the other. Normally I avoid it because of the whole "it has crowds and I'm an introvert" thing, but since it's technically on the way to where I'm going and we're early enough in the season that the crowds aren't too bad, I decide to walk along it.

After a couple blocks I see Ben in all of his white sock and coach's shorts glory standing in line at Beach-a Pizza. It's an outdoor pizza stand that has picnic table seating facing out over the ocean. It dawns on me that I can get in line, buy a slice, and if I sit at the same picnic table, we'll be eating together. That will fulfill my sentencing requirement. Clever me.

I slip into the line and see there are a few people between us. It's not until I'm standing there that I realize I'm still holding the stupid poster. I'd kept it so that I could prove to the girls that I really had stopped by the office, but now it just seems awkward. I'm strategizing what I should do about it when he turns and sees me.

"Hey . . . it's you. Izzy, right?"

"Right," I answer. "And you're Ben."

He smiles. "You remembered."

"Tell me something three times and it sticks."

He lets the people in between us cut in front of him and moves back so that he's next to me. I know it seems small, but this instantly makes me like him more. So many people try to get you to move up to them and cut in front of other people, and I'm never comfortable with that. Of course, I'm not particularly comfortable at the moment standing in line clutching my poster. But you know what I mean.

"Something wrong with the poster?" he asks, pointing at it.

"Nope," I say. "I just picked up another one to hang in the other window."

Apparently he's just as clueless about things as I am, because he buys this as an acceptable excuse.

"Good to see that the word is spreading."

"So what are you up to?" I ask, as if there are a wide variety of reasons why someone would be standing in line at Beach-a Pizza.

"Just getting pizza and a pop."

"A pop?" I ask, confused. "You mean a popsicle?"

"No, a soft drink. Don't you call it 'pop'?"

I laugh. "We say soda."

"Okay, this is good. Now I've learned something," he says. "I'm getting pizza and . . . a soda."

"Very nice," I respond, playing along.

"Pretty soon I'll be just like the locals."

"Well . . . not as long as you eat here."

He looks at me for a second. "What's wrong with Beach-a Pizza?"

25

"You mean besides the name?" I lean closer and whisper. "It tastes like cardboard with ketchup on it."

"It seems pretty popular," he says. "Look at all the people in line."

"Yes, look at them," I reply, still keeping my voice low. "They have pale skin, wear shoes with their bathing suits, and fanny packs. They're wearing fanny packs, Ben! What does that tell you?"

He thinks it over for a moment and shakes his head. "I don't know, what does it tell me?"

"That they're tourists," I say. "Only tourists are waiting here. The people who live in Pearl Beach are not in line. You're living here for the summer. Don't you think you should get pizza where we get it?"

"But you live here," he says. "Why are you in line?"

This one catches me off guard. It's not like I can say, "Because Sophie was on the register and I have to eat with you or be subjected to extended hazing." I pause for a second before blurting, "Because I wanted to rescue you and show you where we go."

"Rescue me?" He likes this. "You're like my knight in shining armor?"

"More like light wash denim . . . but it's something like that."

"Well, you were right about Mama Tacos," he says, reminding me of the horror that was the guacamole-stain recommendation. "That was delicious. I'll trust you again. Where do you think we should go?"

"Luigi's Car Wash," I say.

"I meant for pizza," he says.

"So did I."

"Sounds awful!" He hesitates for a moment. "Let's go!"

It suddenly dawns on me that I may have just asked a guy out on a date.

As we're driving down Ocean Ave. in an old blue Parks and Rec pickup truck, I get my first true up-close look at him since the Bencident. (Sophie can't call it that, but I can.) I'm trying not to stare, but as I give him directions I at least have an excuse to be looking his way.

I will amend my earlier statement in which I said I wasn't sure that all girls would classify him as cute. I think your boy vision would have to be seriously impaired not to rate him at least that high. He has strong features and permanent scruff that gives him a ruggedness I find irresistible. But the clinching feature is still the smile. It's easy and natural, with teeth so bright they might as well be a commercial for the virtues of Wisconsin milk.

"Explain to me why we're getting pizza at a car wash," he says, flashing those same pearly whites.

"It's complicated," I reply. "Back when my parents were growing up, it really was a car wash. But at some point Luigi realized that he could make more money selling pizzas than washing cars, so he decided to convert into a pizza joint."

"But it's still called Luigi's Car Wash?"

"That's the complicated part. Technically it still is a car wash," I try to explain. "It's right on the beach and oceanfront property is really valuable. Developers would love to get rid of Luigi, tear down the building, and put up a condominium or a hotel or something awful like that. But as long as he keeps the name the same and as long they wash a few cars every week, it's protected by an old law that was in effect when he first opened."

Ben laughs and gives me a skeptical look. "I was perfectly happy eating boardwalk pizza, which I have to say sounds way more legit than car wash pizza. Why do I feel like I'm being set up for some kind of practical joke?"

"You're not. I promise."

"Now, before I embarrass myself, you do call it pizza, right?" he asks. "It's not going to be another 'pop' situation, where it turns out I'm using the wrong word again?"

He's funny. I like funny.

"No," I tell him as we pull into the parking lot. "But if you really want to sound like you know what you're doing, just say that you want a couple slices of Big Lu."

"What's Big Lu?"

"It's short for Big Luigi, a pizza with everything on it. It's the house specialty, and trust me when I say that you're going to want to order it."

"You're telling me it's good?"

"No, I'm telling you it's life changing."

"Life-changing car wash pizza?" he says as we get out of the car. "This should be interesting."

Luigi's still has the shape and design of a car wash, which is part of its charm. (It's also part of the legal requirements that protect it.) As we walk up to the counter to order, I'm suddenly extremely self-conscious. I've never been on a date before—and

I'm not sure this would even qualify as one—but I am walking into Luigi's with a guy and I don't know all the protocols. In fact, I don't know any of the protocols. There's no line, so we go straight to the counter.

"I'll have a couple of slices of Big Lu and a—" He almost says "pop," but he catches himself and says "soda."

Then he says something that surprises me.

"And whatever she wants."

I wasn't expecting him to pay for my lunch, but I think it's a check in the "it's kinda, sorta like a date" column.

"I'll have the same," I say.

The cashier rings it up, gives us two cups and a number to take to our table. Ben makes another "is it soda or pop?" joke as we get our drinks, and then we sit down in a booth. I have been in Luigi's a thousand times before, but I have never felt more like a fish out of water in my entire life.

"How long have you lived in Pearl Beach?" he asks.

"Born and raised," I answer. "Third generation. By the way, we usually call it PB."

"More lingo," he says with a nod as he sips his drink. "So far I've learned 'soda,' 'Big Lu,' and 'PB.' Pretty soon I'll be fluent, which is important considering that I'm a native."

I give him a look. "I think you're getting ahead of yourself. You ordered two slices of pizza. That hardly makes you a native."

"No, no, no," he tells me. "It's legit. I was born here."

"You were born in Pearl Beach?" I ask skeptically.

"Nope," he says. "I was born in PB. See, I'm using the lingo."

I laugh. "Now you're messing with me."

"Actually, I'm not. I was born the summer after my father finished law school. This is where Mom grew up, and since his job didn't start until the following January, they came here and stayed with my grandma. That way they could save money and my dad could study for the bar exam. I lived here for the first six months of my life."

"Well then, I guess that means there's an islander in there somewhere," I joke. "We've just got to shake off some of the Wisconsin that's covering it."

"Watch what you say about Wisconsin," he says with mock indignation. "That's America's Dairy Land."

"I didn't mean to imply anything negative."

"You better not. There are a lot of important things that come out of Wisconsin."

"Is that so?" I say playfully. "Like what?"

"Okay," he replies, perhaps a little caught off guard. "I'll list some of them for you."

He pauses for a second, and I impatiently cross my arms.

"Harley-Davidson motorcycles . . . and custard."

"Custard?"

He makes the happy delicious face. "You haven't lived until you've had the custard at Babcock Hall."

"I'll take your word for it."

"And the Green Bay Packers. Everybody loves the Packers."

I shrug.

"And don't forget milk. Without which we would not have our wonderful smiles."

He flashes a smile, and I have to admit that I am sold.

"You've got me there," I say.

I don't know if it's because of the back and forth nature of the conversation or all the endorphins released by the incredible aroma of pizza that fills the air, but I'm actually feeling more relaxed.

"So we'll accept that Wisconsin is amazing and wonderful. But since you're stuck with us for the summer, what exactly does your job with the Parks and Recreation Department entail?" I ask.

"I think I'm responsible for anything that no one else wants to do," he says with a laugh. "There's a lot of scrubbing and cleaning. More than a little mowing. And, starting Monday, I'm one of the counselors for the summer day camp. That should be great—four days a week with a bunch of screaming kids trying to torment me."

"I did that," I tell him.

"You were a counselor?"

"No. I was one of the screaming kids who tormented the counselors. It was a lot of fun."

"The schedule's insane," he says. "Every day it's something different. We've got kick ball, soccer, swimming, and we're even going to the golf course once a week."

"Don't forget Surf Sisters," I say.

"We're going to Surf Sisters?" he asks.

"On Tuesdays campers will learn respect for the ocean, beach safety, and the fundamentals of surfing," I say, quoting the brochure.

"I thought that was at a place called Eddie's Surf . . . something or other."

"Steady Eddie's Surf School," I say.

"That's it."

"Surf Sisters is actually run by two sisters, and Steady Eddie was their dad," I explain. "They are one and the same."

"That's great news," he says with a smile. "Does that mean you're going to be our surfing instructor?"

I try to hide my disappointment as I tell him no.

I leave out the part about how I was supposed to be the instructor but pawned it off on Sophie because I didn't want to deal with all of those screaming kids. Of course, it had never dawned on me that I would want to deal with their dreamy counselor.

"That's too bad," he says. "We could have chased them together."

This development puts me in a funk for a little while, but it's nothing that two slices of Big Lu can't cure. During the rest of the conversation we talk about his hometown and high school. I figure if I let him do most of the talking, I will not put my foot in my mouth, as I've been prone to do in the past. This strategy seems to work, because we keep talking even after we've finished eating, which is pretty cool.

I try to resist my natural instinct to overanalyze every little detail, but I can't help but look for any hint that he might be interested in me. He's good about eye contact; it's not piercing and creepy but he stays engaged. Never once does he make more than a casual glance at the game playing on the big screen TV behind me. Better yet, there are a couple of sharky girls at the next table. They're cute and giggly, and I think more than a little loud on purpose trying to get his attention, but he seems oblivious to them.

"Don't you think?" he says, and I realize that I have no idea what he's talking about. (How's that for irony? My analyzing how engaged he is made me zone out.)

"Totally," I say, hoping that it makes sense based on the question. Fearful of continuing to talk about a subject of which I am unaware, I decide to change the topic. "So how'd you end up here for the summer?"

It didn't seem like a trick question when I asked it, but his expression makes me rethink this. "I'm sorry. I don't mean to pry."

"No, it's nothing secret, just a little sad," he says. "My parents are getting divorced and it's really ugly. There are lawyers and screaming arguments, and my mom was worried that it might scar me for life, so she arranged with Uncle Bob for me to come down here and work with him."

"I'm really sorry to hear that. A few of my friends have had their parents get divorced, and it was hard on them. I'm so lucky that mine are happy together."

"The worst part," he says, "is that my dad is being a total jerk. I don't get it. He's being so mean to her, and I wish I were up there because I want to be there for her. But she thought this would be best for me."

The discussion about his parents brings down the mood of the conversation, and before I can come up with a new topic, he gets a phone call. The conversation is short, and when it's over, he says, "Duty calls."

He takes one last sip of his soda and stands up.

"What's the problem?"

"There's a pavilion at the playground where they like to have birthday parties," he says.

"I know it well," I say. "I believe I celebrated birthday number seven there."

"Apparently some of the kids learned an important lesson about what happens to your digestive system if you eat massive amounts of cake and ice cream immediately before going full speed on the merry-go-round."

"And you've got to clean it up?" I ask with a grimace.

"Like I said, my job is pretty much to do whatever nobody else wants to do." He shrugs. "Let me take you wherever you were headed?"

"It's not far, I can walk," I say. "I don't want to make you late."

"I'm pretty sure it will still be there," he says.

"Okay, I'll take a lift to Surf Sisters."

As we walk out to his truck, I manage to send a clandestine text to Nicole and Sophie. Make sure you can see the parking lot in three minutes. Trust me!

I slide my phone back into my pocket and ignore the vibrating of reply texts no doubt asking for an explanation.

"Thanks for rescuing me from boardwalk pizza," he says as we drive down Ocean. "Luigi's is without a doubt the best pizza I've ever had."

"It was the least I could do," I say. "And thanks for buying me lunch. You didn't have to do that."

"You can buy next time." As he says it he flashes that oh-so-distracting smile, and I'm feeling good.

"Next time." I like the sound of that. Of course, I'm not sure how to read the smile. Is he smiling because he's polite? Is he smiling because he likes being with me? Or is he smiling because he just ate the best pizza in the world?

When he pulls up to Surf Sisters, I look through the windshield and can see that Nicole and Sophie are both looking out the window. They're dumbfounded when they realize that it's me in the truck with Ben, and it takes everything I've got not to react. It also makes me even more self-conscious as I try to come up with the perfect farewell line that will keep him thinking of me.

"Well," I say with a goofy grin, "have fun cleaning up the vomit."

Apparently that's the best I could come up with. My first ever may or may not be a date ends with me turning to a guy and talking about vomit. I am so smooth.

"I'll do my best," he says. "Thanks again."

I get out of the truck, wave good-bye, and watch him drive away.

I'm still not sure what to make of it all, but that does nothing to dampen the feeling of total triumph that I have as I walk into the store. For a moment the two of them stare in disbelief.

"Is there a problem, girls?"

"No," Sophie says, trying to suppress a grin but failing miserably. "Where were you?"

"You know, just eating pizza at Luigi's with Ben. No big."

"Are you serious?" asks Nicole.

I smile and nod. "Absolutely."

"Okay," Sophie says, getting excited. "There are questions that need to be answered. Many questions."

"No, there aren't," I say, trying to project cool for once in my life. "There's just one question that needs to be answered."

"What's that?" she says.

I turn to Nicole, who's working the register. "I'd like an official judgment on this. Which beach girl totally kicks ass."

Nicole grins as she says it. "That would be Izzy Lucas."

And she rings the bell on the register to make it official.

S ince the shop is busy, the girls don't get to grill me for information until after their shift ends and we're all riding to the movie theater. Sophie's driving and Nicole's in the passenger seat. (One perk of being a six-foot-tall girl is that you always get the front seat.) She wedges herself sideways to look at me in the back.

"Explain again how this happened?" she asks.

"First I stopped by the Parks and Rec office to see if I could 'bump into' him there," I say. "And I found out that he was taking his lunch break on the boardwalk."

"I'm surrounded by stalkers," Sophie interjects as she gives me a wink in the rearview mirror.

"So I went walking along the boardwalk and saw him in line at Beach-a Pizza."

"BP?" says Nicole. "That's disgusting."

"Which is exactly what I told him," I continue. "So I suggested that he should try Luigi's and that was that. We were on our way."

"Very nice," says Nicole.

"See what happens when you actually talk to the guy," Sophie says, giving Nicole a raised eyebrow.

"Can we get back to Izzy?" she protests, not wanting another lecture on how she should talk to Cody. "What's Ben like?"

"I don't know," I answer. "I mean, he seems great. He's funny. Kind of goofy but in the totally good way."

"I love that," Nicole says. "Give me cute and goofy over slick and sexy any day."

Sophie gives Nicole another look but decides not to press her on Cody. Instead, she looks at me in the mirror for a second and asks, "Does that mean you're into him?"

I think about it for a moment. "I don't know. Maybe."

Nicole grins. "Her lips say 'maybe,' but the redness in her cheeks says 'hell yeah.'"

We're all laughing as Sophie parks and we get out of the car. "Tell me that you picked this movie because it's supposed to be good," she says to Nicole. "And not because you think 'you know who' will be here."

"He's not going to be here," Nicole says. "He already saw it last Saturday with some of the guys from Interact."

Sophie stops. "And you know this how?"

"I've already been convicted of stalking and as such am protected by double jeopardy," she says. "So lay off."

Sophie and I share a look and shake our heads. Nicole really does need to do something about this.

"All I'm saying is that I pushed Izzy and it paid off," Sophie replies. "I'd like the same good fortune to happen to you."

"Slow down," I say. "We're not sure that it 'paid off' for me. Ben and I had pizza, but I have no idea if he likes me or not. He may just like the pizza."

"Didn't you see any signs?" asks Sophie.

"Yeah," says Nicole. "I've heard there are supposed to be signs."

"The signs were mixed," I reply. "At some points it seemed like he was into me and at others not so much. It doesn't help that his parents are going through an epic divorce. I think it may have soured him a bit on the whole idea of relationships."

We reach the ticket window and Sophie turns to me.

"By the way, you're buying my ticket."

"And why is that?"

"Because you owe me . . . big time."

I think about this for a second. "Because?"

"Because, despite it being a major hassle, I went through the computer and swapped shifts with you every Tuesday for the rest of the summer."

It takes me a moment to realize what she's saying.

"You mean . . ."

"You'll be teaching all the summer campers how to surf, which should give you plenty of opportunities to read signs from Ben."

I wrap her up in a giant hug, and because she's so small it lifts her off the ground.

"You're pretty awesome sometimes, you know that?"

"No," she says. "I'm *incredibly* awesome *all* of the time. And as soon as you two realize that, your lives will improve dramatically."

Needless to say, I am more than happy to buy her ticket.

*O*n Tuesday morning I spend a ridiculous amount of time trying to select my surfing attire. Normally, this is automatic: wet suit in the cold months, spring suit on chilly mornings, bikini and a rash guard when it's hot. My rash guard has two purposes. It's a swim shirt that protects my skin from all the wax and sand on my surfboard. And, bonus, it keeps me from falling out of my bikini top whenever I wipe out.

Of course, *normally* I'm only interested in what's most comfortable and functional for surfing. Today, however, is not normal.

Instead of hitting the waves to find the perfect ride, I'll be teaching a bunch of grade school kids how to surf. That means they'll be staring at me while I do a lot of leaning and bending over. The last thing I want to do is give them a little show-and-tell. But I'll also be in front of Ben, and it wouldn't be the worst thing in the world if I actually looked, you know, cute.

After countless combinations, I finally settle on a pair of rainbow-striped board shorts that have a stylish cut but still cover everything I need covered and a baby blue Surf Sisters rash guard that I put on over a black bikini top. As I take one final look in my bedroom mirror I empathize with all of the women who ask me to help them find a swimsuit. Still, to my surprise, the combination actually looks cute, and in a rare moment of self-confidence I'm willing to say I've gone from flounder to dolphin.

At the beach, Sophie helps me set up before the campers arrive. She's doing a good job of keeping it light and funny so I don't stress out. She can ride you relentlessly, but when you need it, she's nothing but your biggest cheerleader. We're laughing about something when we hear the faint sound of mass whistling approaching us.

I look up just in time to see Ben leading a makeshift platoon of campers over a sand dune and right at us. They are whistling a silly tune as they pretend to march, and it is irresistibly cute.

My guess is that Ben didn't spend nearly as much time worrying about his wardrobe as I did. He's traded in his coach's shorts for a flowery Hawaiian print bathing suit but has maintained the rest of his signature look with a tucked-in polo, white socks, and running shoes. You'd think it was a uniform or a job requirement, except both of the other counselors are wearing swimsuits and T-shirts.

"He's wearing shoes and socks," Sophie says to me. "He's wearing them *on the beach*."

"Yeah," I respond. "I'm going to have to work on that."

I recognize the other counselors from school. The guy's name is Jacob. Even though he's a star soccer player, he runs with the brainy crowd and stays pretty low key. I wouldn't say we're friends, but I've always liked him and we get along well. The girl is a different story.

Kayla is a total alpha, a shark to my dolphin. She lives to make sure that girls like me know that we're not nearly as sparkly as girls like her. For example, just so everyone realizes how unbelievably awesome she is, she's wearing a way too tight Surf City top that shows off her curves—and I imagine also restricts her breathing. Surf City is a megaretail store on Ocean Ave. where girls like Kayla, wearing short-shorts and tank tops, sell overpriced T-shirts and surfboards to tourists who don't know any better. They are our sworn enemies.

"Watch out for that one," Sophie says with a nod toward Kayla. "If she so much as gets a hint you're into Ben, she will totally drop in on you." "Dropping in" is what surfers call it when someone tries to catch a wave that you're already riding.

Although the Kayla development puts a slight damper on my mood, things take a turn for the better when Ben sees me and flashes that smile of his.

Even Sophie can't help but notice. "Well, what he lacks in fashion sense, he makes up for with dimples," she says, accompanied by a friendly nudge of her elbow. "That's my cue to let you two be all alone . . . you know, except for the screaming kids and the conniving camp counselor."

She smiles and gives a friendly wave to Ben and the campers as she walks back up toward the surf shop.

Just as they're about to reach me, Ben holds his hand out like a stop sign. "Campers, halt!"

The kids make exaggerated stops, some even going so far as running into each other in slow motion before crashing onto the sand. Apparently, his goofiness has already infected them.

"I thought you said you weren't going to be teaching this class," he says.

"There was a change in plans," I answer, trying to sound mysterious but probably coming across as clueless.

He thinks about this for a second and nods. "Very nice."

He turns to address the kids, and from the way they hang on his every word I can tell that they love him.

"I want all of you to say hi to Izzy."

"Hi, Izzy!" the kids shout in unison.

"Hi, everyone!" I say back. "Are you ready to learn how to become slammin' surfers?"

There are cheers, and I realize that even if it wasn't for Ben, I should never have tried to avoid this. Kids are great and I love teaching them about the ocean. I can't help but flash back to my own summer camp when I came here for the same lessons. My dad had already taught me the basics, but this was when I really got the bug. It's also when I first started to hang out at Surf Sisters.

"Before we do anything," I continue, "I want you all to repeat these three words. Slip! Slop! Slap!"

"Slip! Slop! Slap!" they shout in unison.

"Who can tell me what these words mean?"

When no one else raises a hand, Ben jumps right in.

"Slip, slop, slap," he says. "That's what happened to me when I tried to stand up in a bathtub this morning."

The kids laugh.

"Good guess," I say. "But not what I was going for. This is why they're important. If you're going to be in the sun for a while, you should always 'slip on a shirt,' 'slop on some sunscreen,' and 'slap on a hat.'"

I open up the two big boxes that Sophie helped me set up and start handing out rash guards, Steady Eddie surf caps, and plenty of sunscreen.

"We love the sun, but we have to respect it," I say. "Too much of it is bad for your skin. Isn't that right, Kayla?"

All eyes turn to Kayla, whose richly tanned skin is a pretty good indication that she does not follow this advice.

"That's right," she says unenthusiastically as she stares daggers at me.

Once everyone is fortified against the sun, I get them all in a big circle so that we can stretch. I don't know if it's coincidence or conniving, but Kayla winds up directly across from Ben so that he has an unobstructed view of her doing her stretches. And, as much as I hate her, even I have to admit she looks pretty spectacular while she's doing them.

Once we're all stretched out, I hold up a thick foam board about three feet long and ask, "Who can tell me what this is?"

Without missing a beat, Ben answers, "A surfboard!"

The kids all laugh because they think he's joking, but I can tell by his expression that he thought he had the right answer. I quickly come to his rescue.

"Ben's trying to trick you guys, isn't he?"

"Yes," they shout, and Ben smiles and plays along.

"This is way too short to be a surfboard, *isn't it*, Ben?"

"Absolutely," he says with a grateful smile. "Way too short. Even for short people like these guys."

"So, who, other than Ben, can tell me what it really is?"

A few of the kids call out, "A boogie board."

"That's right," I answer. "A boogie board. It's also called a body board, and although you use it to ride waves, you don't stand up on it like a surfboard. Do you?"

"No," they reply.

I notice one girl in back is too shy to shout out with the

others. She reminds me of me at her age, so I point to her and ask, "How do you ride a boogie board?" As I ask the question, I rub my hand over my stomach.

"On your belly?" she says with a little uncertainty.

"That's right, you ride it on your belly. Before camp is over we're going to have all of you standing up on surfboards. But for today we're going to just stay on our bellies and ride these. Okay?"

"Okay!" they shout, and this time she shouts with them.

We break the campers into smaller groups and take them out into shallow water a few at a time. This lets them get used to the dynamics of waves and builds their confidence for riding on a board. It's also unbelievably fun.

Most of them pick it up instantly, and I quickly become a fan of the shy girl, whose name is Rebecca. I notice the change in her attitude with every bit of success, and it reminds me even more of the nine-year-old version of me.

The only one who struggles getting the hang of it is Ben. First he has trouble catching a wave, and when he finally does get one, he lies too far up on the board and winds up going face-first into the sand. The kids all get a kick out of this, and the thing that's great about Ben is that he does too. A lot of guys would get embarrassed and try to act cool, but he just goes with the goofy, and the kids love it.

By the middle of the session I am certain that it's more than a crush for me. I really like him and I would love for him to like me. But the problem is that I just can't tell if he's even remotely interested.

He's relaxed when we talk, which makes it seem like he is,

but then he's all goofy with the kids, too, so maybe that's just him. Furthermore, he seems to have no idea that Kayla is a shark in surf clothing and seems mighty comfortable talking to her, too. I don't have the body or confidence to do what she's doing and begin to think that I may be in beyond my depth.

In fact, I don't get a good read on the situation until the lesson is done and we're all carrying our boards back up to the shop. Ben walks next to me.

"This was great," he says. "The kids loved it. I loved it. Obviously, I need a lot of practice and coaching, but it was great."

I can't tell if he's opening the door for me to offer to help him get that practice and coaching or if he's just making conversation. I walk quietly for a moment before I start to stammer, "Well, you know . . . if you really want to get better . . . I could always—"

And that's when Kayla drops in, just like Sophie warned me she would. She sidles right up next to him and grabs him by the elbow with an effortlessness that is as impressive as it is evil.

"Ben, you are so great with these kids," she says, all dimples and boobs. "Don't you think so, Iz?"

I cannot believe that she is calling me "Iz," like we're old friends or something. Of course there's nothing I can do about it but agree.

"Terrific," I say. For a moment she and I lock stares, and I know that war is at hand. Before I can say anything else, one of the campers comes running up to Ben.

"Ben, Ben, Ben," he says excitedly. "You won't believe it. There's this dead fish and its guts are exploded all over the place. It's totally disgusting."

"Well, if it's TOTALLY disgusting," he says with an exaggerated expression, "then I have to see it."

They hurry off and leave me alone with Kayla. Neither of us says another word for the rest of the walk. We're just a shark and a dolphin swimming side by side across the sand.

*Y*ou're my daughter and I love you," my dad says with total tenderness before he flashes an evil grin and adds, "But first I'm going to demolish you, and then I'm going to destroy you."

Welcome to game night with the Lucas family. Always fun, always competitive, always full of trash talk. At the moment we're in the middle of a particularly intense game of Risk, and Dad is about to attack my armies in Greenland. He's feeling good about it until my mom interrupts.

"You know that 'demolish' and 'destroy' mean the same thing," she says, tweaking him.

He stops just as he's about to roll the dice. "What?"

"You can't destroy her if you've already demolished her. Your threat doesn't make sense."

"Donna?" he whines. "I'm going for an intimidation thing, and you are literally raining on my parade."

"You mean 'figuratively,'" she says. "Or is there actual rain falling on a parade I don't know about?"

"You're doing it again," he says, getting flustered. "You're doing it again."

"I'm sorry, but I think if you want to be a global dictator, the least you can do is use proper grammar."

My parents totally crack me up. They're both teachers at Pearl Beach High School. Mom is the chair of the English Department, hence the grammar, and Dad teaches history and coaches cross-country, which explains the competitiveness. At school I might have a slight tendency to avoid them, but they're actually very cool and fun to hang out with. During the summer we usually play board games around the kitchen table a couple nights a week.

"What if I say this?" he offers, having fun with it. "First I'm going to invade your country, and then I'm going to destroy it?"

He looks at her hopefully, but she just shrugs and replies, "It's not great."

"Why? What's wrong with it?"

"Why invade the country if you're going to destroy it? I think you may mean that you're going to invade the country and destroy her army, but that's not what you said. Your command of pronouns is about as strong as your armies in northern Africa."

He's trying to think up a comeback when the doorbell rings. "Saved by the bell," he says. "Literally."

"Thank you," she replies. "In that instance 'literally' is correct."

She stands up and adds, "I'll go answer the door so you can keep up your attacks on Greenland and the English language."

"English teachers," he says under his breath as he shoots me a wink.

Just as he's about to roll the dice, I hear a familiar voice talking to Mom at the door and signal Dad to stop.

"Wait a second. Is that Ben?"

"Ben?" my father asks. "Who's Ben?"

Suddenly visions of embarrassment dance through my head.

I turn to him and give my most desperate face. "Don't be you. Don't tell bad jokes. Don't tell embarrassing stories. Just once, try to be normal."

"I am offended," he says indignantly. "I have no idea what you're talking about."

I give him a look and he returns it in kind.

"Really?" I ask.

"Really."

I hear them walking toward the kitchen and I know I'm running out of time. "If you're good, I'll promise not to attack you in northern Africa and we can gang up on Mom in Asia."

"Deal," he says with a grin.

We shake on it just before Mom walks into the room with Ben.

"Hi, Izzy," he says sheepishly.

"Hey, Ben," I say, trying to figure out why he might be here. "Mom, Dad, this is Ben. He's down for the summer from Wisconsin. Ben, these are my parents."

"Nice to meet you," he says. "I'm sorry to interrupt your game."

"That's okay," says Mom. "We were just about to take a break."

"We were?" asks my father, no doubt disappointed that his plans for global domination keep getting interrupted.

"We were," she says, "so that you and I could head over to the Islander and get some ice cream."

"That's right," he replies, suddenly pleased. "We absolutely were going to get some ice cream."

Without missing a beat Mom picks up her purse and beelines for the door with Dad right behind her. Just before he leaves, though, he turns around and pulls out his phone to take a picture.

"Dad?" I say, suddenly worried. "What are you doing?"

He takes a picture of the game board and gives me a look. "Just in case someone accidentally 'bumps' into the table while I'm gone, I want to make sure we can put all the pieces back where they're supposed to be."

Rather than reply, I just shake my head and let them leave.

"I really am sorry to just drop in like this," Ben says once they're gone. "But I don't know your phone number and I need to ask a favor."

"Sure," I say, trying to sound confident and cool, neither of which remotely describes my current state of being. "But if you didn't know my phone number, how'd you figure out where I live?"

"I stopped by the shop to see if you were working, and one of your friends was there. She told me how to find you."

"Would that be the really tall one?"

"No, it was the one who says I wear the wrong clothes on the beach."

I cringe. "You heard that."

"She has the kind of voice that carries," he says. "But it's okay. It didn't hurt my feelings or anything. I really don't know what to wear on the beach. And I did think that the boogie board was a surfboard."

"I know."

"And I call things by the wrong name."

"Yeah."

"If I'm going to spend the summer here, I don't want to feel like I'm an alien from some far off planet."

"Okay, but what's the favor?"

"Can you teach me all that stuff? Can you teach me what to wear? Where to go? How to tell the difference between a surfboard and a boogie board?"

"Sure," I say. "I'd be happy to."

"Really?"

"Absolutely. When's your next day off?"

"Saturday," he says.

"Perfect," I tell him. "I'm off this Saturday too. Why don't we meet here at eleven?"

There's that smile, and then he says the most remarkable thing of all.

"It's a date."

On Saturday morning I wake up early to surf the stretch of beach closest to my house. The waves are better down by the pier, but I'm not really looking for a workout. I just want to clear my mind and have a chill start to the day.

As I paddle out I keep thinking about something that Nicole said to me last night. She came over to the house to hang out and, big shocker, talk turned to Ben. Considering our mutual cluelessness about boys, it was pretty much a blind-leading-the-blind conversation. That is, until she said, "The girl you are on a surfboard is the girl you have to be with him."

At first I laughed at the whole profound quality of it. But the more I thought about it, the more I realized she was on to something. My problem is that the girl I am on a surfboard has literally been surfing longer than she's been walking, while the girl I am with boys has barely taken baby steps. I have no idea how to convert one into the other.

I try to figure it out as I sit on the board, dangling my legs in the water. Unfortunately, my brainstorming session is as flat as the surf. This morning the ocean looks like a lake, and after fifteen minutes with little more than a ripple, I decide to call it a day. But just as I start to bail, the surf gods surprise me with a sudden gift. I turn to take one last look and see a swell forming in the distance. It's going to be big and it's all for me.

My board is already lined up perfectly, so all I have to do is lie flat on my belly and start paddling. I go slowly at first and then pick up the pace when it gets close. As I feel the wave come up beneath me, I try to study my technique. Maybe it's as simple as Nicole said, and all I have to do is look for hints of how I am on the surfboard to figure out how I should be with Ben.

I feel a rush as the wave catches the board, and I get up on my feet. I analyze every detail—the face of the wave, the placement of my feet, and the way my hand reaches back toward the white water breaking off the crest. I adjust my weight to test my center of gravity and bend my knees to lower my butt closer to the deck. I study everything . . . for about three seconds.

Then I pearl.

Pearling is what you call it when the nose of your board digs under the water and throws you flying over the front. This particular one is a textbook example, and before I even realize what's happening, I slam face-first into the water. It's more disorienting than scary. One moment I'm riding a wave and the next I'm getting slapped around by Mother Nature. When I'm underwater it feels like a weird combination of slow motion and superspeed as the force of the wave pushes me down from the surface.

I get kicked around for a few seconds until it passes over me. Then I wade up to the tide line and plop down on the sand to catch my breath. The back of my shoulder stings where it scraped against some shells, and there's a dull throb around my ankle because it got yanked by the tether line attached to the surfboard. But overall my body isn't hurt nearly as much as my pride.

I'm not embarrassed because I wiped out. Everybody does that. It's just that I did it like some newbie trying to catch her first wave. I'm not even sure what went wrong. Since I was so carefully analyzing each step, you'd think I'd be able to figure it out. But as I run through my mental checklist, it seems like I was doing everything right.

That's when it hits me.

The reason I pearled is *because* I was analyzing each step. I was thinking too much. Normally I don't think at all. I just do it. I mean, you can't fight a wave; you can only go where it takes you. Maybe boys are the same way. Instead of analyzing every little detail and looking for signals with Ben, I should just see where it takes me. I should just be myself.

Okay, so this might not be the most original realization, but it sure is new for me. Normally when I'm around guys, I'm trying to be anyone but me. But I remind myself that Ben's the one who suggested hanging out today and that he's the one who used the phrase "It's a date." He might actually be into me.

That thought gives me a rare burst of confidence as I walk home with my board under my arm. Earlier I was worried about how the day would unfold, but now I'm thinking it might work out fine. Of course, that could just be because I bumped my head pretty bad when I was underwater, but I'm going to go with it.

It also helps that I've eliminated wardrobe drama this time. Unlike the day when I taught the campers, I don't need to spend time obsessing about what I should wear. Nicole and I took care of that last night. I picked out a loose pink halter to wear over the top of my bathing suit and a pair of old denim shorts that seem cool but not in a trying too hard sort of way.

As I look at myself in the mirror I feel . . . cautiously optimistic. I also feel a throbbing in my shoulder. I twist to see if there's any noticeable swelling but stop when I hear footsteps on the porch. My room's in the front of the house, which means I'm always the first to know when someone's coming to the door. It sucks when you're trying to sleep in on a Saturday morning, but it's great at times like this, when you want to make sure you're the one answering it instead of your parents.

I move out into the hall and wait for Ben to knock.

And I wait.

And I wait.

Through the door I can hear the sounds of deep breathing and loud footsteps walking from one side of the porch to the other. It sounds like he's panting and pacing, which doesn't really make sense. It's not like he can be nervous about hanging out with me. Or can he be?

I peek through the window and can't believe my eyes.

"Dad!" I exclaim as I fling the door open.

My father's doing huge lunges across the porch and checking

his pulse by holding three fingers against his wrist. He's also wearing running shorts that are a little too short for my comfort level, a sweat-covered T-shirt, and a smiley face bandanna. I did not make that last part up. He's actually wearing a smiley face bandanna.

"What are you doing?" I ask.

"Cooling down," he says between deep breaths. "At my age you've got to stretch to keep from tightening up."

I think about adding a tip that at his age he should also rethink the concept of short-shorts, but there's not time. I check my watch and it's exactly eleven o'clock. Ben's going to be here any second.

"Do you have to stretch here?" I ask.

"I guess I could do it in front of the Bakers' house, but I think that would look a little strange."

"Spoiler alert: It looks strange anywhere," I say as I scan the neighborhood for Ben. "And why are you wearing a bandanna with a smiley face? Did you lose a bet?"

Dad stops for a moment and gives me a confused look. "Is there something going on that I should know about?"

"No, there most definitely is not," I say. "Now, would you please get inside before you ruin it?"

At first he's completely baffled, but then a look of comprehension comes over him.

"Too late." He nods down the block to where Ben is walking toward our house. "I think I figured out why you're stressed. His name is Ben, right?"

"Why do you want to know?"

"Howdy, Ben!" he calls out.

Howdy? Seriously? When did we become cowboys?

"Howdy, Mr. Lucas," Ben says as he reaches the walkway. "Hi, Izzy."

"Hi," I respond, trying to smile at him while simultaneously giving my dad the cue to disappear.

Dad doesn't seem to get the hint, because he's continuing to stretch and has now moved on from lunges to deep knee bends.

"Just ignore me," he says, as if that were possible. "I have a whole stretching routine I have to do after I run."

"Me too," Ben says. "It drives my teammates crazy."

"Teammates?" my dad says.

"I run cross-country at my school."

"What a small world!" Dad says. "I coach cross-country at PB High."

Do you ever wish that life were like a DVR? I do. That way I could hit pause and rewind this in hopes of it playing out a different way.

"We should run together," Dad suggests.

"That would be great," Ben replies. "I signed up for a 10K next month and I need to train for it."

"The Rocket Run?"

"That's it."

"I'm running it too," my dad says. "We can train together and then keep each other company during the race."

I mean, this is seriously not how I had envisioned the day unfolding. But just when I think it can't get any worse, Ben says three words that break my heart.

"It's a date."

When he said it to me about our day together, I took it to

mean that it was an actual *date*. But now I'm beginning to wonder if it's just something he says.

Finally Dad finishes stretching and asks, "So what do you two have planned for today?"

"A major makeover," Ben says. "Izzy's going to teach me the ways of Pearl Beach. She's going to help me blend in with the natives."

I am totally ready for Dad to finish me off with some joke like "How would she know?" But that's not what he says.

"So you're a runner . . . and you're smart," he says. "That's a good combination. You guys have fun."

It may sound hokey, but in person, in the moment, it's sweet. Once Dad is inside, Ben turns to me and rubs his hands together in anticipation.

"So where do we begin?"

"That depends," I reply. "How much of a transformation are you looking for?"

"Total witness relocation program," he says. "Wardrobe, attitude, everything."

"Well, then," I say with a smile, "we better get some ice cream."

*T*he Islander has been serving ice cream on the boardwalk for as long as there has been a boardwalk. It has entrances on both the beach and street sides, and there is a double counter in the middle of the shop that faces each way. This counter looks like an island, which is how the shop got its name. But because PB actually is an island, locals co-opted it and they like to wear the shop's "Islander" T-shirts as a sign of civic pride.

I order my usual, a waffle cone with two scoops of mint chocolate chip, and Ben gets a junior sundae with hot fudge and whipped cream on rocky road. There is a row of booths against the wall, and we take the one in the middle.

"I'm always up for dessert," he says. "But I don't see how a sundae is going to give me insight into Pearl Beach. You know, we actually have ice cream back home in Wisconsin. That whole 'America's Dairy Land' thing isn't just for the license plates."

"We're not here because of the ice cream," I say.

I turn sideways so that my back is pressed against the wall and stretch my legs out on my side of the booth. He gets the hint and does likewise. Now we're looking right at the counter.

"We're here for the view," I explain.

"What's so special about a view of an ice cream counter?"

"There are two sides to Pearl Beach," I tell him. "The tourist side and the local side. You can't have one without the other. We need the tourists and the tourists need us."

"Okay," he says. "That makes sense."

"But our beach and their beach are different," I say. "They're coming here for something they've seen in movies and on post-cards. It's kind of like the theme park version and not the real one."

"You're starting to lose me."

"I'll give you an example. Have you been to the candy shop down by the arcade?" I ask. "The one with the big mixer machines that twist taffy?"

"Yeah," he says. "I went in there when I was handing out post-ers. It's really cool."

"Did they offer you a sample of the saltwater taffy?"

"Two," he says with a guilty smile. "They were delicious."

"Do you know why they call it saltwater taffy?"

He looks at me like it's a trick question. "Because it's made with salt water?"

"No," I say. "It's just regular taffy made with fresh water."

"Then why do they call it that?"

"Because over a hundred years ago there was a candy shop on a boardwalk in New Jersey that got flooded in a storm. All the taffy got seawater on it, so the man at the counter joked that it was now 'saltwater' taffy. He was *joking*, but when people heard about it, they started buying it up. They figured saltwater taffy must be something that you can only get at the beach. And from that point on all boardwalks are expected to have saltwater taffy."

"So you're saying that the beach is full of con artists taking advantage of tourists?"

"Hardly," I reply. "You like the taffy. It's delicious. And people expect it to be here. They want to come to the beach and see the pretty candy being made in the big machines. They want to buy a decorative box of it to give to their grandma. There's nothing wrong with that. But while tourists think of it as something to do with the beach, we think of it as something to do with tourists. It's fake. That's true of almost everything on the boardwalk."

"So the locals don't come down here?" he asks.

"Not much. Some of the kids do when they're scamming for a quick summer vacation romance, but for the most part, the locals only come down here for two things: work and . . ."

"Ice cream," he says, putting it together.

I nod.

"The Islander is just that good. Now, if you look toward the boardwalk entrance, most of the people you'll see coming off the beach are tourists. But if you look toward Ocean Ave., you'll see the locals. This table is where the worlds collide. It is the perfect place to study them side by side and see how they're different."

Ben takes it all in and understands what I'm talking about.

"Okay," he says, turning toward me. "This is kind of brilliant."

"And don't forget the ice cream is *amazing*."

He takes a spoonful and nods his agreement. "Yes, it is."

We spend a half hour people watching, and Ben quickly picks up on some of the basic differences. He starts off with the obvious ones, like clothes and sunburns, but eventually starts to pick up on the more subtle things, like attitude.

"All right," he says. "I get the thing about the shoes and socks."

"Sophie will be so relieved."

"But here's one thing I don't get." He nods toward the beach side. "All of these people are on vacation." Then he nods to the street side and continues. "But these people all seem more relaxed."

I couldn't be prouder. This was the reason we started here.

"You've got it," I say as I stand up. "You've figured out step one. That means it's time to move on."

I start walking out toward the boardwalk and he follows me.

"But I haven't figured out anything," he says. "I just noticed the difference. I don't know why they're different."

We keep talking as we snake our way through the clumps of people on the boardwalk. "You don't have to know why. You just have to know that it's true. We all have different theories on why."

"Really? What's yours?"

"My theory is unimportant," I tell him.

"Maybe so," he says. "But I want to hear it anyway. I don't just want to figure out what the beach is about."

"What do you mean?"

He looks at me. "I'd like to figure you out too. I find you . . . *intriguing.*"

I worry that this makes me blush, so I look down as I smile.

"Okay," I say. "Come over here and look out at the ocean."

We walk over to the railing that overlooks the water.

"I think it's because tourists are like waves. But maybe that's just me. I always think everything is somehow related to surfing."

"How are tourists like waves?"

"When a wave comes at the beach it looks like the *water* is coming toward the land."

"Isn't it?"

"Not really. It's mostly an optical illusion. The wave is a force of energy that travels through the water and makes it rise and fall. It also pitches forward and falls back a little, but the actual seawater basically stays in the same place. And once the wave is gone, the water is all back where it started. Tourists do the same thing. They come rushing toward town and it's all so very exciting, but they're not here for long. That means they have to squeeze everything into that short period of time. They're so rushed that they're willing to go into a gift shop and buy shells with real money when all they have to do is walk along the beach and pick them up for free. That's loony tunes. So to me they're like waves that come crashing on the shore, and we're like the water. They have fun. They rise and fall. But it's not relaxing. And once they're gone, we go back to normal, like nothing ever happened."

"That's . . . deep," he says, taking it all in. "Are you always so philosophical?"

"Hardly. I just spend a lot of time thinking about waves."

"Okay, so what's our next stop?"

"Next we are going behind enemy lines," I say as we start walking down the boardwalk again. "But you have to promise me that under no circumstances will you buy anything while we're there."

"If it's another ice cream shop, I might not be able to resist. That junior sundae just triggered the hunger without fully satisfying it."

"It has nothing to do with food, but I mean it. You *have* to promise."

"All right, I promise not to buy anything," he says. "But where am I not buying anything?"

Just saying the name brings a scowl to my face. "Surf City."

Surf City is huge. It's a surf shop on steroids. And like steroids, everything about it is phony, especially the girls. Their boobs are big, their tank tops are small, and their knowledge of surfing is comically inept. Take for example the girl at the door who greets us in Hawaiian. You know, because even though we're five thousand miles away from Hawaii, it just sounds so surfy.

"Mahalo!"

Of course she has no idea that *mahalo* means "thank you" and not "hello."

"Ma-hello to you, too," I say back, with a tinge of snark as I shake my head.

I lead Ben up to a second-floor landing so we can fully survey the landscape. The lower level is filled with swimwear, clothing, and accessories while the upper has surfboards in every color of the rainbow. Every inch of it's gleaming, and everywhere you look there's another walking, talking Malibu Barbie.

"Welcome to the belly of the beast," I say as I look out over it. "Pure evil."

Ben takes it all in for a second and turns to me. I can tell he's conflicted about something but doesn't know how to say it.

"What's wrong?" I ask. "Spit it out."

"You love surfing, right?"

"More than you know."

He looks out across the store again and then back at me. "Then why isn't this your favorite place on earth? I mean, the name says it all. This is Surf City."

I don't reply with words so much as I emit a low growl.

"Okay, let me rephrase that," he says. "I know this place is like the worst place in the world, but since I'm just a cheesehead from Wisconsin, could you help me develop the right vocabulary to fully describe how awful it is?"

"I'd be happy to. First of all, it's owned by a faceless corporation and only exists to make money. It just happens to be that they make it selling surfboards. There's no love of the ocean or surfing in its DNA. I mean, just look at the boards. They're arranged by color, like that's the most important feature. It's like if you went into a bookstore and all the books were arranged according to how many pages they had.

"No one's concerned about matching customers with the right one. They just want you to buy any of them. And to be honest, the boards are mostly here to create an artificial atmosphere so they can sell you overpriced swimsuits, Hawaiian shirts, and sunglasses. Or, best of all, a bunch of Surf City T-shirts with their logo everywhere so you can go back home and become a human billboard as you tell everyone about your 'radical adventure hanging ten and riding gnarly waves.'"

When I reach the end of my rant, I realize that it was a little more passionate than I had intended. But Ben takes it all in stride and makes a joke out of it.

"So, you're saying you *don't* like it?"

"Yes," I say with a laugh. "I'm saying I don't like it. But it's not about what I like or don't like. It's about showing you how to blend in among the locals. And if you look around, you'll notice that there aren't any here. Only tourists. See the fanny packs and the sunburns?"

"And the white socks."

"Pulled all the way up," I add, shaking my head.

"I wish you told me yesterday before I went and bought all those Surf City T-shirts."

He's joking, but I still give him my "don't mess with me" look. And, while I don't like to brag, my "don't mess with me" look is quite impressive.

"But you said that they're *evil*. How is any of this more evil than selling saltwater taffy? That's just as fake and you're okay with it."

"Seven dollars for a decorative gift box of candy is a lot different from seven hundred for a longboard," I say.

"Seven hundred dollars?" he says with a comical laugh. "You can't be serious."

"Take a look."

We walk over to a row of blue longboards, and he looks at the price tags. He shakes his head in disbelief.

"And the worst part isn't even the money," I say. "This is way too much surfboard for a beginner. But they'll never tell you that. They'll just let you walk out the store and totally bomb in the water. They'd never tell you that you can get a used fish for about seventy-five bucks that's much better to learn on."

"A used fish?"

"It's a type of surfboard," I say. "But we'll save that lesson for later. We're still taking baby steps."

He laughs and we start to leave (escape?) when we pass the store's Wall of Fame. It features action photos of some of the surfers who make up the Surf City Surf Team and a display case full of their trophies.

"Impressive," says Ben.

"Yeah. As much as I hate to admit it, their team is amazing," I concede. "They win most of the tournaments in the state."

"Like King of the Beach?" he says, referring to the annual Pearl Beach tournament.

"How'd you know about King of the Beach?" I ask.

"It's sponsored by Parks and Recreation," he says. "I will be working there later this summer."

"Surf City has won both trophies," I say. "That one's for the

top team and that one's for the grand champion. Bailey Kossoff
has won the grand champion trophy two years in a row."

"Is he a local guy?"

I shake my head. "No. They sponsor guys from around the
state. That's how they make sure to win."

"Does Surf Sisters have a team?" he asks.

I shake my head. "There's no money for it. These guys are like
the New York Yankees. They can sign anyone who's really good."

"I bet they can't sign you."

"Well, no, they couldn't, but since I don't surf in contests, it
doesn't make much of a difference."

"Why don't you?"

"It's just not my thing," I say. "I like to keep my surfing
between me and the ocean. No spectators, no judges."

He raises a skeptical eyebrow but lets the topic slide.

So far the day seems to be going great. I still don't have
any idea if he's into me or if he's just looking for a friend, but I
feel more comfortable with Ben than I've ever felt with a guy.
He laughs at my jokes, and when I try to explain why I think
tourists are like waves and Surf City is evil, he doesn't look at
me like I'm a lunatic or something. But now it's time for the
big test.

Now we're going to Surf Sisters.

*S*urf City is owned by an evil, faceless corporation," he says as
we walk along Ocean Ave. "But you said there's actually a pair of
sisters who owns Surf Sisters, right?"

"Mickey and Mo. They're the best."

"Mickey and Mo sound more like surf brothers than sisters."

"That's because the guys they used to beat in all the surf contests thirty years ago were too embarrassed to say they were getting waxed by Michelle and Maureen."

"So, unlike you, they were willing to compete in contests?"

I give him a look, and he holds up his hands in surrender.

"Anyway," I say, changing the subject back, "their dad was a legendary lifeguard and surfer."

"Steady Eddie," he says.

"That's right, Steady Eddie. Lifeguarding doesn't pay much, so he started up Steady Eddie's Surf School to give lessons to people staying at the hotels along the boardwalk. Mickey and Mo's mother wasn't in the picture, so they were always part of the deal. They were the first girls in this area to make names for themselves as surfers, and they were determined to make sure it was easier for the next generation."

"Which is why they opened the shop, right?"

"It just seemed like the logical next step. They turned their house into a shop, and when Steady Eddie passed away, they kept the surf school going to honor his memory. It's part business, part civic duty, part family memorial."

"So the shop was actually the house where they grew up," he says. "Okay, I see why that beats some corporate megastore."

"I was hoping you would."

Sophie and Nicole are both working today, but they've sworn to be on their best behavior when we arrive. Sophie's on register while Nicole's walking around making sure all the customers are finding what they're looking for. Both seem to be keeping an eye on the door as we enter.

Even though they saw Ben when he first came to the shop and again when he was with the campers, they've never officially met him, so I take care of the introductions.

"Ben, meet Sophie and Nicole," I say. "Guys, this is Ben."

They exchange hellos, and when I see Sophie about to talk, I panic for a millisecond that she might revert to her normal self and say something outlandish just to see how he reacts. But she keeps her promise to behave.

"What brings you to the shop today, Ben?" she asks.

"I want to get some new shoes and socks to wear on the beach," he says. "Maybe knee-high socks and something in a boot. Is there such a thing as a beach boot?"

The girls both laugh, and suddenly any potential awkwardness is gone.

"Actually," he continues, "I'm getting some hard-core beach tutoring from Izzy, and I think that means I need some wardrobe adjustments."

"Looking for anything in particular?" asks Nicole.

"I'm guessing I need some new trunks."

They both look at each other in total confusion.

"Board shorts," I say, translating. "They speak a different version of English in Wisconsin."

They laugh some more, but Ben doesn't seem to mind.

"You don't say 'trunks' either?" asks Ben. "It's like 'pop' all over again."

Because the shop is a converted house, it has a homey feel that's very different from Surf City. The staff even picked up Mickey and Mo's habit of referring to the different rooms by what they once were. That's why surfboards are in the garage, women's swimwear is in the family room, and accessories are in the kitchen, where the counter and shelf space are perfect for displaying everything from sunblock and sunglasses to key chains and waterproof wallets.

"We're going to the dining room," I tell the girls.

"We're eating again?" Ben asks.

"No," I tell him. "The dining room is where we put everything that's on sale."

"That's good," he says. "Despite its obvious glamour and prestige, the Parks and Recreation Department doesn't pay particularly well."

"Don't worry," says Sophie. "We've all got employee discounts."

"Yeah," adds Nicole. "We'll take care of you."

I smile because this makes me think that he's passed his first test with them. This is confirmed about fifteen minutes later when Ben carries an armful of clothing into a fitting room and Sophie and Nicole rush over to me like football players about to tackle a quarterback.

"We approve," Sophie says with a firm whisper.

"Definitely," adds Nicole. "By the way, you look really cute today."

"Thank you."

"You owe me so bad," Sophie adds. "Not only am I the one who made you eat with him, but I'm also the one who swapped shifts with you for the rest of the summer. Don't forget about that."

"I already paid you back. Don't forget who bought your ticket at the movie."

"I think this is worth more than a movie. This deserves—"

She's interrupted when Ben comes out of the fitting room wearing a pair of navy blue board shorts. They look great, but we're all a little distracted by the fact that he's shirtless and—surprise, surprise—his muscles and abs come fully loaded. (Thank you, cross-country.) The three of us are literally speechless, a reaction that he mistakes for disapproval.

"They don't look good?" he asks, pointing at the shorts.

"No," I say with a cough. "They look . . . great."

"Yeah," Sophie adds. "Nice trunks."

The mention of trunks makes him smile, unleashing the dimples again. "I know, I know. I promise I'll get the hang of it all."

He is totally oblivious to his current overall hotness factor, which only makes him that much more appealing. He goes back into the fitting room, and the others turn to me and we're speechless again.

"She's right," Nicole finally says. "That's worth way more than a movie."

It takes everything we've got not to bust out laughing. I can honestly say I have never felt the way I feel at this particular moment. I know it sounds pathetic, but it's making me a bit dizzy. I'm having trouble processing the whole thing.

By the time we're done, he's picked up another pair of board shorts, two Surf Sisters T-shirts, and a pair of inexpensive but comfortable flip-flops.

"Give us some catwalk action," Sophie says. "Let's see how it plays."

Ben goes along with this and walks back and forth in front

of the register, accenting it with some goofy fashion poses. When he's done, he turns to the three of us and asks, "So what do you think?"

"I'd believe he was an islander," says Nicole.

"It won't be official until he loses the tan line from his socks," adds Sophie. "But he's definitely getting there."

"I can hardly believe it," I say.

He takes it to mean that I can't believe how well he's got the look down. And while that's true, it also means that I can't believe this is happening to me. The cynic in me is waiting for the bubble to burst.

After we leave the shop, we head down to the beach and walk barefoot along the waterline. I point out some shells and a shark's tooth, but for the moment the lessons are over. I just want to enjoy . . . this.

Whatever "this" is.

It is the most romantic moment in my life, which is a bit of a problem because for all I know I'm just his shopping buddy. I mean, he really seems to like me and we've spent the day together, but I don't know how to know for sure. It would be great if he held my hand as we walk along the beach, but his hands are full because he's carrying two Surf Sisters shopping bags.

I decide to add a little stop.

"Let me teach you something," I say. "Stop, look out at the water, and wiggle your feet like this."

I wiggle my feet side to side and they start to sink into the wet sand. He does the same, and we both settle in about ankle deep.

"I like it," he says.

"It's cool, isn't it?" I reply. "I always love to do that when I'm walking along the water's edge."

We spend a quiet moment looking out over the ocean. It's peaceful and nice, but inside my head I'm going a million miles a minute. Finally I snap and blurt out, "So, do you have a girlfriend back home in Wisconsin?"

It is very unsmooth and made worse by the fact that it is not followed with a quick denial. His face looks a little pained, and I wish I could erase the question.

"I'm sorry," I say. "It's none of my business."

"I don't mind," he says. "I don't have a girlfriend . . . anymore. I did for a long time. For over a year. But we broke up during spring break."

That sounds pretty recent considering they dated for so long. I should stop asking questions, but I can't help myself. "Did you break up because you were coming here for the summer and she didn't want to try long distance?"

"That may have been part of it," he says. "But there were a bunch of little things. I think a lot of it has to do with my parents. I mean, I always thought they were a perfect couple, happy and in love with each other. Then it turned out that they weren't. It made me realize that things aren't always how they seem. I started to question what was going on with Beth and me, and eventually I decided that we weren't right for each other either."

Beth and Ben. Ugh. They even sound perfect together.

"I'm sorry. It really isn't any of my business."

"No, it's okay," he says. "Actually, it's kind of nice to have someone I can talk to about it. Things were so crazy at home, I didn't even tell my parents until a month after it happened. And my guy friends were useless. They don't usually have much to offer when it comes to relationships."

I have killed the mood and totally lost control of this conversation. I have done the boy-girl version of pearling and it's my own fault. Yet I can't seem to make myself pull out of it. I just have to know whom I'm competing with.

"What's Beth like? I bet she's pretty."

"She's really pretty," he says, in an automatic way that I could never imagine a guy saying in reference to me. "And smart. And funny. Everyone thought we were perfect together."

I would like to go on the record here and declare that I completely hate Beth.

"But that's history," he says with a trace of melancholy. "She's in Wisconsin and I'm in Florida."

Izzy Lucas, door prize.

I really have no idea what to say next, so I just stand there and try to imagine how I can possibly compete with the girl he just described.

"It's easy to talk to you," he continues. "You're the kind of girl I can just be myself with. That's nice."

And the final verdict is in.

"Easy to talk to," "kind of girl," and "nice" are all codes I know how to decipher. I'm the confidante, the girl he feels comfortable talking to about the girl he really likes. Unfortunately, this falls into the category of "been here, done this." My heart feels like it's sinking into my stomach just like my feet sank into the sand.

*T*hat's it?" an exasperated Sophie exclaims when I finish recapping my day with Ben. "That's the end of the story?"

"That's it," I say.

We're sitting in a booth at Mama Tacos sharing a plate of nachos.

"You bailed too early," she says.

"I hung in there as long as I could," I reply.

Nicole has an order of chips and guacamole and slides into the booth next to me.

"I still think he's totally into you," Sophie says.

"He sees me the way *every* guy sees me," I say. "As the one who makes for a really good friend and has a great personality. Besides, I think his parents getting divorced has turned him against the whole concept."

"The concept of what? Marriage?" Sophie asks. "I'm not saying he wants to settle down for life, but I think he's interested. And if he is spooked because of what's going on with his parents, then you're going to have to be superbrave like my girl Nicole over here."

She nods toward Nicole right as she chomps down on a huge guac-and-salsa-covered chip.

"What makes Nicole courageous?" Then it hits me. "Wait a second—did you talk to Cody?"

Nicole grins and nods as she finishes the chip.

"I want details!" I say.

"It's not that big a deal," she says.

"Liar, liar, skinny jeans on fire," says Sophie. "It's a huge deal."

"Tell me," I say. "What finally inspired you to break out of your years-long silence?"

She looks me right in the eye and says, "You."

"How's that?"

"I've never seen you as happy as you looked with Ben," she says. "I thought maybe that could happen for me. So I just called him up and asked him if he wanted to catch a movie. Just like that. No plan. No script. No stalking."

My cheeks hurt from how much I'm smiling. "Oh my God! What did he say?"

She almost blushes at the answer. "Yes."

I really am happy for Nicole. She has liked Cody forever, and it is amazing that she had the courage to ask him out. But I'd be lying if I didn't say that a part of me was dying inside. I inspired her because I looked so happy, but the happiness was all based on hope. Not reality. I was happy because I didn't know better, and that makes me feel like some tourist who just bought a surfboard for seven hundred dollars.

Over the next two weeks I see Ben twice for summer camp. I'm polite, but I try to keep the conversation to a minimum. I just can't shake the sting of the conversation we had. Normally, I don't mind being the confidante, but with Ben it's different. I need more.

At the surfing class he comes up to me before we stretch and asks, "Do you think we can do another lesson this week? I still feel like a fish out of water around here."

I shrug and tell him, "It's hard to say. I've got a lot going on with my parents this week."

"Okay," he replies, sounding a little disappointed. "Maybe next week."

"Sure, we'll see."

I continue using my evasive skills the next week, however, and when he makes a joke about calling something by the wrong name, I just give a halfhearted laugh.

"Right. That's funny."

I feel like a total drama queen about it, but it's just so hard. I like him so much and am utterly embarrassed by my inability to navigate these waters. At the end of the lesson I almost go over to him to talk, but I notice that he's talking to Kayla and I hear her invite him to a party. I've lived here my whole life and have never been invited to one of the cool-kid parties. I take it as the final sign that we belong in different circles and that I should just move along.

That's what I'm thinking about on the last day of June as I paddle out on my board. It's early and beautiful and I am safe here, in my special place, with no one around to get in the way. These waters I can navigate perfectly.

The waves are great and it is liberating to ride them one after another. It's like the surf gods are trying to make up for my heartbreak. My last ride in is perfect, and when it finally dies out, all I have to do is step off the board into the shallow water. I am fully relaxed.

And then I hear clapping.

"I knew you were good, but I didn't know you were that good."

I look up at the beach and see Ben sitting there. He stands up, and I have no idea how long he's been watching me.

"I really think you should compete in some of these contests," he continues. "I know it's not your thing but . . . wow."

"How long were you there?"

"For about forty-five minutes," he says.

How did I not see him there? I wonder as I walk up toward him.

"What are you doing here?"

"I've got seventy-five dollars," he replies, holding up his wallet. "I want to learn how to surf. I thought you might help me get—what did you call it—a used fish? Is that right?"

"Yeah," I say. "That's what it's called."

"Great. Where do we find one?"

"You could check online or I can ask around at the shop to see if anyone knows of one for sale."

He walks right up to me and stops. "Did I do something wrong?" he asks. "Because if I did, I'm sorry."

"No," I say curtly. "You're perfect."

"Then why are you avoiding me? I thought you were going to teach me about the beach. I don't want to look online for a surfboard. I want you to help me find one. I want you to teach me how to surf. I want to hang out with you."

I close my eyes tightly and can feel the burn of the salt water. "I can't do that."

"Why not?"

"Because . . . I'm busy. I've got work . . . and—"

"I'll work around your schedule," he offers. "Besides . . . I thought we were friends."

"'Friends,'" I say. "Why does that sound so impersonal? Friends."

"I take my friendships very seriously," he replies.

"Of course you do," I say. "Friends are the kind of people you talk to about other girls, right?"

"Is that what this is about? I'm sorry I talked to you about Beth," he says. "But if you remember, you were the one who asked me about her. I never would have brought her up, but you asked and I'm not going to lie to you."

"And what about your new friends, like Kayla?" I ask. "I heard her invite you to a party. Did you go?"

"Yes," he says. "For about thirty minutes, just to be polite."

"Is that what this is?" I ask. "You're being polite?"

"No, this is me trying to figure out why you keep avoiding me. I don't understand."

"I know," I say. "It doesn't make any sense. I'm really sorry, but I have to head back home so I can go to work. I'm opening the shop today."

Luckily I'm still dripping wet from the ocean, so he can't tell that there are tears mixed in with the water on my face. I force a smile and start to walk past him toward my street.

"I knew it was a boogie board," he blurts out.

"What?"

"When you held it up at camp. I knew it was a boogie board. But I always give a wrong answer so that the kids don't feel bad if they don't know something."

"Then why did you act like you didn't know later on?"

"I was flustered. I wanted to have an excuse to talk to you," he says. "I figured if I looked pathetic enough, you might feel sorry for me and help."

"You were flustered?" I say. "Because of me?"

"Wasn't it obvious?"

"No. I'm not very good at picking up signs."

He turns right to me and says, "Let's see if you can pick up on this one."

Even though I'm dripping wet and carrying a surfboard, he wraps one arm around my waist and the other around my shoulder and kisses me. To say the least, I'm caught off guard, but I drop my surfboard and start to kiss him back.

It is the first kiss of my life, and on a scale of one to ten I'd have to rate it at least a fifteen. I know I don't have much to go on, but I have spent a great deal of time thinking about it and it far exceeds my wildest hopes.

There's a cool breeze coming off the water, the sky is bursting with color and light, and my feet sink into the sand as I lose myself in his lips. I feel like I have caught the longest, sweetest wave, and I want to ride it for as long as possible before it crashes against the shore.

July

*I*t's Tuesday morning and in about fifteen minutes Ben and the summer campers will arrive for their weekly lesson. This will be the first time the kids are going to try to stand up on their boards, and I've recruited Nicole and Sophie to help me demonstrate good technique. It will also be the first time I've seen Ben since the kiss, so I'm hoping they'll help me with that, too.

Since we've already established that I'm useless at picking up signs, I figure it can't hurt to have my own signal-deciphering support staff. Of course that means I have to tell them about the kiss, which I haven't done yet. I drop that bomb while we're carrying all of the gear down from the shop to the beach.

"By the way," I say as if early morning romantic encounters on the beach were just part of my every day. "Did I mention the passionate kiss I had with Ben?"

At first they think I'm joking, but then they see the expression on my face.

"Seriously?" Sophie says with total disbelief. "That seriously happened?"

I nod.

"When?" asks Nicole. "This morning? Last night?"

"Yesterday . . . *morning*," I say sheepishly.

"And we're only hearing about this now? We were with you all yesterday afternoon. How did it not come up?"

The truth is I didn't tell them yesterday because I wasn't sure what to make of it. I'm still not. I know it was awesome and wonderful and the most romantic moment of my life. But it almost feels like it was part of a movie I saw and not something that actually happened to me.

"Details," Sophie says, more as a demand than a request. "Right now."

"Okay," I respond. "But we have to keep setting up. The kids *and Ben* will be here soon."

I tell them everything as we lay a dozen soft boards out on the sand. After a day to analyze and obsess over every detail, it's refreshing to actually tell the story. Hearing it aloud reinforces the fact that it really did happen and wasn't just my imagination. I tell them about catching the last wave and walking up onto the beach. They both eat up the part about Ben sitting in the sand clapping.

"Cute, cute, cute," Nicole says with a broad smile. "So very cute."

And although I'm somewhat embarrassed by the melodramatic tone of my conversation with him, I give them an honest recounting of what was said. By the time I get to the kiss, they are eating out of the palm of my hand.

"And . . . ," Nicole says when I finish.

"And what?" I ask.

"And . . . what happened next?" Sophie asks.

"You heard the part where we kissed, right? That was kind of the big finish."

They look cheated.

"There's got to be more!" Sophie claims. "Did he just vanish into thin air? Didn't you say anything?"

"I'm sure I said something, but my head was spinning way too much for me to remember what it was. I do seem to recall that we were both in a sort of stunned 'I don't know what to make of what just happened' silence during the walk back up from the beach to my house."

"Was there any sort of follow-up moment?" Nicole asks hopefully

I think about it and nod. "There was a part when I sort of manipulated the situation so that we could kiss again."

"And yet you left that out?" Sophie asks, frustrated. "You know you're terrible at telling this story."

"How did you manipulate it?" asks Nicole.

"When we reached the house, we went around into the back-yard and I asked him to help me put my board back on the rack. I told him it had to go on the top pegs but had trouble reaching that high by myself."

Nicole laughs. "Why did you tell him it needed to be up there?"

I am almost too embarrassed to answer.

"I said it needed to be in direct sunlight to keep any conden-sation from contracting the foam core."

They both look at each other and then back at me.

"That doesn't make any sense," Nicole says. "It's like you just made up words."

"I know that and you know that, but he doesn't know that,"

I explain. "It's not like I could say I wanted him to do it because he's tall and I was looking for an excuse to brush up against him."

"Did it work?" asks Sophie. "Did you brush up against him?"

I smile at the memory and nod. "It was electric. I turned and looked up at him, and I was just about to kiss him again when . . ."

". . . yeah . . . ," they say eagerly.

". . . my dad came out from the house to go on his morning run."

They sag. "Argghhhh."

"That's when it got awkward. Dad said something like, 'Hey Ben, what are you doing here?' And I sort of panicked."

"Oh my God," Sophie gasps. "What did you say?"

"I told him that Ben had stopped by so the two of them could go running together."

Sophie and Nicole both laugh out loud.

"You did not," says Sophie.

"No, that's exactly what I did. Because, you know, I'm so smooth."

"And Ben went along with it?" asks Nicole.

"He didn't really have much of a choice. They ran eight miles. By the time they got back, he had to go chaperone the campers on a field trip to the Kennedy Space Center and there was no chance to follow up."

"So you haven't seen him since it happened?" asks Nicole.

"The first time will be in a few minutes when he arrives here. I figure it should be a very romantic follow-up. What with all the screaming kids and of course my favorite person on the planet, Kayla McIntyre."

"Forget about Kayla," Sophie says. "He's already picked you

over her. She lost. You won. Game over. You're his summer romance."

"It was one kiss," I say, trying to maintain some semblance of reality. "In my world one kiss is a huge deal, but in the regular world I don't know that it qualifies as a summer romance."

"Do not sell yourself short," says Nicole. "You always do that. It was a kiss with purpose."

"It was a kiss that he had to run eight miles for," I reply. "How bad is that?"

"No," she says. "It was a kiss that he thought was worth running eight miles for. How *awesome* is that?"

"The tall girl makes a valid point," says Sophie. "He likes you. And when you didn't get the signs he was sending, he built you a billboard."

"Okay, maybe he does like me," I concede. "But he's just broken up with a longtime girlfriend, and he's all freaked out about his parents' divorce. I'm not sure he's looking for a full-fledged summer romance."

"Well, whatever he's looking for," Sophie says, pointing toward the beach access, "we're about to find out."

I turn and see Ben marching the kids our way. He's acting like his normal goofy self, which is a good start, but while he's wearing his sunglasses I can't really read his expression.

"Do not sell yourself short," Nicole reminds me just before they get within earshot. "You are totally worthy of long distance running."

I appreciate the pep talk, but I'm still in full panic mode right up until the moment he reaches us and flashes that smile.

It's a huge relief. I realize that part of me was worried that he completely regretted what had happened and that he was going to act differently around me. I still don't know what there is between us, but at least now I know there's nothing awkward about it, so that's a big step.

Kayla is her normal self, gorgeous and obnoxious (gorbnoxious?) all at once. She's got a new bathing suit that truly showcases her (not so) secret weapons, but today I have a secret weapon of my own—Sophie. Wherever Kayla goes, Sophie is right by her side acting like they're BFFs, roommates, and sorority sisters all rolled into one. This makes it impossible for her to flirt with Ben. When we line up to stretch, Sophie slides in front of Kayla so that she obstructs Ben's view of her. And when it's time to pick demonstration partners, Sophie latches on to her arm and exclaims, "We have to be partners, Kayla! We just have to!"

Despite all the subterfuge and mental distractions, the big news of the morning is the lesson. We keep the soft boards—large, padded surfboards—on the sand and practice our paddling and pop-up techniques. Then we hit the water and put them into practice. I can't express how exciting it is to see the kids' faces light up the first time they get up on their feet and ride a wave. Even though we're only in three feet of water, it's exhilarating for them.

My favorite is Rebecca, the shy girl I noticed the first day. She has continued to come out of her shell a little more each week. Today she stays up on the board the longest of anyone, and I can see in her the same spark I had when I was her age at this camp.

Throughout it all, Ben and I exchange quick glances and

whispered comments. Our hands touch a couple of times as we help kids get up on their boards, and once when I'm not looking his way, he uses a boogie board to splash me, which gets a big laugh from everyone. Even with my compromised sign-reading ability, it all seems kind of flirty.

We finally have a brief moment right after the lesson when the kids are taking an orange slice and bottled water break. I look over and see that Kayla is still dealing with Hurricane Sophie, which means she won't be able to drop in on me again like she usually does.

"They did great today," I say.

"*You* did great today," he replies. "The way you love it so much connects with them. They want to feel the same way because it's so real."

There's an awkward pause, so I just jump headfirst into the situation.

"Speaking of real . . . ," I say, unleashing the worst segue in history, "did that *really* happen yesterday?"

He smiles and nods. "It did. In fact, I think it was maybe going to happen again when we were interrupted."

"By 'interrupted' you mean when you had to take an eight-mile detour with my dad?"

"Kinda, yeah," he says. "I have to say I did not see that coming. I was hoping that maybe we could talk about it. . . . You know, without so many people around."

"That can be arranged."

"How about after work?"

"Sure. My shift ends at six thirty."

"Great, I'll meet you at the shop," he says. "You're not going to make me go running with your dad again?"

I shake my head. "I promise."

"Good, 'cause I'm planning on wearing my flip-flops so I blend in with the locals. And those things really make you blister around the three-mile mark."

Our eyes linger for a moment, and I say, "See you at six thirty."

"See you then."

He rushes off to make sure the kids pick up all their orange peels and water bottles, and I start stacking up the surfboards to carry back up to the shop. I see Kayla finally break free of Sophie and head our way, but she's too late. Today's score is Dolphin 1, Shark 0. And the dolphin is now in it to win it.

Although Sophie and Nicole seem to think that all the signs they saw on the beach were positive, I'm still approaching the situation with total caution. All I really know is that Ben's coming to talk with me after work. Maybe he's planning to say that the kiss was a mistake, or that while he likes me, he doesn't *like* me like me. It's all so hard to figure out.

I spend most of the day watching the clock, and at 6:13 I'm in the middle of my "do you see yourself as a shark or a dolphin?" routine with a girl looking for a bikini when Ben comes into the store. He smiles and waves, and since I don't want to be rude to the customer, I respond on the sly with a half smile and a raised eyebrow that I hope looks cool and not like a nervous twitch.

"Which do you like best?" the girl asks, holding up two swimsuits.

I give her my undivided attention, consider both suits, and point to the one in her left hand. "That one."

She scrunches up her face. "I think I like the other one better."

I resist the urge to say, "Then why did you ask me?" and instead go with, "That one looks cute too. Why don't you try it on?"

She heads for the changing room, and I turn back to look for Ben. Only now he's gone. I scan the shop and half worry that maybe I'm just imagining him now. (Imaginary boyfriend—that does kind of sound like me.)

Sophie sees my distress as she walks over. "Badger Ben just went out to the garage," she says, referring to the room where we keep all the surfboards.

"'Badger' Ben?"

"You shot down all the dairy nicknames, so I thought I'd try something else. In addition to being America's Dairy Land, Wisconsin is known as the Badger State. I figure Badger Ben has alliteration and a nice ring to it."

I don't pretend to understand what it is with Sophie and nicknames, but I'm a little too anxious at the moment to get into it. "How did he seem?"

"Like he was about to break your heart," she says. "He's probably going to tell you that he never wants to see you again and he's running off to marry Kayla."

I gasp before I realize she's joking.

"You might want to turn down the nervous knob," she says,

with a friendly pat on the shoulder. "Listen to the music. I picked this playlist specifically to help you mellow out."

In the shop we usually play a steady blend of beach, Hawaiian, and reggae music, and after a while you stop hearing it and it disappears into the background of your brain. But now that I listen, I realize that Bob Marley is singing one of my favorite tunes: "Don't worry about a thing, 'cause every little thing gonna be all right. . . ."

"Okay," I say after I get the hint, and take a couple of deep breaths. "I'll calm down."

"Good, because you're much better when you're relaxed. You're not one of those 'performs well under pressure' kind of girls."

"Gee thanks, Coach. Good to know I can always get a pep talk."

"I'm just keeping it real."

"By the way," I add, "'Badger Ben' is a no go."

She shrugs. "I knew it the second I said it, but you gotta try these things out to be sure."

Fifteen minutes later my shift is over and the girl has finally decided on a bikini. It goes without saying that she picked the first one I had recommended. I remind myself that it's important for her to be comfortable with her purchase, so I don't mind the other five we had to go through before we got back to it.

Once she's made her purchase, I am free to go and head over to the garage. It's been my favorite part of the shop ever since I was a kid and I'd come to look at all the boards and try to figure out which one was made just for me. We don't have nearly the number that Surf City has in its inventory, but all of ours are choice. About half of them are custom made in the area. These cost a little more, but they are beyond sweet.

Personally, I'm saving up to buy my very own M & M, which is what we call the boards that Mickey and Mo shape themselves. They only make about a dozen a year, so they're pretty hard to come by.

Speaking of Mo, when I get to the garage, I see her in back talking to Ben. She's in her midfifties, but she looks much younger than that. A life spent surfing, swimming, and kayaking has kept her extremely fit. It also keeps her hair wet a lot of the time, which is why she usually just pulls it back in a ponytail.

Of the two sisters, I'm closer to her. This is no knock on Mickey; it's just that Mo and I have more in common. Mickey's loud and in your face like Sophie, but Mo hangs around the edges like I do. We surf alike too. Both of us favor a long, smooth style rather than a more athletic and aggressive one.

She's showing Ben a display case that serves as a tribute to Steady Eddie, her father. It has all sorts of artifacts including surfing trophies, a lifesaving medal, and even his torpedo buoy, which is the big float that lifeguards carried back in the day.

"He won every surf contest in the state," she says, beaming with pride.

"What about King of the Beach?" Ben asks, referring to our local contest. "Did he win that one too?"

Mo laughs. "Seven times—more than anyone."

"Awesome," says Ben. "Where's the trophy for that?"

"At Surf City," she says. "It always goes to the current champion."

"That's kind of unfair," says Ben.

"I don't know," she replies. "It's in their store, but Dad's name is on it seven times. Mickey and I think of it as covertly advertising our store over there."

"Why don't you ask her who's won it the second most times?" I say, interrupting.

"We're in the middle of a conversation, Izzy," she says, deflecting the comment.

"Go ahead and ask her," I say again.

"Who won the second most times?" he asks.

She's reluctant to answer, but Ben and I wait her out, and she finally concedes, "Mickey and I have each won it four times."

"You were King of the Beach?" Ben asks.

She nods.

"The only two girls to ever win it," I add, because I know that Mo won't.

"That means between you two and your dad, you guys have your name engraved on it fifteen times."

"I never thought of it that way, but I guess so." Mo is uncomfortable receiving praise, so she redirects the conversation. "Ben, why don't you show Izzy what you learned?"

"Oh, yeah. Watch this, Iz." One by one he points to a row of surfboards, identifying each one by type as he goes. "This is a shortboard, this is an egg, this is a fish, and this one . . . is . . . a gun?"

"That's right, a gun," Mo says. "Now which one is the quad?"

"The fish," he says, pointing toward it. "Because it has four fins."

"Perfect."

"Very impressive," I say.

Feeling good about his surfboard IQ, he turns to Mo and adds, "I can do more than identify. I also know that you have to keep them in direct sunlight so that the condensation doesn't contract the foam."

Mo starts to correct him, but I shake her off and she lets it slide. Instead she turns to me and says, "I understand you're going to be teaching Ben the fine art." She always refers to surfing as "the fine art."

"Yes, I am," I say.

She gives us the once-over and nods her approval. "Good choice."

I don't know if she's saying that I'm a good choice as a teacher for him or if he's a good choice as a guy for me. Knowing Mo, it's probably a combination of both.

"I'll be happy to take any pointers that you may have too," he tells her. "After all, you are a four-time King of the Beach. Or is it Queen?"

"King works," she says with more than a little pride. She thinks about it and says, "My advice is that you should remember to fall in love with your heart and not with your brain. . . ."

I start to stammer something about it being way too early to use the *L* word, but catch myself when she continues.

"So pick a board that speaks to you right here." She taps him in the center of the chest. "And always listen to what Izzy tells you. The girl has the gift."

"I'll do that," he says.

Mo smiles and leaves us in the garage. For the first time since my dad interrupted us yesterday morning, we are alone. I look at him. He looks at me. And I realize I have no idea what to say. You'd think that since I've been obsessing over this moment for the last six hours, I might have come up with an opening line.

"Hi." (Clever, huh?)

"Hi," he says. "Is your shift over?"

"Yep," I say. "Although I do have to be home for dinner in about an hour."

He thinks this over for a moment. "An hour, huh? That doesn't really leave us enough time to run the eight miles I was hoping to get in, so do you want to just go out on the pier and look at the ocean instead?"

"It's one of my favorite things in the world."

The Pearl Beach Fishing Pier is rare in that it's equally popular with tourists and locals alike. It stretches out from the southern end of the boardwalk and is exactly one quarter mile long. When Ben and I get there, it's low tide and the beach is at its widest. That means we have to walk nearly a third of the length of the pier before we're actually over the water. There are people fishing from both sides for most of the way, but none at the far end. There's also no railing at the end, which allows boats to tie off and lets us sit down on the edge and dangle our feet over the water.

"It's pretty," Ben says, looking out at endless ocean.

"It's better than pretty," I say as I close my eyes and feel the sea mist against my face. "It's perfect."

There's that word again—"perfect." It's the same word I used to describe him yesterday morning, and I wonder if he makes the connection.

We're both quiet for a little while, and I can tell he's thinking of what to say. I decide to beat him to the punch.

"I'm pretty sure I know why you wanted to talk," I offer. "And I'd just like to apologize for all the melodramatic baggage I laid on you yesterday. I also want to apologize for giving you the cold shoulder lately. You deserve better."

"First of all, you don't need to apologize for anything," he says. "And secondly, that's not what I wanted to talk about."

I take a deep breath. This is it.

"What do you want to talk about?"

"You've told me great things about the beach and surfing. You've told me where to eat and how to dress."

"But . . . ," I say. "This sounds like it's leading to a 'but.'"

I open my eyes and turn to him. He's looking right at me.

"But," he says, "you've told me almost nothing about *yourself*. So, if you don't mind, I'd like to talk about you."

This catches me off guard. Completely off guard.

"What do you mean?"

"I mean you know all kinds of things about me. You know about my parents getting divorced. You know about me breaking up with my ex-girlfriend. You know about my school and my uncle and that I run cross-country. But the only thing I know about you is that your favorite ice cream flavor is mint chocolate chip."

"That's probably the most interesting thing about me."

He shakes his head. "You should think more of yourself, Izzy. I'm sure there are an endless number of interesting things about you, and I'd like to know some of them."

I rack my brain trying to think of any worth telling, but I come up blank.

"I'm sorry. It's all just so . . . ordinary."

"That cannot be," he protests.

"Okay, I'll prove it. You've met my parents and I'm an only child, so that means you know my entire family. I get good grades at school, but I'm pretty anonymous when I walk through the halls. That's partly by choice and partly due to the high school version of Darwin's natural selection. I haven't told you about breaking up with my ex-boyfriend because I've never had a boyfriend. So, now you're all caught up."

"You've never had a boyfriend?"

I find this particular bit of information to be supremely embarrassing, so I turn away and look back at the water as I answer. "No."

"Why not?" he asks. "What's the problem?"

"I guess I'm just a loser," I say sharply.

"No. I mean, what's the problem with the boys in this town? How is it possible that you've never had a boyfriend? Does the salt water get in their brains? Does the sun make them stupid?"

"You've seen Kayla," I say. "My school is loaded with girls who look like that."

He thinks about this for a moment. "Okay, I'll admit that Kayla is hot—"

"You think?" I say sarcastically.

"But she's not in your league. You're smarter, funnier, and way more interesting."

"All things that a girl wants to hear. I'm sure she goes to bed every night cursing my really good personality."

"You do have a really good personality," he says. "But if you want me to be shallow, I'll point out that you're also better looking than her."

I give him the look. "That's completely untrue and you know it."

"That's funny, because I don't know that," he says. "I do know that she asked me to go to a party tonight. And I know that I turned her down so I could hang out with you."

I'm not sure if I'll ever have another such opportunity in the future, so I savor this for a moment before I respond.

"Really?"

"Really, and I'll prove it," he says, throwing my line right back at me. He covers his eyes with his left hand. "Ask me to describe Kayla."

I'm skeptical of where this is going, but I don't have much choice. "Describe Kayla."

"Big boobs. Long legs. Great hair."

I haven't mentioned it yet, but he's right—Kayla's hair is spectacular. "Okay," I reply. "You're kind of proving my point."

He shakes his head but still keeps his hand over his eyes. "Now ask me to describe you."

I don't really see how this can turn out well, so I don't say anything. He doesn't let that stop him.

"You have a wrinkle in your chin," he says.

"Wow, a chin wrinkle sounds way better than big boobs."

"You have this *amazing* wrinkle in your chin," he says, ignoring my sarcasm, "that only appears when you smile. It's so irresistible that I keep telling stupid jokes just so that you'll laugh and I can see it again."

I reflexively run my finger along my chin.

"And your eyes defy description," he continues. "When I met you, I thought they were blue. Then, when we went to Luigi's, I could have sworn they were brown. And yesterday morning . . . I'm certain they were green. Every time I see you, the first thing I look at are your eyes so I can see what color they are."

Let me reiterate that this type of conversation is new to me, and it has me feeling a little breathless.

"And when you get embarrassed your cheeks turn red." He uncovers his eyes and looks right at me. "Like they're doing right now."

Of course the fact that he says this makes me blush that much more.

"The first time I saw it was when I asked you how the poster looked and you started to say 'awful' but tried to change it to 'awesome,' and it came out 'awfslome.'"

"You noticed that?"

He nods. "I notice everything about you."

"Well, I can't help but notice that all the things you just pointed out—wrinkly chin, inconsistent eye color, and the oh so sexy blushing—are in fact flaws. So again I say that you're kind of proving my point."

"You cannot believe that," he says. "You know they're not flaws."

"Well, I admit that you manage to present them in a way that's kind of amazing, but—"

"Maybe this analogy will work for you. Before you got to the garage, Mo showed me all the different types of surfboards. She really opened my eyes. Who knew there were so many?"

"I knew," I joke, but he ignores it.

"Girls like Kayla are like factory boards. Shiny. Smooth. Pretty. They look great but they look alike."

"And girls like me?" I ask.

"There aren't *girls* like you, Izzy. There is *a girl* like you, singular. You're like this custom board that Mo showed me. She shaped it herself, and it has all these little details and indentations that make it special and unique. They're features, not flaws."

I look at him and am totally speechless. On the list of the greatest things that anyone has ever said to me, this is the entire list. Nothing else is even close.

"I don't know what to say."

"Well, you could say something about who you are. For once don't make me do all the talking."

"I'm really not trying to be difficult; I just can't think of anything."

"Tell me why you won't surf in a contest."

"I already did. It's just not my scene."

"Sorry, wrong answer," he says as he makes a game show buzzer noise. "There's got to be more to it than that. Is it because you're shy? Is it because you think you'll lose?"

"Maybe . . . but there's more to it than that," I try to explain.

I think about this for a moment, and he waits patiently for an answer. I look out at the water and try to put it all into words.

"For me surfing is completely pure. It's just me and the water and my board. It's almost spiritual. Actually, it *is* spiritual. There's no one watching, no one judging. It doesn't matter who's popular or who's pretty, and it's not about being better than anybody else. It's just about the quest for perfection."

"And what do you mean by perfection?"

"Think about everything that goes into creating a wave: the gravitational pull of the moon, the wind and weather thousands of miles away in the middle of the ocean, the contours of the ocean floor. It's an amazing cosmic event that is hidden from sight until the last possible moment. The wave only breaks the surface for such a short period of time, and perfection is the tuning fork that rings in your heart when you catch it the moment it comes to life and ride it until the last bit of it disappears. It's the feeling of knowing that the forces of nature all came together and you were there to fully appreciate every last bit of it."

He considers this for a moment, and this time I wait patiently.

"Was that perfection yesterday morning?" he asks. "When you caught that last wave?"

I close my eyes and think back to the wave. "Absolutely."

"And did it ruin it for you when you found out that I saw you do it? Did my being there make it *im*perfect?"

"No," I answer. "Of course not."

"Then why would other people ruin it? I think you should get over this fear. Better yet, I think you should compete in the

King of the Beach contest. It's not like girls don't enter. Mickey and Mo both won it. Why not you?"

"Because," I say, as though that alone were enough of an answer.

"That's it? 'Because'? That's not a good enough excuse."

"It should be," I reply a little prickly. "You wanted to know something about me and I told you. And the first thing you're doing is telling me to change that thing. It's not a fear. It's just the way I'm wired. You watching me surf is different from a crowd of people watching me. It's the most personal thing I can share. I don't think you understand that."

"I don't think you have any idea how great it is to watch you. I don't even understand surfing and I think it's amazing. Yesterday morning, watching you, that was mind blowing. Without a doubt it was the best forty-five minutes I've had since I've gotten here."

"Really?"

"There is nothing I can do as well as you can surf. When I first got here, I thought surfing was a hobby. Then, after a few weeks of talking to you, I began to think of it as a sport. But yesterday, when I was watching you, I realized that it's an art. You're an artist, Izzy."

You can now add this to the list I just mentioned of the most amazing things anyone's ever said to me.

"You think so?"

"I know so."

"Okay," I say shyly. "Then that's one thing that you know about me. But I'm not looking to share that with the world, okay?"

"Okay," he says. "I'll stop pushing you."

We both share a smile, and he reaches over and slips his hand into mine. I feel a charge crackle through my body. Neither of us says anything for a moment, and I give his hand a little squeeze in return.

"Now I want you to tell me something," I say.

"Anything."

"Why did you kiss me yesterday?"

He thinks about it for a moment before he answers. "Because I was tired of imagining what it would be like. I just had to know."

"You'd been imagining it?" I ask. "Imagining kissing me?"

He nods. "Big time."

"Since when?"

"Since I met you."

"Right," I say with a laugh. "When I had the guacamole stain on my shirt?"

"I like guacamole and I respect a girl who can pull it off as a fashion statement."

I turn to look at him, and the sea breeze blows my hair in every direction. He reaches up and gently moves it out of my face, and I tuck it between my neck and shoulder.

"And what was it like?" I continue. "Kissing me?"

He flashes the smile I see in my mind whenever I think about him.

"Even better than I had imagined. Which is saying something, because I had set the anticipation bar pretty high."

"Do you . . . maybe . . . want to try it again?"

"I . . . do," he says, but with some hesitation. "I . . . really . . . do."

"Why do I sense another 'but' coming up?"

"It's already July first and I go back to Wisconsin on August twenty-fifth. That's—"

"Fifty-five days," I interrupt.

"Wow, you came up with that quickly."

"I've already done the math. All of it. Fifty-five days, seven weekends, six more summer camp classes." I shrug. "You're not the only one who's been imagining."

This makes him smile.

"I want to kiss you very much," he says. "But if I do, I know that it will hurt unbearably bad fifty-five days from now. Maybe worse than anything's ever hurt before. And that makes me wonder what I should do."

Now I turn my whole body and lean forward so that I am just inches from his face. "What *you* should do? Don't I have a say in this?"

"Of course you do," he answers. "What do you think we should do?"

"I think it's like a wave," I say. "But that's just me. I always think everything's like surfing."

He has a perplexed look on his face. "How is it like a wave?"

"Consider all the cosmic forces that have brought us to the end of this pier. Your parents, my job, your uncle, summer camp. All of these unseen forces have led us here, and the chance that we have is only going to last for a brief period of time. Just like a wave. I say we catch it as soon as we can and ride it until the very last part dissolves into the sand. I say that we shoot . . . for perfection."

I don't wait for him to respond. Instead I reach around, put my hand on the back of his neck, and pull him gently toward me as I begin to kiss him. I can taste the salt air on his lips, and when I close my eyes I lose myself in those lips. It is wonderful and exciting. It's more than I ever would have dreamed could have happened. But no matter how hard I try, I can't ignore the clock that starts in my head. Even as I kiss him I can hear it ticking away.

Fifty-five days and counting.

I want you . . . to name which five members of the Continental Congress were selected to write the Declaration of Independence."

I blink, rub the sleep out of my eyes, and try to refocus. Much to my horror I realize that it's not a nightmare. Uncle Sam really is accosting me in the kitchen. Okay, it's my father in an Uncle Sam costume, but it's still pretty nightmarish.

"What?" I mumble with a sleepy yawn.

"I want you," he says, exaggerating the pose to look like the famous Uncle Sam poster, "to name which five members of the Continental Congress were selected to write the Declaration of Independence."

Normally, I make it a rule to ignore my father when he's in costume. And you'd be surprised by the frequency with which I have to invoke this rule. But that's impossible at the moment because he's blocking my access to the refrigerator.

"I just want to get some milk for my cereal," I moan. "Why does there have to be a quiz?"

"Because it's the Fourth of July and your father's an American history teacher," he says, as though that were a reasonable explanation. "C'mon. Give me the names."

I can tell that he's not giving up, so I rack my brain. "I'm pretty sure one was Thomas Jefferson."

"Yes," he says, no doubt perturbed that I'm only "pretty sure."

"And you've gotta figure that Ben Franklin was there, right?"

"He was."

He waits for more, and all I do is shrug.

"That's it?"

"It's seven in the morning and I'm in the middle of summer vacation," I say. "You should be happy that I got that many."

He shakes his head in total disappointment. "That's two out of five. That's only forty percent. Do you find forty percent acceptable?"

"I'm only getting two percent milk, so yeah," I say with a wicked smile. "That leaves thirty-eight percent for later."

Rather than continue our back and forth history lesson, I wedge my way past him, grab the milk and orange juice, and head for the table.

"John Adams, Robert Livingston, and Roger Sherman were the others," he says. "In case you were wondering."

"Thanks," I answer as I pour the milk over my cereal. "But I wasn't."

Despite my current—and I would argue quite defensible—lack of excitement, Fourth of July is a huge deal in Pearl Beach. It's the busiest day of the year for tourists, and we really give them their money's worth. The celebration starts off in the morning with the Patriots Parade, continues all afternoon with live music at the bandshell, and concludes with a huge fireworks display over the pier.

I don't want to be a buzz kill for my dad, so I try to engage in some conversation. "Is your band marching in the parade this year?"

"Yes," he says with glee, unwilling to let my mood dampen his enthusiasm. "And we're playing the two o'clock set at the bandshell."

I swallow a spoonful of cereal and chuckle. "You love saying that you're playing a 'set,' don't you?"

"I almost said that we had a 'gig,' but I thought you might give me a hard time about it."

"I definitely would have."

Every year on the Fourth of July my dad and a bunch of other guys he knows form a band they call the Founding Fathers. It's perfect not only because he gets to dress up as Uncle Sam, but also because it blends three of his greatest loves: music, American history, and bad puns.

"Are you going to sing my song?" I ask, giving him my best doe eyes.

My song is "Isabel," an old country song by John Denver that my father used to sing to me when he'd put me to bed.

"I don't know," he says, playing hardball. "Our set's only for thirty minutes and we've got a lot of songs."

"Seriously? That's your answer?"

He nods and we have a little stare off before I finally relent.

"Massachusetts, Connecticut, New York, Pennsylvania, and Virginia."

"And why are you suddenly listing states?"

"Because those are the colonies that John Adams, Roger Sherman, Robert Livingston, Ben Franklin, and Thomas Jefferson represented in the Continental Congress."

"You knew all along."

"Of course I did. You've only made me watch *1776* about a thousand times."

"Then why'd you act like you didn't know?"

I give him a look. "Because I don't want to encourage you to give me pop quizzes every morning."

He smiles broadly. "That's my girl."

"Now what about my song?" I ask.

"I guess you'll have to come and find out," he answers. But as he walks out of the kitchen I can hear him start to sing, "Isabel is watching like a princess from the mountains . . ."

Today would be the perfect day to hang out with Ben, except we're both busy for huge chunks of it. He's marching with the campers in the parade and working at the bandshell during the concert. Meanwhile, I'm going in early to help set up at Surf Sisters and working the late shift tonight. If I'm lucky, I'll get out in time to catch some of the fireworks. I'm pretty sure our paths will cross a few times during the festivities, but there are no guarantees as to when.

I ride my bike to the shop, and when I get there, I'm surprised to see Nicole standing in the parking lot wearing her band uniform.

"You know I'm all about seeing you in the funny hat, but shouldn't you be lining up for the parade?"

"I've got about twenty minutes," she says.

I lock my bike to the rack and reply, "I'm sure we've got the inventory all covered. You should go hang out with the drum line. And by drum line I mean you should go hang out with Cody."

"I will," she says. "But Mickey called me first thing and asked me to come in. She said that she wanted to talk to the whole staff."

Mickey and Mo must be concerned about something, because the Fourth is our biggest sales day of the year. I assume they want to make sure that everyone's ready. But when I walk into the shop and see them talking in hushed tones, I begin to worry that something's wrong. Typically they're upbeat, but there are no smiles today.

Mickey steps forward first and does a quick head count to make sure we're all here. Including the two of them, there are ten of us in total, and while I'm closest to Sophie and Nicole, I think of everyone as my extended family.

"We really hate to do this today," Mickey says. "The Fourth is such a big day for the beach, and we know how much of a zoo it can be. But there are some developments that are about to become public, and we want to make sure that you hear them from us first."

Now I am really worried. Mickey is getting teary and has trouble continuing, so Mo puts an arm around her and picks up where she left off.

"After thirty-three years of doing what we love . . . we are sorry to announce that . . . this is going to be the last summer for Surf Sisters. We're closing down the shop at the end of September."

She continues speaking, but I literally do not hear another word while my mind tries to process what she has just said. I know this sounds melodramatic, but I can't overemphasize how important the shop has been to me. I look around and realize that everyone else is equally stunned. This is our place. This cannot be happening.

"What are you talking about?" Sophie blurts out.

"Like I said," Mo continues, "we didn't want to tell you like this, but you're family to us, and word has leaked out and we're sure you'll hear about it."

"How is this even possible?" one of the girls asks. "I know we don't get the crowds that Surf City does, but business seems like it's been good."

"It's more complicated than that," Mickey says, clearing her throat. "A developer is going to build a new resort, and the bank sees this as a chance to make a lot of money. We've tried everything we can think of, but there's really nothing we can do about it. We will, however, do everything we can to help you all find new jobs."

We sit there in stunned silence for a moment, and an idea comes to me.

"What about Luigi's Car Wash?" I say. "Luigi's was able to stay open because it had been here so long. Doesn't the same law protect us?"

They share a look and turn back to us.

"We thought the same thing," Mo says. "We even got our lawyer to file paperwork with the city. But it turns out we opened four months too late to qualify."

I can't believe this would happen at the very moment I was happier than ever before. It's like if one part of my life goes well, then another has to go off the rails. I look around the shop and suddenly years' worth of memories start to flood through my mind. I can't even begin to imagine what this is like for the two of them. They grew up here. They've spent their lives building a business here. And it's going to become some ridiculous hotel.

"What can we do?" I ask.

"I'm glad you asked that," Mickey says. "We know there's a lot of sadness about this, but we don't want our last memories of Surf Sisters to be sad. We want to have an incredible last summer. And you're the key to that. We have accepted that this is going to happen, and we're going to have fun. We want you to have fun too. If you can't have fun at the beach during the summer, then you're really doing something wrong."

"And that fun starts tonight," Mo says. "We're closing a couple hours earlier than planned, and we're going to set up beach chairs on the roof so we can watch the fireworks, just like we used to with Dad. You're all invited."

Suddenly I think about Ben, and I must make an expression, because Mo notices it.

"What is it, Izzy?"

It seems inappropriate to ask, but I don't know what else to say. "I was just wondering if I could bring a date."

For the first time all morning, there are smiles around the room.

"We would love it if you brought a date."

$\mathcal{I}$n the world of parades, ours is on the homemade end of the spectrum. We don't have giant balloons like the Thanksgiving Day Parade in New York, and our floats aren't lush and intricate like those in the Rose Parade on New Year's Day. Instead we've got some marching bands, people from different civic groups, old guys in antique cars, and about a dozen pickup trucks pulling flatbed trailers decorated with plastic fringe, chicken wire, and tissue paper. The grand finale is the high school drama teacher dressed as George Washington waving from the back of a fire truck with all its lights flashing. It is beyond corny, and I wouldn't miss it for the world.

Sophie, my mother, and I stake out a spot right at the corner where the route turns off Seagate and onto Ocean Ave. This is the halfway point of the parade as it makes its way from the high school parking lot to the bandshell, and because they have to slow down and wait at the turn, most of the bands play a full song here.

While we're waiting for the parade to begin, we tell Mom about Surf Sisters, and she's almost as bummed as we are. This funk hangs over us until we catch sight of Dad's band coming our way. The Founding Fathers are playing some Dixieland jazz number, and what they lack in precision and synchronicity they more than make up for with enthusiasm and ridiculous costumes.

My dad plays trombone, and I swear he picked it because it's the goofiest looking instrument. He exaggerates his marching when he sees us, and it's impossible not to laugh at him. We all shout and wave, and he responds with a wink and a long, drawn out blast from the trombone.

"Has he always been like that?" I ask my mom.

"Always," she says. "He did the exact same thing when I waved at him during this parade back when he was in the high school band and I was your age."

Sophie and I laugh at this, but as I watch Mom watching him, I can tell she's flashing back in time for an instant. She smiles and I notice her cheeks have the same blush that Ben described in mine. It dawns on me that there was a time when my mom felt exactly the same way about Dad that I feel about Ben. I wonder if she had as many questions as I do or if she was one of those girls who had all the answers.

Our next highlight is when Sophie's little brother marches by with the Cub Scouts. Unlike my father, there's nothing silly about him. He's the pack's flag bearer and takes his responsibility with full patriotic seriousness.

"Way to go Anthony!" shouts Sophie.

He looks over at us and gives us a very grown-up nod. We respond with wild applause and cheering, and he can't help but break into a little smile.

Behind the scouts is a group of Shriners in miniaturized sports cars. The tassels from their fez hats flap in the wind behind them as they race by and make figure eights in the street.

Next up is my least favorite float. It's sponsored by Surf City and features Bailey Kossoff, the reigning champion of the King of the Beach surf contest. He's sitting on a throne next to a fake palm tree, wearing board shorts, a royal cape, and a king's crown.

I've got nothing against him. I think he's an amazing surfer, but I could live without all the Surf City bimbos in their bikinis who surround him and wave to the crowd. Of course Kayla is one of the girls, and when my mother sees her, she says something completely unexpected.

"I know I'm a teacher and I'm not supposed to talk about a student," she says. "But since this is summer vacation and it's just us girls, let me tell you something. I cannot stand that girl."

This is completely out of character for Mom. I don't think I've ever heard her say anything negative about a student in front of me.

"I'm serious," she says. "Her mom was the same way when we were growing up. I tell you, the broom does not fall far from the witch tree."

Sophie eats it up. "I've missed hanging out with you, Mrs. Lucas."

"I've missed you, too, Sophie," Mom says with a smile. "We should do this more often."

I wonder if Mom made this unprecedented move because she has somehow become aware of my current situation. I don't doubt that Kayla's going to keep flirting with Ben, and my mother probably wants to give me a little boost. Before I can give it much thought though, we hear the sound of approaching snare drums.

"Here comes our girl!" Sophie says, pointing at the band.

Nicole may not always like the fact that she's six feet tall, but it sure does help us pick her out of crowds.

"Check it out—she's right next to Cody," I say, noticing the lineup. "Maybe there's something to be said for intervention-worthy stalking."

Mom gives us a look but decides not to ask.

The band marches to the cadence from the drums until they come to a stop right in front of us. They are about to play a song, and since they've played the same six or seven songs at every football game we've ever attended, Sophie and I try to predict which one this will be.

"'Hawaii Five-O,'" she guesses.

"'A Little Less Conversation,'" I counter.

We only have to hear the first few notes before I'm flashing a broad smile and basking in the glow of victory. "Nailed it."

The Pearl Beach High School Marching Panthers have been playing "A Little Less Conversation" for as long as anyone can remember. I wouldn't be surprised if they began playing it the day after Elvis released the song. This is not a complaint, mind you. They play it because they completely knock it out of the park every time.

Just as we do at football games, we all sing along. It builds to a climax when we shout, "Come on, come on! . . . Come on, come on! . . . Come on, come on!" That's when the trumpets reach their crescendo and the whole band starts marching again at our urging.

I really kind of love everything about Pearl Beach, if you haven't noticed.

This is the first time I've seen Nicole perform since she switched to drums, and you'd never know that she hasn't been playing them her whole life. She is so focused she doesn't even notice us jumping up and down waving at her.

There are more Shriners—this group is on tiny motorcycles—and then the mayor rides by waving at everyone from the back

PULLED UNDER

of an antique car. Next we see Ben and the kids from summer camp marching alongside the float for the Parks and Recreation Department.

The kids are wearing various athletic uniforms and carrying sports gear to represent the many activities that the department sponsors. Apparently, though, some of them have gotten tired and handed their gear off to Ben. At the moment he's carrying a surfboard, a baseball bat, a football helmet, and a bag of golf clubs. Considering that they're only halfway through the route, you've got to wonder how much more he can carry.

"He's going to pass out before the end of the parade," jokes my mom.

I don't know the proper protocol when your boyfriend (can I call him that? I think so) marches past you in a parade, so I just smile and do a coy fingers only wave when I see him. He's trying to say something to me, but I can't hear him over the revving engines from the tiny motorcycles.

"What?" I ask.

He rushes over to us, short of breath and frantic. "I need your help. Can you take this?" he says as he hands me the surfboard.

"You want me to take it to the shop and hold it for you?"

He gives me an incredulous look. "No, I want you to carry it alongside me and march in the parade."

"You want *me* . . . in the parade?"

He looks desperate. "Yes!"

"You really don't get the whole 'introvert' thing, do you?"

Before he can answer, he has to chase after a kid dressed as a football player who's wandering off in the wrong direction.

115

I stand on the curb frozen by fear. I'm totally mortified by the idea of marching in a parade in front of, you know, people. That's when I feel a hand push me from behind and make the decision for me. I stumble out into the street and it's too late—I am in the parade. I turn around expecting to see that it was Sophie but am surprised to discover that it's my mom.

"He asked you to help and he's really cute," she says. "Have fun."

Fun?

I'm a little bit like a deer caught in the headlights until I see Rebecca, the shy girl from the surfing class. She's dressed in a soccer uniform, holding a ball in one hand and waving to the spectators with the other.

"Hey, Izzy," she says when she sees me there. "Isn't this great?"

I'm not sure, but I think I just got schooled by the nine-year-old version of me.

"You bet," I say. "Why don't you walk with me?"

Rebecca and I walk together for a couple of blocks and I begin to feel less self-conscious. Once that happens, I help Ben corral the kids, and we start doing a little routine in which we stop, stutter step, and start marching again all in unison. They get a kick out of it, and it stops them from wandering off so much. By the time we reach the bandshell, we've got the step down and I'm actually enjoying myself.

"Thank you," he says as we reach the parking lot. He just drops all the gear that's been handed to him.

"You're welcome," I say.

I give him a moment to catch his breath, and once he does, I ask, "Do you have time for lunch?"

He looks around at the mass of kids. "I need to wait here until their parents pick them up."

I think it through. "How about if I get the food and meet you back here? Hopefully by then you'll be free."

"That sounds great," he says.

I head over to Angie's Subs. Luckily Angie's daughter is a friend and she helps me sidestep the mob. I order a foot-long Italian Special with extra Peruvian sauce (I don't know what's in Peruvian sauce, but wow!), and twenty minutes later Ben and I are splitting it in the arctic chill that is the Parks and Rec office. He clears off some space at the end of his desk, and we set up our little dining area.

"What would you like to drink?" he says as he holds up two bottles of water. "Water or water?"

I play along and scratch my chin as I consider my choice. "Water, please."

"Excellent choice." He hands me one of the bottles and sits down across from me. "So what do you think of my fancy desk?" He raps the metal top with his knuckle.

"I like it," I say. "It's not only cheap, it's also messy."

"It's not messy," he says defensively. "This may look disorganized, but all of these stacks mean something to me. That one's for summer camp. That one has all the permission slips, and those two are for the King of the Beach and the Sand Castle Dance.

"By the way, in case you change your mind"—he takes a sheet of paper off one of the piles and dangles it in front of me—"here's an application for the King of the Beach."

I know he's trying to be supportive, but the thought of

competing in the King of the Beach is simply terrifying to me. I wish he'd stop pushing it. The Sand Castle Dance, however, is a completely different matter.

"Enough with the King of the Beach," I say, ignoring it. "You have a better chance getting me interested in the Sand Castle Dance. It's kind of like our summer prom and a pretty big deal for us."

He nods as he swallows a bite of his sandwich. "I know. I hope I can get a good date. You think Kayla would go with me?"

"That's not even funny," I say as I slug him in the shoulder.

"Ow, ow, ow," he says, rubbing it. "I was only joking."

"Well, now you know better than to tell stupid jokes."

He rubs it some more, and I realize I packed a harder punch than I had intended.

"Do you know why I am working so hard preparing for the Sand Castle Dance?"

"No," I say. "And I'm not sure I care."

"You should care. I'm working so hard because I made a deal with my boss. If I take care of all the prep—which includes finding the band and arranging the decorations—then I don't have to work that night. I get to spend the whole evening at the dance with . . . wait for it . . . *my girlfriend.*"

I just let that word linger in the air for a moment. It's got kind of a musical ring to it.

"How do you know I want to go?" I say. "The word on the street this year is that it's being planned by a guy who doesn't know what he's doing. It's probably going to be lame."

He gives me a look. "I'm going to let that slide. But only because you got this incredible sandwich."

"Speaking of dates," I say, trying out yet another unskillful segue, "what are your plans for fireworks tonight?"

"Some oohing, some aahing, nothing special planned," he says. "I thought you had to work."

"About that . . ."

I tell him all about Surf Sisters and the surprise announcement. He seems truly upset that the store's going to close, and I can tell he's trying to figure out a solution. He's not going to come up with one, but he wins points with me for trying. I also tell him about the plan to watch the fireworks from the roof of the shop.

"So, you wanna be my date?"

"You and me on a date?" he says playfully. "In front of all the girls at Surf Sisters?"

"Yes."

"Gee, that doesn't sound the least bit intimidating. Isn't there somewhere we could watch where I'd feel less out of place? You know, like in a pit of wild panthers or something like that?"

I lean across the desk and wag a finger in his face. "I just marched in a parade for you. A parade through crowds of people! Don't even get me started about feeling out of place."

"Okay, okay," he says. "I'll do it."

I hear a new band being announced at the bandshell and I panic.

"What time is it?"

"Two o'clock," he says.

"We gotta go."

"I've still got ten minutes for my lunch break," he replies.

"The Founding Fathers are playing," I reply. "I don't want to miss my song."

We hurry out of the office and get to the bandshell just as they start to play it.

"Isabel is watching like a princess from the mountains . . ."

Ben smiles when he realizes what's going on. "Very nice," he says. "Your dad has a good voice."

We listen for a while, and even though I've heard it countless times, this is the first time I take notice of one particular line.

"With a whisper of her sadness in the passing of the summer . . ."

As a girl I'd always focused on the princess line, but now the idea of sadness and the passing of summer has new meaning. That's in the future though. Right now, I'm just going to focus on enjoying it.

*D*uring my shift at Surf Sisters I have moments of nostalgia, sadness, laughter, and anger. We all do. It's just impossible for us to believe that such an important part of our life is coming to an end. Mickey and Mo try to keep our spirits up, but it's hard to separate the job part from the surfing and the friendship parts. In a way we're lucky that it's the Fourth because we're so busy dealing with customers, we don't have much time to dwell on the negative.

Ben arrives right before closing. He's made a point of going home and switching out of his work clothes and is now rocking the whole islander look with a pair of khaki shorts, a graphic tee, and flip-flops.

"Badger Ben sure doesn't look like he's from Wisconsin any-more," Sophie jokes with a friendly nudge.

I give her a look. "I thought we decided 'Badger Ben' didn't work."

She nods. "I just thought I'd give it one last try."

He walks over to me, does a double check of everyone in the room, and whispers conspiratorially, "I'm the only dude here. Are you sure this is okay?"

Despite his best efforts to keep these concerns quiet, Mo has overheard him. She comes up from behind and whispers into his ear, "She's sure."

Startled, Ben turns around to see her smiling.

"We always like to have a couple guys around," she continues, "just in case any menial jobs come along."

I think this is Mo's way of testing him. A lot of boys might get defensive or feel intimidated. But Ben just goes with the flow and plays along.

"Well, if that's the case," he says, "I think my vast experi-ence doing menial chores for Parks and Rec makes me more than qualified. Do you have any playground vomit that needs cleaning up?"

"No," she says, pleased by his response. "But the night's still young, so you might want to check in with me later."

Despite this confidence, I'm sure Ben feels a little more comfortable when a few more guys show up. This includes Mickey's husband and—surprise, surprise—Nicole's longtime crush, Cody Bell.

"Did Nicole invite him?" Sophie asks.

"She must have," I say. "Probably today at the parade."

Sophie beams with pride. "Aren't my girls growing up?"

I shoot her a look and hope that Ben hasn't overheard. Sophie, meanwhile, walks over toward Nicole and Cody. From past experience I know that's she going in as a wingman to make sure that Nicole doesn't get too nervous.

"What was that about?" Ben asks.

"Just Sophie being Sophie," I say before I quickly change the subject. "Wanna see the roof?"

"Sure."

I guide Ben into the storeroom, where I pull a set of folding stairs down from the ceiling. A generation ago these led to the attic, but the roof has been remodeled and includes a full wooden deck with a wraparound railing and spectacular 360-degree views.

"I get to go up here every two hours to update the surf report," I tell him as we reach the top and open the door to the deck. "My reward is the view."

"Okay, wow!" he says when he steps out and sees what I'm talking about.

Night has fallen over the ocean; the lights along the board-walk and the pier are coming alive as the moon casts a silvery wash across the water. It is incredibly romantic, and when I see that we are all alone, I sneak a quick but meaningful kiss.

"That's why you wanted to be the first ones up?" he says.

My smile confirms my guilt, although I admit to nothing.

"I don't know what you're talking about," I say. "So what did you think of Independence Day Pearl Beach style?"

"Different from Wisconsin, that's for sure."

"How do you guys celebrate up there? Milking cows? Churning butter?" I joke.

"I'm going to ignore that because today you came to my rescue," he says. "I know you're not a big fan of being in the spotlight, so marching in a parade could not have been fun."

"Fun? No, it was not fun. It was *terrifying*." I'm only half joking, but we both laugh.

"I do appreciate it."

Pretty soon everyone else makes their way up onto the roof, and we all enjoy some yummy teriyaki chicken skewers that Mickey's husband picked up at Chicken Stix, a kebab shack a couple blocks down the beach. As you'd expect from a Surf Sisters get-together, it's pretty low key and mellow. The funny thing is that no one is talking about the one thing that's on everybody's mind. Then, a few minutes before the fireworks are scheduled to begin, Mickey takes a sip from her glass of wine and addresses us all.

"We'd like to thank you for coming tonight. Back when Mo and I were young girls—way before there was an actual deck up here—our dad would bring us out on the roof every Fourth of July. We'd lie with our backs against the wooden shingles and watch the fireworks go off. We thought we had the best view on the island, and I think you'd have to agree that we were right. So, as we celebrate this tradition one final time, I'd like to propose a toast to the man who started it."

She holds up her glass, and everyone else holds up whatever they're drinking. (For me it's sweet tea.) "To Steady Eddie."

"Steady Eddie," everyone says with enthusiasm.

"King of the Beach," adds Mo.

It's the last part that punches me in the gut. I think about the Surf City float in the parade with its King of the Beach sitting on a throne surrounded by Kayla and her friends. It represents the opposite of everything that Steady Eddie embodied. The opposite of everything I believe in. This is the thought that nags me as we watch the fireworks.

The show lasts for about twenty minutes and really lives up to its billing as *spectacular*. I love the way the colored lights reflect off the water. Standing on the roof, I see that the boardwalk sparkles almost as much. It's great, but even still, I can't get rid of that nagging feeling.

"What are you thinking?" Ben asks toward the end.

"That it looks beautiful," I respond.

"No, I mean, what are you thinking about?" He gives me a look that says he knows something is on my mind. "Be honest—is it a problem that I'm here?"

Apparently, I'm not only bad at reading signs but also at giving them.

"Absolutely not," I say, trying to speak loud enough so that he can hear but soft enough so that no one else can. "It's amazing that you're here. Amazing."

"Are you sure? 'Cause it doesn't look like it."

"I'm more than sure. It's just that I'm upset about all of this." I gesture to the others on the deck with us. "I wish there was something I could do."

He goes to say something, but then he stops himself. Instead, he just looks at me and smiles. Then he puts his arm around my shoulder and squeezes me in closer for a moment.

Maybe it's the nostalgic display of fireworks, or maybe it's the wonderful realization that I, shy Izzy Lucas, am cuddling with my fabuloso boyfriend—I still can't believe that part—that makes me wonder what it would be like if I actually was the type of person who had the courage to compete in the King of the Beach. Better yet, what if all of us girls entered and shredded the waves as one last great send-off for Surf Sisters?

"What are you smiling about?" Ben asks.

I didn't realize I was smiling, but I dare not even say it aloud. Instead I answer, "Nothing . . . everything."

Moments later, the grand finale starts to blanket the sky with color and light, and the noise drowns out any possibility of him pursuing the subject further. Surprisingly, I can't shake the daydream of all of us competing. As a team. As Surf Sisters.

"Hmmmm," I say out loud for no particular reason.

As I look at the fireworks, my mind keeps turning it over. Then, when the final ribbons of color fade into the night and the smoke and smell of powder waft over us, I wonder if this is something we should do. I have found a boyfriend. I have marched in a parade. Could I possibly compete in the King of the Beach? Could all of us? We could go out with a fight. Our very own grand finale.

The party has reached its end, and people are beginning to hug one another and say good-bye. I start to breathe faster as I wage an internal debate. There's no way to go to the register to get a verdict on this one. I have to make this decision all on my own. And as it is with most decisions you dread, the difficulty isn't so much figuring out the answer, which is obvious, but deciding if you can face the consequences.

"Wait!" I say as the others start to leave. They all stop what they're doing and all eyes turn to me. I freeze for a moment as I reconsider my decision one last time.

"What's the matter, Iz?" asks Mo.

"What's the matter?" I say, incredulous. "The store's closing. That's the matter."

Her eyes are watery and consoling at the same time. "I know, sweetie."

"We can't just let it happen," I say. "We can't just keep coming to work and act like we're happy as we count the days until it's over. It's not fair to Steady Eddie and it's not fair to you."

Mo wraps me in a hug as tears run down her face. "I don't know what else we can do," she says.

"I know," I say with a deep breath. Then it hits me. I want to do this for Surf Sisters, but I also want to do it for me. I'm tired of standing off to the side. I'm ready to be noticed. "We can win the King of the Beach and get your trophies back."

Over the next week I develop a new routine in my daily life. Today fits the profile perfectly. It starts in the morning when I wake up early and head to the beach with my surfboard under my arm. This may not seem like a change, considering that I surf most mornings anyway, but now my approach is totally different. First of all, these sessions are not about finding my Zen place and becoming one with the ocean. They are full-out training sessions. I'm working to build endurance and strength.

I'm practicing technique and I'm challenging myself to develop the moves I'll need to do to get the judges to notice me.

Secondly, I've started to surf the pier. Every break, which is what surfers call a specific location, is unique. The more you surf it the better you know its secrets. The King of the Beach is held at the pier, and by the time the contest begins, I want to know each and every inch of it. The problem with surfing there, however, is that it's the most popular break on Pearl Beach. This means there are always other surfers there, even in the early morning hours, and I have to work on my "surfs well with others" skills.

The other girls from the shop are coming down to the pier too, but we are keeping our plans on the down low. One thing—the only thing?—working in our favor is the element of surprise. Surf City has walked away with the team championship every year for more than a decade. On the morning of the competition, their only concern will be figuring out which one of their guys is going to win the individual crown. We don't want them to be just overconfident about the team title. We want them to think it's automatic.

That means we don't arrive together. We don't wear any Surf Sisters gear. And we never talk about the contest. In fact, we don't really talk much at all. Well, except for one of us.

"So," Sophie says as we sit side by side straddling our boards and waiting for the next set. "Have you told Ben that you love him yet?"

I don't even dignify this with so much as a glance in her direction.

"It's obvious that you feel that way," she continues. "You love, love, love him."

"Stop it," I say, still trying to ignore her.

"Have you said that you can't imagine being without him and that you're going to follow him back to Wisconsin so you can live on a big dairy farm together?"

"Do you mind?" I say, finally turning to her. "I'm trying to surf here."

She nods. "And I'm trying to make you better at it."

I flash her my skeptical eyes. "How does annoying me make me better?"

"I'm not only annoying you, I'm also teaching you the importance of not letting anyone distract you. You know . . . like I just did."

"What are you talking about?"

Before I even finish my question, she has turned and is paddling. By the time I figure out what's happening, it's already too late. There's a beautiful wave coming, and she has completely shut me out and stolen my position. Normally I surf by myself or with my dad, and there are no distractions. That won't be the case during the King of the Beach, as Sophie reminds me fifteen minutes later when we're back in the lineup.

"There's no margin for error," she says. "Wave selection plays a big part in who wins and who doesn't. You can't afford to miss any good ones because you're distracted."

I nod my agreement and remind her that we need to keep the talking to a minimum.

After my morning session I go home and crash in my bed for a power nap. Of course, before I do that I check to see if I have any texts from Ben. Even when he's working with the campers, he usually manages to send off a steady stream during the day.

After my nap I head in to Surf Sisters and work my shift. Mickey and Mo have put me on the same shift almost every day. They said it was to help me establish my workout routine, but I think secretly they're trying to have my hours line up with Ben's as much as possible. (See what I mean? They totally rock.)

The vibe at the shop is completely different from the way it was a week ago. Everyone is excited about Surf Sisters competing in the King of the Beach. I think the important part is that it gives us something positive to think about and takes our minds off the fact that the store is closing. Even the fact that we're keeping it a secret gives the whole thing a spy vs. spy feel.

There is one massive problem, however, that nobody's talking about. I know I'm certainly not going to bring it up. But . . . even though I'm the one who came up with the idea and I enjoy our secret sisterhood and backroom plotting, I don't see how we can possibly win the contest.

The Surf City team isn't just good. It's amazing.

Consider this little nugget. Surf City sponsors ten of the twenty highest rated surfers in the state. A team can submit up to eight surfers in the competition. That means two of the best surfers in all of Florida won't even make it on their team. Meanwhile, Mickey and Mo are the only people on our team who have even been in a tournament before. And, while I don't doubt their greatness, the two of them are over fifty and haven't competed in decades.

It is this sobering thought that's going through my mind as I pull down the folding stairs and climb up onto the roof of the store. Every two hours I'm responsible for updating the surf report we put up on our Web site and on the sign that hangs outside our door. That means I get to go up on the roof with my binoculars, check the waves, and read the thermometer and wind gauge. It's like I'm a TV weather girl, except without the hair spray and a perky nickname.

I'm looking through the binoculars when I hear a voice.

"How's it looking?"

I turn around and see that Mo has followed me up.

"Not great. The waves are one to two feet, ankle to knee high. Small, clean lines crumbling through. The wind is five to ten knots north-northeast."

"Oh, to live in Hawaii," she says, bringing a smile to both of us. "But I guess the struggle makes us appreciate it that much more."

She's talking about the fact that Florida waves are nothing compared to their relatives in California and Hawaii. I love it here, but if you want to surf in the Sunshine State you have to work at it and learn how to make a lot out of a little.

"My dad and I have talked about going out there as a graduation present," I say. "The plan is basically to live in a tent on the North Shore of Oahu and surf until we drop."

"You gotta love dads who teach their girls to surf," she says with an appreciative nod. "But don't forget that these waves gave the world Kelly Slater." Born and raised in Florida, Kelly Slater is considered by many to be the greatest surfer of all time. I've got his poster on my wall.

"What brings you roof-side?" I ask.

"The view," she replies, "and you."

"Why me?"

It dawns on me that we're in virtually the exact same spot that we were standing on the night of the Fourth, when she had tears in her eyes and I got the ball rolling on this whole competition thing.

"The last few days I've been out on the pier watching you girls practice," she says.

"Really? I haven't seen you there."

"We're supposed to be keeping it on the down low, so I've been hiding out," she says with a shrug. "But there's one thing that can't be hidden—your talent. I don't think you have any idea how good you are."

"Really?"

"Really," she says.

"How good do you think I am?"

"Beyond slamming. Way better than I was at your age."

I give her a skeptical smile. "Nice try."

"What do you mean?"

"You're trying to build me up for the contest," I say.

She shakes her head. "No, I'm trying to make sure you appreciate your talent. That you understand that it exists."

Praise like this coming from Mo means a lot. Other than my father, she's taught me more about surfing than anyone.

"That's hard to believe, but thanks," I tell her. "You don't know how much that means to me coming from you."

"That's the part I thought you'd like hearing," she says, changing the tone of the conversation. "Now I'm going to tell you something that you won't."

I brace myself.

"In a few months Surf Sisters will no longer be here. But you will still only be sixteen years old. You have a future in this sport."

"What's the part that I don't want to hear?"

She pauses for a moment before saying it. "Surf City doesn't have a single ranked girl on their team. Once they see what you've got, they'd be fools not to jump at the chance to sponsor you . . . and you'd be a fool not to take it."

I cannot believe what I'm hearing. This is like Santa Claus coming down your chimney and telling you that there's no such thing as Christmas. Mo cannot be telling me to join up with Surf City.

"There's no way I would ever do that. Not with them. The only reason I'm even competing in the first place is because I want to beat them."

"Well, that's too bad," she says. "You shouldn't be surfing because of them. And you shouldn't be surfing because of us. You should be doing it for you. I've been watching you and I've noticed a complete evolution in your style. You've found a spark and you should see where it takes you. You know what I think about their store. But there's no denying that their team is outstanding . . . just like you."

"You're right," I say, more confused than anything. "I don't want to hear this."

I don't wait for a response. I just walk past her and head back down the stairs.

*I*t was completely out of left field," I say as I tell Ben about my conversation with Mo. "In a weird way it felt like she was dumping me."

"Don't be ridiculous," Ben says as he tries to scrape the wax off an old surfboard. "Mo loves you. The last thing she'd do is dump you."

Despite my mood regarding Mo and our conversation, this brings us to the best part of my new daily routine. If I'm not training or working at the shop, then the odds are pretty good that I'm with Ben. We've done something together every night this week. We've gone bowling (I was pathetic), played putt putt (I beat him on the last hole and was surprisingly obnoxious about it), and just hung out and watched TV. (He's already got me hooked on British mystery shows.)

We've also started basic surfing lessons. For the first few he borrowed Black Beauty, which is what my dad calls his favorite shortboard, and now Ben's purchased one of his own. It's an old quad fish that he dubbed Blue Boy in keeping with my dad's naming tradition. It's been a while since Blue Boy has been in the water, so I'm teaching him how to strip off the old wax and start anew. He's got it lying across two sawhorses and is bent over, hard at work.

"How's this?" he asks as he scrapes the last bit.

"Good," I say, inspecting it. "Very good."

I hand him a bar of Mr. Zog's that I picked up at the shop.

"Now start to apply the base coat. Make straight lines from one rail to the other directly perpendicular to the stringer." The rails are the side edges, and the stringer is a thin strip of wood that runs down the center of the board and makes it stronger.

"Like this?" he asks as he carefully rubs the bar of wax across the board.

"Exactly," I say.

I like watching him work. He does this little thing where he bites the left side of his lower lip when he concentrates, and it's beyond cute. It's also a sure sign that he is trying to do it perfectly. It's a total contrast to the goofy way he is around the kids during camp.

"You know Mo was just looking out for you," he says. "She doesn't want you in denial. She wants to make sure you can move on after the summer."

When he says this I realize why the conversation with Mo is bothering me so much. It's not just the fact that she thinks I would represent Surf City. It's the fact that she is already encouraging me to find something new after the summer. She's trying to make it all right for me to replace Surf Sisters. And the problem is, if she can persuade me, then so can Ben.

"Is that something you can relate to?" I ask pointedly.

He starts to answer but stops when he realizes that I've set a trap.

"They're two very different things," he says, choosing his words carefully. "But, yes, I can relate to worrying about you in September."

I put my hand on his hand to stop him for a moment, and he looks up at me.

"When the time comes for you to go back home, do not be like Mo. Don't encourage me to meet another boy and replace you. I knew what I was getting into when I kissed you on the pier. I'm a big girl and I know that September will come. But we said this was going to be like the perfect wave. We're going to ride it until the very end and not worry about the next one."

He stands upright and carefully looks at me. I can tell he's debating what he should say next. In my brain I know that he will go home and find someone new. And, theoretically, I know that I will also find someone. But, in my heart, I can't bear the thought right now.

"Okay," he says quietly. "I promise I won't."

Then, completely out of nowhere, I start to cry. Not big sobs, but steady tears that slide down my cheeks one by one. The fact that I'm embarrassed about this emotional display only makes me cry that much more.

We're on opposite sides of the surfboard, so he reaches across and holds my hand as he navigates his way around the sawhorse and wraps me in his arms. I cry a little harder as I bury my face in his chest, and he gently strokes my back. I start to apologize for being such a drama queen, but he just shushes me and holds me tighter.

"It's okay, baby."

Just hearing him say that fills me with this warmth. In a weird way I've never felt worse and better at the same time. I close my eyes and listen to the sound of his heart beating.

*O*kay, I'd like to officially apologize for *whatever* that was earlier," I say as we walk along the beach a few hours later. There's only a sliver of a moon hanging over the water, but stars fill the night sky and it's stunning.

"You don't have to apologize," he says. "You're allowed to show emotion. That's part of the package."

"Well, it was both unexpected and unprecedented," I explain.

"Although I will say that there was a sort of emotional cleansing quality to the whole thing."

"Is that your way of saying you feel better now?" he asks.

"Well, if you want the SparkNotes version, yes."

"I am perfectly happy with the SparkNotes version," he says. "But also more than willing to go into greater detail if that makes you happier."

I stop and put my hands on my hips in mock protest. "Are you saying that it doesn't matter or just that you don't care?"

"Neither," he answers as he skillfully snakes a hand through my arm and pulls me closer to him. "I'm saying that I'm here for you however you need me to be."

I give him a playful nod and counter, "You're a slick talker, Ben Taylor. You always seem to say just the right thing."

"And is that a problem?"

"It kind of is."

"Let me get this straight," he replies, looking down at me. "Are you now criticizing me for *not* saying the wrong thing?"

"The female mind is quite the riddle," I joke. "Besides, I'm not criticizing you. I'm just keeping you on your toes."

"How about I keep you on your toes instead?"

He wraps his arms around my waist and lifts me ever so slightly, so that now I'm on my tiptoes—the perfect kissing height. At first I think it's going to be a peck, but our lips linger and I close my eyes. The instant it's over, I pick up the conversation where I left off.

"See what I mean? You always say the right thing. That's suspicious, don't you think?"

I break free from his arms and sprint ahead of him.

"Where are you going?"

"I thought you were a runner," I call back. "Yet I'm the one winning the race to the lifeguard stand!"

Up ahead of us is a lifeguard stand. It looks like a giant high chair that's twelve feet tall and made out of bright orange two-by-fours. I've got a good head start, but he quickly closes the gap and we both get there at the same time.

"I won," I say, catching my breath.

"Hardly," he laughs. "It was a tie and you cheated more than a little bit."

"That's not what I meant. I won because I got you right where I want you," I say as I climb up into the seat. It is big and roomy enough for a lifeguard to sit with all of his gear. Or, in other words, it's the perfect size for two people to squeeze into.

"So this was your plan all along," Ben says as he climbs up and slides in next to me.

"Bwahahaha," I reply with an evil master villain's laugh. "And you, Ben Taylor, were just my puppet."

This high up, there's a cool night breeze that makes it perfect for snuggling. I've known that couples do this and I have always imagined what it would be like. (Spoiler alert: It's awesome!) Ben puts his arm around me and I slide up next to him, and we just snap together perfectly like pieces in a jigsaw puzzle.

"Are we even allowed to be up here?" he asks.

"Of course we are," I say. "It's for lifeguards during the day, couples at night. It really fits right into the whole 'reduce, reuse, recycle' philosophy that we encourage here at the beach. Very multipurpose and good for the environment."

I rest my head on his shoulder and look out at the sea. More than a minute passes without either one of us saying a word. We just listen to the slow and steady music of the waves washing up on the beach and then pulling back into the ocean. Everything at this moment is perfect. So of course that means I have to screw it up.

"Can I ask you something?"

"There's an ominous beginning," he says.

"Whose idea was it to break up?"

"What are you talking about?" he asks. "We're not breaking up."

"No. I mean between you and Beth. Whose idea was it to break up?"

He lets go of me and turns so that his back is against the side of the chair. I may not be fluent in body language, but I can tell he's not thrilled with the question. "Why would you even ask that? Everything about this moment is perfect. Excuse me, *was* perfect."

"I know."

"So why would you ask that?"

"I told you. The female mind is complex."

"It's not a joke, Izzy."

"And I'm not joking. I know it doesn't make sense to you, but this is all new to me. I've never had a boyfriend. Nothing even close to one. That means you know every single thing about my past relationship history. So when we're sitting like this and everything's perfect, you know what's going on in my mind."

"Trust me when I say that I have no idea what's going on in your mind."

"Okay, that's a fair point," I answer. "But all I know about Beth is that she was beautiful and wonderful and everyone thought you two were a perfect couple."

"And after I told you that, you ignored me for two weeks," he says. "In fact, just a few blocks up from this very spot you told me that you couldn't be the girl I talked to about other girls."

"Things are different now," I reply. "And to be honest, since the only things I know about Beth are how wonderful she is, a little part of me could stand to hear how it ended."

I really don't know what it is about me that takes perfect moments and twists them into psychodramas, but I can't help it. I am who I am.

There's just enough moonlight on his face for me to tell that he's biting the left side of his lower lip. He's in deep thought mode, so I stop talking. Finally, after what seems like forever, he responds.

"It was my idea. We were out by the lake. She was talking about the prom and how important it was and how it would be this signature moment in our relationship. I mean, I know it's a big deal, but it is just a dance. She was obsessed with what table we were going to sit at, where we were going to go for photographs, and I just couldn't get excited about it. Maybe it's because I was in a pissy mood about my parents, but I just couldn't. Then, somewhere in the middle of it all, I just knew it was over."

He stops for a moment and takes a deep breath.

"Some of my friends said that I should've just hung on until it was time for me to come to Florida, but I couldn't do that to her. She didn't deserve to be strung along. So I told her that I was really sorry but I couldn't go to the prom with her and that we couldn't see each other anymore."

"You dumped her right before the prom?" I say, almost feeling sorry for her.

He nods. "I know. I'm a terrible person."

"You're not a terrible person," I say. "The timing was unfortunate, but if that's how you felt, you did the right thing."

"Just for the record, Beth did not agree with your take on it. She made sure everyone knew how much it was not the right thing. I can't blame her, I guess. Somehow she did manage to bounce back and find a guy who was more than happy to sit at the right table and smile his way through God knows how many pictures. He's a good guy, actually. I hope it works for them."

There's a pause. Which means of course that I have to keep pressing the issue.

"How did you know it was over?" I ask. "You said that in the middle of it all you just knew."

He turns his head to the side and shakes it in disbelief. "You really want me to tell you this stuff?"

I nod. "I know. I can't help it."

"Somewhere in the middle of all the discussion it dawned on me that it really was more than a dance for her. She sounded like my sister did when she was planning her wedding. And that's when I realized that Beth was actually in love with me. We weren't just dating. It wasn't just some high school thing. She loved me."

"And you weren't in love with her?"

"No," he says. "I might have been in love with the idea of her. I might have loved the attention. But I didn't love her, and it seemed incredibly unfair for me to let someone love me when I didn't feel the same way in return."

Now here's a problem.

I have no doubt that I am completely in love with Ben. Not the idea of him. Not the concept of him. Him. I've even wondered if I should tell him. But now I think the smart thing to do is to keep that secret to myself. Instead, I lie to him for the first and hopefully only time.

"Lucky for us we don't have to worry about that," I say, trying to sound convincing. "We both know that this is just for the summer."

He doesn't really answer. Instead he just kind of nods, and I lay my head on his shoulder again. It takes a moment, but he puts his arm around me.

It's quiet for a while and we just sit there. I can't help but think I'm doing everything wrong in this relationship. I don't know why I asked about Beth, but the truth is I really felt like I needed to know that stuff. I put my hand over to rest it on his chest, but he pulls back, and I worry that he's about to tell me that I'm just not worth the headache. But instead, he says something completely unexpected.

"Is that a body?"

"What?"

"Over there," he says, pointing down the beach about a hundred feet. "I just saw that dark shadow move. I think it might be a body."

I look, and when I see it, I know instantly what it is.

"Ooh, ooh, ooh, it's not a body," I say, trying to contain my excitement. "Follow me."

I quickly climb down the lifeguard stand, and he's right behind me.

"I just saw it move again," he says as he tries to keep up. "What is it?"

I stop and turn to him. "A turtle!"

I grab him by the hand and we race down the beach together until we get close. We slow down and stop when we're about fifteen feet away from where a massive sea turtle is slowly dragging herself across the sand. She's three feet long and weighs nearly two hundred pounds.

We keep our distance, and I put my finger over my lips and say, "Only whisper, and don't cross her path."

He nods and replies, "She's huge."

"She's a loggerhead coming ashore to lay her eggs."

A bank of clouds drifts by and reveals the moon, its light dancing across the turtle's red and brown shell.

"She's going to lay them over there," I say, pointing toward the sand dunes. "Don't disturb her and don't let her see any lights, like your phone; it can confuse her."

"Okay."

We spend the next thirty minutes watching her. It's a lumbering crawl up onto the edge of the dunes, and you can't help but marvel at her determination. When she starts to scrape away an area with her front flippers, I tug on Ben's hand and we quietly loop around to get a closer look. She uses her hind flippers to dig a nest and then fills it with dozens of ping-pong-ball-sized eggs.

"Oh my God!" Ben whispers, being careful not to disturb her. "It's amazing."

I nod in agreement.

Once she's done laying eggs, she uses her flippers to cover the nest back up, and then she begins the laborious task of dragging herself back to the ocean. We keep watching, but we move far enough away so that we can talk at regular volume.

"She was born here in Pearl Beach," I say.

Ben gives me a skeptical look. "How could you possibly know that?"

"Because sea turtles always come back to the same beach where they were born. It's in their DNA."

He thinks about this for a moment and then says, "Like me."

"What do you mean?" I ask.

"I came back to the beach where I was born too."

I laugh. "That's true. You did."

"What will happen with the eggs?"

"In about six weeks they'll hatch, and the little turtles will poke out of the sand and look for the moon. That's the key."

"What do you mean?"

"That's how they find their way," I explain. "During hatching season all the houses on the beach keep their lights off. That way the babies can find the reflection of the moon on the water and know where to go. Then they'll scramble back toward the ocean and disappear."

"That sounds amazing," he says. "We've got to come and watch."

"Will you still be here then?" I ask.

I didn't mean it as anything more than a basic question. But, given the conversations of tonight, it carries some emotional baggage.

"Yes," he says quietly. "That should be my last week."

I've already been enough of a drama queen for one night, so I decide it's time for me to put on the brave face. I take his hand in mine and our fingers intertwine.

"Perfect," I say. "We'll come out and watch them together. You're going to love it."

I'm a total moron," I say as I slip on a blue cami and look at it in the fitting room mirror.

"You're being too hard on yourself," Nicole calls out from the next stall. "I'm sure you're exaggerating."

"I don't think so," I reply. "I cried. I grilled him about breaking up with his girlfriend. Twice. It was basically a horror movie."

"And then you were saved by a sea turtle," she says. "Now there's a twist on the normal environmental dynamic."

"No kidding. Who knows how much damage I could have done if she hadn't rescued me?"

"Let me see the outfit," she says.

I step out and she looks it over. I'm wearing a lace shirt over the cami and a pair of white jeans.

"It's nice," she says. "But I like it more with the skirt than the jeans."

"That's a relief. I was worried the jeans would look better and then I'd have to make it through a whole meal without spilling anything on them."

"But it's okay to spill something on the skirt?" she asks with a raised eyebrow.

"No, but the white denim is just asking for it. That looks amazing on you, by the way."

Nic's trying on a floral baby doll dress with black leggings that really take advantage of her height.

"You sure? They're not too tight?"

I shake my head. "You know what Sophie says."

"There's no such thing as too tight," we both answer in unison.

The one drawback of life on Pearl Beach is that the nearest mall is almost an hour away. The two of us have made the trip because we've found ourselves in an unexpected situation. Namely, for the first time in our lives we have boyfriends. As a result we're both looking for a little wardrobe pick-me-up. Of course we don't have much money to spend, so we're only looking on the sale racks.

"It was a lot easier when I stuck to dark colors and solids," Nicole says. "You know, in order to blend in while I stalked him."

"Good times," I say as we head back into our stalls. "Speaking of which, how are things now that you and Cody actually talk?"

"Way more fun," she says. "Although we're taking it kind of slow. We only go out once, maybe twice a week."

"Are you okay with that?"

"Absolutely," she says. "The slow helps because it's all so new to me. I feel like I need relationship training wheels."

"That makes two of us. I don't think I can count on that turtle rescuing me every time I start to spiral out of control."

"Yeah, not so much."

We step back out and now she is wearing a graphic tank top and a high-low skirt that looked like nothing special on the rack but incredible on her.

"I should never shop for clothes with you," I say.

"Why?"

"Because of the whole six-foot-supermodel thing. I feel like Stumpy McGee."

"Who's Stumpy McGee?" she says with a laugh.

"I don't know. I just made her up. But he cannot pull off any of the looks that you've been rocking."

"Well, you're not Stumpy McGee because everything you've tried on looks adorable. Besides, I could never get away with wearing those," she says, pointing at the pair of boyfriend jeans I'm trying on.

"Sure you could," I say. "Except on you'd they'd be capris."

We both laugh and I realize that this is the beauty of having a lifelong best friend. You can give each other garbage, boost each other's confidence, and look out for each other all in consecutive sentences.

I remember learning how to ride a bike, and I'm still learning how to drive. (I've got my permit, but I do not feel a rush to get my license.) But I don't remember learning how to surf. It was too long ago, and that's a shame because if I did remember, it might help me teach Ben. Today is his first lesson on his new board, and he wants to make it memorable.

"It's time we go out where the grown-ups surf," he says.

Up until now, he's been using my dad's board and I've done the same lessons with him that I do with the summer campers. We've stayed in shallow water, and he's only caught waves after they've broken. It's a great way to learn, but now he's ready to go out beyond the white water. At least, he thinks he's ready. Just in case he's not, I'm right alongside him reminding him of each step along the way.

First we wade out into the water until it's waist deep, and then we lie out on our boards and start paddling. The part that surprises people the most is how hard it is to paddle. It looks like it should be easy, but it's not. You have to get used to balancing, and you have to work hard to go against the tide.

"Don't forget to duck dive," I tell him.

Duck diving is what you do when you paddle into a wave that's coming right at you. The way you're supposed to do it is to speed up right until you're about two feet away and then push the board down under the water and let the wave pass over you. If you forget, the wave slams your board into you.

Apparently he didn't hear me, because he forgets.

"My bad," he says. "I was supposed to do something there, wasn't I?"

"Duck dive!" I say, louder this time as another wave approaches. Now he picks up speed, and although it's not particularly graceful, he manages to get under the wave and pop out on the other side.

"Like that?" he asks.

I ignore the lack of grace and focus on the positive. "Yes. But next time try holding the rails tighter and push down with your whole body."

"Got it," he says.

We dive under a couple more waves before we get out beyond the break to where the water is calm. The look on his face is priceless. He is loving it.

"Now you need to straddle your board like this," I say, demonstrating.

"Do I look at the ocean or at the beach?" he asks.

"Did you not listen to any of the lessons I gave you?"

"I tried," he says. "But it's hard to pay attention because you're so pretty."

This makes me laugh. "You look out at the ocean until you see the wave you want. Then you turn and start paddling."

"Got it," he says.

I look over at him and see that he's struggling to find the right balance. His butt keeps sliding from one side of the board to the other and he overcorrects to keep from falling off.

"Don't worry. You'll get the hang of it."

He squirms a little more and then finally settles into position. Kind of.

"This is . . . what's the word you use . . . 'radical'?"

"I think they stopped using that a couple decades ago," I say. "But I know the feeling. Now remember, you don't have to stand up the first couple times. You can catch the wave and ride it lying down. It's good practice and helps you get the hang of it."

"Are you kidding me?" he scoffs. "I did not rescue Blue Boy

from some old garage just so I could ride him lying on my stomach. We are ready to hang ten."

"Do you even know what hanging ten means?" I ask with a laugh.

He shakes his head. "Come to think of it, I don't. But there's not enough time for you to tell me because I believe this wave is for me."

It's a great dramatic moment. Or at least it would be if he successfully turned and caught the wave. Unfortunately, all he does is turn and slide off the board. Six times in a row. Once he finally gets the turn down, he goes through a brutal thirty minutes in which he tries to catch wave after wave only to watch each one pull away and leave him behind.

"What am I doing wrong?" he asks.

"The moment the wave lifts your board, you're natural instinct is to lean back, but you should actually lean forward."

He nods. "It's harder than it looks."

"Much harder," I say. "Do you want to take a break? We could paddle in and rest or maybe practice some more in the white water."

He shakes his head defiantly. "I am not paddling back. I am riding in."

"Okay . . ."

"I mean it," he says, trying to psych himself up. "I'm going to ride in . . . standing up."

Fifteen minutes later he actually catches a wave for about ten seconds. When he loses it, I worry that he'll be frustrated, but the opposite happens. He's more jacked than ever.

"That time I really felt it," he says. "I think I've figured it out. I did what you said and it worked. I just have to force myself to commit to it. I have to force myself to continue leaning forward."

That's what he does on the next wave and I am beyond thrilled as he catches it and takes off toward the beach. There are a couple times when he almost loses it, but I can see the exact moment when he latches on for good.

It's a thing of beauty.

And then he tries to stand up. Which is not a thing of beauty.

He actually makes it farther than I would have guessed. He's wobbly but he manages to find his balance, kind of like a baby when it's taking its first steps and keeps its butt real low. Then he tries to straighten out his legs and stand all the way up, and when he does, he leans too far forward and pearls. The tip of the board digs into the water and throws him into the air. He slams face first into the ocean and disappears for a moment before standing up in shallow water.

I instantly catch the next wave and ride it right to him.

"Are you okay?" I ask anxiously.

"I'm not okay, I'm great," he says.

Then he turns and I see his face. There's a gash under his right eye that's bleeding and makes me gasp.

"What's wrong?" he asks. "Is my nose broken?"

"No. Your nose looks fine," I say. "But you've got a bad cut under your eye."

"Cool," he says, oblivious to any pain. "Did you see that ride? It was wicked fun. I totally get why you're addicted to this. Let's get back out there."

"Maybe we should, you know, take care of the cut first."

"Really? Can't we stay just a little bit longer?"

"Oh my God," I exclaim.

"What is it?" he asks.

"You're already hooked."

I hear the knock and I bolt into action.

"I've got it!"

I hurry down the hall, but before I open the door, I pause, take a breath, and run my fingers through my hair. It's important not to seem anxious and frantic. Especially at times like this, when you *are* anxious and frantic.

"Hi," I say as I crack the door open to reveal a smiling Ben.

"Hey," he says in his superspecial dreamy way. The swelling in his cheek has gone down, and I no longer worry that I've destroyed the masterpiece that is his face.

I lean out and whisper, "You know you don't have to do this. It's not too late to run away."

"I want to," he says. "Besides, I brought these."

He holds up a small bouquet of flowers, and I fling the door open.

"You got me flowers?" I'll admit it. There's a hint of giddy in my voice.

"Actually," he responds with a cringe, "they're for your mother. I wanted to thank her for inviting me to dinner."

"Hmmm," I say, with raised eyebrows. "So that's how you're going to play it. And here I thought you always knew the right thing to say."

We walk down the hall toward the kitchen.

"Ben's here!" I announce. "He brought flowers."

"For me?" Dad says, looking up from the pot of spaghetti he's stirring.

"No," I respond. "They're for . . . Mom."

Dad cocks his head to the side and wags a wooden spoon at us, splattering some red sauce across the stove. "You better watch it, son. That woman's married and she'll break your heart."

My mother comes in from the dining room shaking her head. "Would you two give the boy a break? Sometimes I feel like I live with wild animals."

Without missing a beat, Dad and I both do jungle animal noises, which only makes her shake her head that much more. She ignores us and takes the flowers from Ben.

"Thank you, Ben. They're lovely."

"Thanks for inviting me," Ben says.

She motions to Dad and me. "It certainly would have been understandable if you had declined. How's that cut?"

"Better," he says. "Thanks for that, too."

Mom was the one who treated the cut when we got back to the house. She checks to make sure it's healing okay.

"Needless to say, living with these two has made it necessary for me to develop basic first aid skills."

Dad and I do the jungle noises again, and Mom just shakes her head.

Even though Ben's been hanging out at the house on a regular basis and has eaten with us on multiple occasions, this is the first time he's "officially" been invited for dinner. My mother has some old school South in her, and she wants to make sure he knows that he's welcome in our house. She's even insisting that we eat in the dining room instead of the kitchen like we usually do.

At first I didn't get it, but judging by the flowers and the fact that Ben wore nice khakis and a button-down shirt, I think that she may have been onto something I missed. Once we put the flowers in the vase and finish setting the table, I have to admit that it does feel special.

Ever the English teacher, Mom asks him, "Have you had to do any summer reading for school?"

I start to answer no for him because I haven't seen him near a book, but he surprises me.

"I just finished *The Grapes of Wrath* a few nights ago. It was great. Steinbeck's my favorite author."

"I didn't know that," I say.

"Which part? That I just finished *The Grapes of Wrath*? Or that Steinbeck is my favorite author?"

"Either."

He shrugs. "You never asked."

"I love Steinbeck too," says my mother. "Although I prefer *Of Mice and Men*."

"That book's too sad for me," he says.

"You don't think *The Grapes of Wrath* is sad?" she asks.

"Incredibly sad," he says. "But somehow it has a sense of hopefulness about it."

I look across the table at my mother, and the only way to accurately describe her reaction is to say that she is actually swooning.

"Why, yes it does," she says, with a glow to her cheeks. "There certainly is a lucky English teacher up in Madison, Wisconsin."

"Did I miss the memo about book club?" I ask.

"No," says Dad. "It's not really book club. He's just kissing up to your mother."

Ben shoots Mom a look. "I'm not kissing up. I really do like Steinbeck."

"I know," she says. "We can talk books later."

"Great," he says.

The conversation continues, and a few minutes later Ben finishes a bite of spaghetti and goes to say something but stops.

"What is it?" I ask.

"I was going to say how great the spaghetti is, but then I realized your dad would just think I was kissing up to him, too."

"No, no, no. Feel free to compliment the spaghetti," Dad says. "That's totally different."

"How is that different?" I ask.

"Because unlike the collected works of John Steinbeck, the epic greatness of my spaghetti sauce is indisputable. Go ahead, son, kiss away."

"I want to make it when I go back home, so can you tell me what jar it comes in?"

My mother and I burst out laughing, and Dad's eyes open wide in horror.

"A jar? You think I make spaghetti sauce out of a jar? I'll have you know my mother was born in Italy. And not the one in Epcot. The real one."

Dad loves giving people a hard time. He calls it "bustin' their chops," but I refuse to use that term because I'm not some high school boy in the 1980s. But the truth is, he loves it even more when someone is willing to bust his right back.

"I'm just kidding," Ben says. "It's delicious. Is it your mom's recipe?"

"Actually, no," Dad says, bursting with pride. "I invented it."

"I think 'developed' would be a more appropriate usage," the English teacher across the table from me says. "'Invention' usually implies some sort of groundbreaking shift or advancement."

"Like I said," Dad replies with his booming voice, "I 'invented' it."

Mom and I laugh because we know that Dad has just begun. He could talk about his sauce for hours.

"I've spent years perfecting it. It is perfect, don't you think, Ben?"

"'Perfect' is exactly the word I would use."

"And I've never written the recipe down. I keep it all up here." He taps his right temple. "I make it for my team the night before every big race."

"Then let's hope it pays off tomorrow."

"It most definitely will."

While the inspiration for the meal may have been good manners, the menu selection was all about carbo-loading. Tomorrow Ben and Dad are driving to Cocoa Beach for the Rocket Run, a 10K road race whose name was inspired by the nearby space center. They've trained together a couple times a week and have turned it into some sort of male bonding thing.

"The trick is that you have to make sure the sauce is not too heavy. My mom's sauce is great, but if you ate it the night before a race, it would slow you down. This is light but still has enough kick to make it worthwhile."

"Too bad it doesn't come in a jar," Ben says after another forkful. "I'm sure my team back home in Madison would love it."

"I can teach you to make it," Dad says out of the blue. "You've just got to promise not to tell anyone else. We'll keep it between you and me."

"I promise."

Ben's happy. Dad's happy. I, however, am . . . not happy.

"Excuse me?" I say.

"What's the matter?" asks my dad.

"When I asked you how to make it, you said that I couldn't be trusted."

"That's because you're terrible with secrets," explains my father. "But I trust Ben."

I know this started out as a joke, but there's a part of me that is semi-offended here. I really did ask him to teach me, and he really did refuse.

"What makes you so sure you can trust him?"

Dad looks at me as if it should be obvious. "Well, I've already trusted him to take care of the thing that I love the most in the world. I think he can handle a spaghetti recipe."

I'm glad that my dad loves me so much, but seriously. "I'm not just some *thing* you trusted him with. I'm your daughter."

The three of them are quiet for a moment, and then I hear Ben trying to hold back a laugh. He fights it for as long as he can, but then it finally erupts.

"What's so funny?" I ask him.

"I don't think he was talking about you, Izzy."

I look at their faces and can tell that he's right.

"Then what was he talking about?"

"His surfboard. He trusted me with his surfboard."

"Black Beauty is the thing you love most in the world?" I say, with all the outrage I can muster while laughing.

"I'm sorry, baby," Dad says. "I thought you knew."

Now Ben is really losing it, and I realize that I've never seen him laugh this hard. He's like a kid having a good time, and it dawns on me that this is the thing he's been missing. Maybe it's even the thing he thought he'd never get again. His family is breaking apart, and there will never be any dinners like this where his mom and dad are sitting around the table telling jokes and giving him a hard time.

The rest of the meal is filled with funny stories and new insights. For example, I learn that in college he's hoping to major in English—another swoon from my mother—and that he's terrified of roller coasters—more chop busting from my father.

Originally I was thinking we might go out after dinner to catch a movie, but instead I suggest he get a taste of the über-competitive cage match that is our family game night.

"The game is charades," Dad says as we move to the living room. "Lucas-style charades."

"What's Lucas-style?" Ben asks me.

"Lucas-style is when your parents are both teachers and they like to take everything that's fun and turn it into something that's educational and maybe a little less fun. Like at my fifth-grade birthday party, where instead of Pin the Tail on the Donkey, we played Pin the Beard on the Civil War General.

"It was one of those big bushy beards," Dad tries to explain to Ben. "But it just didn't translate."

"No, it didn't," I say.

"And how do you do Lucas-style charades?" Ben asks.

"The categories have more of an Advanced English and AP American History vibe," I answer him. "Instead of TV shows and celebrities, we've got categories like Underappreciated Authors, Historic Battlefields, and my personal favorite, Politicians of the Nineteenth Century."

"Those were good clues," Dad says rehashing a sore spot from a past game. "I was pretending to 'fill' the cups and get 'more' of them. Fill . . . more. Millard Fillmore."

"Those clues are only obvious to you," I say.

"Well, today you don't have to worry about my clues," Dad says. "That's because this is a battle of the sexes—Mom and you against Ben and me."

And, then, as if gender supremacy wasn't enough, he raises the stakes just a little bit more and says, "Winning team picks what flavor ice cream we get from the Islander."

"You're on!" I say, in a growl that would make a professional wrestler proud.

Ben lights up as we break up into teams, and I can tell he really needs some family time. When it's time to play, I'm up first, and I pull "William Shakespeare" out of the hat.

"We got this," I say to Mom as I get into position.

Dad hits the stopwatch and signals me to go.

I do the signs for "writer" and "second word" and start shaking side to side. Ben and Dad laugh hysterically, but I ignore them.

My mom starts shouting out answers. "Twist. Shimmy. Shake."

I signal that she's right with "shake" and move on to the next part of the word. I pretend to throw a spear, and it takes her a moment to figure it out, but then she gets it.

"Shake . . . spear. William Shakespeare!"

Dad hits the stopwatch and announces our time. "Twenty-three seconds."

Mom and I high-five. We feel pretty confident, and I can already taste the mint chocolate chip ice cream I plan on selecting.

Ben's up next and draws a name from the hat. Since I'm the timekeeper, he shows it to me, and I see that it's "J. D. Salinger."

"This round's all ours," I assure my mom. "No way they'll beat twenty-three seconds."

"Ignore that," Dad says, trying to encourage Ben. "I trust you with my recipe and I trust you with my clues."

Ben thinks for a moment and finally decides on his plan. "Okay," he says. "I'm ready."

I signal him to go. He does the sign for writer and then squats like a baseball catcher and holds up his glove.

"J. D. Salinger!" screams my dad.

I hit the stopwatch and look down at the number.

"How fast?" asks Dad.

I shake my head. "Seven seconds . . . but it doesn't count."

"What do you mean, 'it doesn't count'?" asks Dad.

"You cheated," I say.

"How did we cheat?" asks Ben.

"I don't know how, but I know you did."

"What do you mean?"

"All you did was squat. How is that J. D. Salinger?"

They both look right at me, and at the exact same moment say, *The Catcher in the Rye.*"

That's when I realize that they didn't cheat. Even scarier, they're totally in sync with each other.

"Oh my God," I say, turning to my mom.

She says exactly what I'm thinking. "We've created a monster."

What follows is the most intense game of charades I've ever played—and, in my family, that's saying something. Ben and Dad make a great team, but Mom and I keep it close. We finally lose it with Politicians of the Nineteenth Century. That category always kills me. I draw a blank trying to act out "Ulysses S. Grant," and Ben somehow gets "Zachary Taylor" from my dad pretending to sew.

"It's a Taylor, like a tailor," he says, trying to explain.

Even though we play competitively, we don't really take it seriously, and I feel a deeper connection with Ben than I did before. I never realized how important it was for me that he get along well with my family.

"As the champions, we get to pick the ice cream flavor," Dad announces. "And as our MVP, you get to make the decision for us, Ben. What flavor do you want?"

Ben thinks about this for a moment and says, "Mint chocolate chip."

"No," Dad says, as though he's just suffered the ultimate betrayal. "You're picking that because it's Izzy's favorite flavor."

"It is?" he says, playing dumb as he shoots me a wink. "I'm picking it because it's my favorite flavor."

"The whole point of winning is so you can rub the loser's nose in it after the competition," says Dad.

"It really is hard to believe they let you coach children," says my mom. "Come on, let's go get the ice cream. I'll let you be as obnoxious as you want the whole car ride over."

"You will?" says Dad. "That's really sweet. That Zachary Taylor hint was amazing, wasn't it?"

Mom and Dad leave and, for twenty minutes at least, I get to be alone with Ben.

"So now you know what game night is like," I say.

"It was a lot of fun," he says.

I walk over to him and wrap my arms around his waist. "I guess you deserve a victory kiss."

"I would think so," he says.

We kiss for a moment and everything seems good. Unfortunately, that moment does not last.

"I need to tell you something," he says, pulling back. "I didn't want to do it in front of your parents, but I got a call from my mother right before I came over here."

"Is everything okay?"

He shakes his head. "The divorce is getting uglier, and now they're arguing about custody rights. My mom wants me to be with her all the time, but my dad wants to split custody so that I'd go back and forth between them."

"Well, that's good that your dad still wants to be part of your life, isn't it?"

He thinks about it for a moment and seems sadder than I've ever seen him. "Maybe if that were the reason. But he doesn't really want me around. I think he just wants to make sure she doesn't win and to make it so that he won't have to pay as much in child support."

Once again I am so grateful that my parents are happily married.

"Anyway," he says, "the judge wants to talk to me."

Now it dawns on me.

"What does that mean?" I ask.

"I have to fly up to Wisconsin," he says. "I leave on Sunday."

Now I really panic. "You're coming back, aren't you?"

"Yes."

I breathe a sigh of relief and ask, "How long will you be gone?"

"A week."

Even though we never talk about it directly, I always know exactly how many days there are until Ben's supposed to leave at the end of the summer. At the moment I have exactly thirty-one days. My plan is to use each one of them carefully, and now I am going to lose seven just like that.

"Seven days . . . ," I say softly.

"I know," he says.

"That's not fair."

I look at him and realize that I am being totally selfish. He's losing seven days too, but during that time he has to meet with a judge and pick one parent over the other.

"But even worse, it's not fair to you," I say as I give him a hug. "I'm sorry you have to go through this."

He rests his head against my shoulder, and I think I hear the faint whispers of him crying.

I swap my Saturday shift with Nicole so I can go watch Dad and Ben at the Rocket Run, and then on Sunday I get Sophie to drive Ben and me to the airport. His uncle was going to do it, but I'm trying to get all the time with him I can. To say the least, my mood is a little down, and there are extended quiet periods on the ride.

"The surf contest is just a few weeks away," says Sophie, trying to generate any sort of conversation. "We're going to get a lot of practice in while you're gone."

I expect Ben to respond, but he doesn't. He just bites his lower lip, lost in thought. He's concentrating, but I have no idea about what.

"Is something wrong?" I ask.

He turns to face me in the backseat. "Parks and Rec is sponsoring the surf contest," he says.

"Right?"

"And I work for Parks and Rec."

"Okay."

"It wouldn't be right if I used that position to give you an advantage. Ethically, I mean."

"Of course not," I say.

Sophie raises her hand partway. "Are we sure about that?"

"Yes," I say, slapping her hand down. "Of course we are."

"I was just checking."

"We don't want you to cheat for us, Ben," I tell him.

"Right," he says with a smile. "But it wouldn't be cheating if I told you that it is a good idea to read the rules. I tell that to everyone when they pick up an entrance form."

Sophie shoots me a look in the mirror, and both of us are wondering where this is going.

"And since you know that I am a lawyer's son and was taught to read everything carefully—and, by everything, I mean . . . every . . . single . . . word—then unlike other people who just ignore it, you might take that advice to heart."

He stops there and we share a look. I have no idea what he's getting at, but I do know that he's trying to give us a little help. I also know that, for the moment at least, that's as far as he's willing to go.

"Well, my boyfriend is going out of town," I say. "So I have plenty of free time this week, and I was planning on reading through the contest rules very carefully."

He smiles and nods. "And you're going to do that before you turn in your entrance form?"

I nod. "Absolutely."

The car is quiet for a moment.

"Okay," Sophie says. "That was . . . weird . . . but we're here. So why don't I drop the two of you off? Izzy, I'll come back around and pick you up in twenty minutes."

"Thanks," I say as I reach forward and clasp her on the shoulder.

"I know, I know, I'm amazing," she says, and although she's joking, it's completely true.

Ben and I get out and things are pretty quiet. He doesn't have to check his bag, so once he picks up a boarding pass, we walk over to the security line. It's killing me and he's only going away for seven days. I can't imagine how it will be in four weeks when we come back here and he'll be going away permanently.

We stand there for a little while and just silently hold hands. Then, when it's time for him to go, he gives me a kiss and a hug that linger longer than I expect.

"Good luck," I tell him. "I'll be thinking about you the whole time. Especially on the day you see the judge. It's going to be all right."

He nods and gives me another kiss.

"I'm going to miss you so much," he says.

One more hug and then he walks away and gets in line.

"I meant what I said," he says as he turns back. "Read every word."

"I will," I say, trying to put on a brave face.

I watch him walk away, and although I know he can't hear me, I just have to say it aloud, so I whisper.

"I love you."

August

$\mathcal{I}$'m pathetic.

I know this. But knowing it and being able to do something about it are two totally different things. It's been five days since Ben left, and no matter where I go, I'm constantly reminded of him. Right now we're closing up the shop, and as I lock the front door, I notice the poster he brought in the first day we met. Just the sight of it makes me want to cry, so you can guess how much fun I've been to be around. Nevertheless, Sophie and Nicole have not wavered in their repeated attempts to lift my spirits. You have to love their tenacity.

"Ladies, the dance floor is ours," Sophie announces as she turns up the volume on the sound system. "Let's crank it."

Sophie is obsessed with nineties dance music, and she loves to blast it while we clean up. As a result, she's gotten Nicole and me hooked too. The first song on the playlist is another example of how she keeps trying to make me smile.

> Right about now, the funk soul brother
> Check it out now, the funk soul brother

Despite the fact that it is basically just the same two lines repeated over and over and that its name is completely baffling,

I love "The Rockafeller Skank." I know, it makes no sense, but the beat is irresistible. Which is no doubt why Sophie is leading off with it.

Sophie sings along behind the counter as she sorts the day's receipts, and Nicole busts a shoulder shimmy and dances with the push broom while she sweeps the floor. I, however, maintain my groove-free status as I mope and restock the clothing racks.

"Who's up for Mama Tacos tonight?" Sophie asks, raising her voice but still moving to the beat. "I could destroy some nachos."

"Count me in," says Nicole. "How 'bout you, Iz?"

I shake my head and mumble some excuse that gets drowned out by the electronic rhythm.

"What?" she says, this time raising her voice.

I try again, but they don't hear me.

Finally I just blurt out, "No thanks!"

Sophie presses stop. The room goes quiet, and suddenly our fun little surf shop becomes one of those cop show interrogation rooms.

"Why not?"

"I'm just not very hungry," I say defensively. "And I've got to get up early to train."

"Which is it?" asks Nicole.

"What do you mean?"

"You gave us two excuses," she says as she stops sweeping. "Which one's the real one?"

"First of all, they're not 'excuses.' They're answers. And both happen to be real."

Nicole turns to look at Sophie; they share a brief psychic-twins moment. Then she turns back to me and says, "You're shutting us out, Izzy. I don't know why, but you are."

"Just because I'm not in the mood for nachos? That means I'm shutting you out?"

"Now you're 'not in the mood.' That's excuse number three. Who are you trying to convince? Us or you?"

She walks over until she's standing just across the rack from me. "You haven't hung out with us once this week. We get that you're busy when you're with Ben. We'll cut you that slack. But since he's out of town, we thought the three of us would do some stuff together."

"Yeah," says Sophie. "We kind of figured we could cheer you up."

"I don't need cheering up," I say curtly. "I'm fine."

Nicole goes to reply, but instead she just shakes her head and resumes sweeping. "Whatever."

"What is it?"

"I've known you forever," she says. "Whatever this is, it's not *fine*."

"Well, you're entitled to your opinion."

She looks at me and nods. "And you disagree?"

"Very much so."

"Then why don't we take this to the register."

I cannot stress how much I am not in the mood for having my love life taken to the register. "Let's not. The last thing I need right now is the two of you ganging up on me."

"Excuse me," says Sophie. "You feel terrible. We understand that. But if you think we would 'gang up' on you, then we've got real problems, because that's not who we are."

I know she's right and I regret saying it, but the truth is there's nothing they can say that will make me feel better. Plus, I worry if I tell them *everything* that's on my mind, it will only make things worse.

"It was a poor choice of words," I offer. "I apologize."

"It's *us*," says Nicole. "You don't need to apologize. You just need to talk."

I don't respond. I just keep rehanging shirts that were left in the fitting rooms. I figure they'll give up, blast some music, and let me get back to my mope-a-thon. But they wait me out. There's no music or questions, just the sound of the hangers as I slide them on the rack. Finally, I give in.

"You really want to know what's bothering me?" I say.

"We really do," says Sophie.

"He's only been gone for five days and I'm fully mental. What happens a month from now when he's gone for good? And what happens a month after that when this shop closes? What am I going to do? Where am I going to go? I can't just sit in my room and cry all the time."

"Is that what you've been doing, sweetie?" asks Sophie. "Have you been crying in your room at night?"

"Maybe," I grudgingly admit. "But I'm serious. What should I do? I can't figure it out."

I look at them and wait for answers. I can see that Nicole is carefully considering her words before responding, "I don't know."

I wait for more, but she doesn't say anything else. "'I don't know'? That's your answer?"

"That's the truth," she says. "I don't know what you should do. But I do know that whatever it is, you're going to do it with me. You'll be with me at school and wherever it is that we decide to hang out once this place is gone, and we'll figure it out together."

"It's awful," Sophie adds. "Ben's great and he's totally into you. You're such a cute couple, so we get that it's not fair. But don't forget that you were already awesome before he came into your life. And you'll still be awesome after he goes back home. Maybe even more so because he's opened up parts of you that we've never seen."

I raise a skeptical eyebrow. "Like what?"

"Like the fact that pre-Ben Izzy would never have entered the King of the Beach," says Nicole. "She should've, but she wouldn't have. Ben gave you confidence. He made it so you believe in yourself."

This is something that I had not thought of. "You might be right about that."

"Of course we are," says Sophie. "We're your best friends. We know things about you that you don't even know about you."

"Is that so?" I ask, amused.

"Yes, it is," she says. "Like for instance, right now I know that you've still only told us part of what's bothering you. We already knew that you missed him and were unsure about the future. This is not that kind of moping. This goes deeper. What else is it?"

Somehow the vibe has gone from interrogation room to confessional. They really are great friends, and I know that I can tell them anything. Still, I have to take a couple of deep breaths before I can say it.

"I love him."

They raise their eyebrows at this announcement, but neither says anything, so I continue.

"It's not a crush. I don't just like him. I am *in love* with him. And I know that I have no experience and don't know what I'm talking about. But I also know what I know. I love him and I can't even tell him."

"Why not?" asks Nicole.

"He broke up with his last girlfriend because she was in love with him and he didn't feel the same way in return. He said he didn't think it was fair to her. I can't take that chance. It's bad enough that I'm going to lose him at the end of the month."

It's amazing how relieved I am to have that off my chest. I can't tell Ben, but I can tell the two of them. Saying it out loud makes it seem real and not just something floating around in my mind.

"If you really feel that way, then I think you should tell him," Sophie says. "You should at least give him the chance to say it back to you. But that's for you to decide, not us. That's well beyond the powers of whoever controls the register."

"Does that mean you're ruling in my favor?" I ask.

"You're guilty of shutting out your best friends. There's no doubt about that. But I'm going to let you off with a warning and a reminder that we're your biggest fans. All we ever want to do is make things better."

"Okay, I know that. I won't forget." I'm relieved to have shared my secret and relieved that she's not going to make me do something stupid. "I also appreciate the fact that you resisted your recent trend of overstepping your bounds when you're on the register."

"I'm not done yet," she says.

I shake my head and turn to Nicole. "I knew it was too good to be true."

"This court also finds you guilty of another crime, and I'm afraid it's one that cannot simply be ignored."

"And what is that?" I ask.

"Failure to dance to 'The Rockafeller Skank.'"

This makes me laugh for the first time all week. "Please tell me it's another warning."

"Oh, no, no, no," she says. "We are going to stay here until we see . . . the Albatross. And don't just go through the motions. We want to see it performed with the passion and pageantry it deserves."

The Albatross is a goofy, over-the-top dance we came up with one night when we were doing inventory. It involves strutting around while holding your arms fully extended like wings. It's exactly the type of thing that you do when you're being silly with your friends, yet under no circumstance would you do anywhere else.

Sophie presses play and the music starts blaring again.

They just stand there with their arms crossed, looking at me expectantly.

"No way," I say. "You can stare at me all you want," I continue. "Because I am not going to do this."

They turn the music up even louder.

That's it. I can fight it no longer.

At first I just tease it a little and bounce my knees, then I bust out a big smile and the arms extend as I start the strut. They clap and holler, and pretty soon the three of us are grooving. It's fun and a great emotional release. I get so into it that I even close my eyes, which is dangerous when performing the Albatross.

We're startled out of our little moment when the music shuts off abruptly. We look to the counter and see Mo standing by the sound system. I'd totally forgotten that she was working in the garage.

"Sorry to interrupt your party," she says, clearly enjoying the moment, "but I need you guys to come out to the garage."

We follow her outside and are surprised to see that Mickey is there too. Today was her day off, which means she must have come in through the back door while we were busy.

"What's up?" asks Sophie.

"The King of the Beach is coming up," says Mickey, "and we thought we should have a team meeting."

Even though there can be as many as eight competitors on a team, so far the Surf Sisters squad is just the five of us. None of the other girls at the shop really surf much, and despite my attempts to secretly recruit during my practice sessions at the pier, so far I have struck out.

"That's a good idea," I say. "You want to go over practice schedules?"

"Actually, we thought we might start off by giving you guys some M&M's."

"None for me," answers Nicole. "I try to eat just a few, but then I start craving more, and before you know it I've polished off an entire family-sized bag. It's not pretty."

The sisters share a look and chuckle.

"We're not talking about the candy," says Mickey.

It takes a moment, but I'm the first one to figure it out. "Oh my God! Oh my God! Oh my God!" I say as I begin to tremble with excitement. "Do you mean . . . ?"

Mo looks at me and nods. "We figure it's the least we can do. We may not have the best team at the contest, but you can bet we're going to have the best-looking boards."

Now I notice that there are three gift-wrapped surfboards lined up against the back wall. They're giving us hand-shaped, custom made Mickey and Mo—M & M—surfboards. (This is me hyperventilating.)

"Those M&Ms?" Sophie says, pointing at them and practically crying. "You mean those M&M's?"

The sisters laugh even more, tickled by our excitement. "Consider them your bonus for years of hard work and dedication."

Nicole's the last one to catch on, but when she does, her reaction may be best of all. She doesn't say a word. She just squeals as she runs over to them, her long arms flailing in excitement.

"We wanted you to have them for the contest," Mickey says. "But we figured you'd need some time to break them in."

"Go ahead," says Mo. "Open them up."

We tackle the wrapping paper like human paper shredders and unveil three gorgeous and gleaming surfboards. Each one has an original design and color scheme. Sophie's is cosmic seventies psychedelic, perfect for her retro tastes, while Nicole's has a pattern that looks like a stylized sea turtle's shell, no doubt because she's our most ardent environmentalist. They're both beautiful, but mine . . . mine is the prettiest of them all.

"I absolutely love it," I say. "It's breathtaking."

My board has a swirl of colors that radiate from the center like the fingers of a hurricane. The colors look like little tiles in a mosaic and alternate between shades of green, blue, and brown. The phrase "The Eye of the Storm" is written in the center.

"I'm particularly pleased with how that one turned out," says Mickey. "I took a couple of pictures for our portfolio."

I look up at her and shake my head in awe. "It's a work of art, Mickey. How'd you come up with the design?"

"I didn't," she says with a smirk. "It was your boyfriend."

"Ben? Did this?"

"He actually wanted to buy you a custom board," Mo starts to explain. "He asked if we could work out a payment plan because he said he wouldn't have enough money until the end of the summer, but that he really wanted you to have it in time for the contest. He said he even knew what he wanted the design on the board to be."

I look over at Sophie and Nicole, and they smile warmly at the thought of Ben doing this.

"We told him that we had already planned on giving you boards for the contest," adds Mickey. "But we were curious to see his design."

"That's when he handed me this," Mo says as she holds up a sheet of paper with the design sketched out on it. "I thought it was great."

"I wonder why he wanted this design in particular," I say.

She shrugs. "So do we. He told us that you would know."

I have no idea.

I look down at it. It is mesmerizing. It seemingly changes color depending on how you look at it or how the light hits it. That's when I realize what it is, and I'm so caught off guard that I reach up and cover my mouth.

"What?" asks Nicole.

I shake my head. "I can't. It's too . . . mushy."

"That means you have to tell us!" Sophie says. "We could stand some mushy."

I look at them and say, "It's the color of my eyes."

I have a love-hate relationship with video chatting. I love, love, love the fact that I can see Ben even though he's 1,347 miles away. (Yes, I figured out the exact distance between our houses because, well, you know.) But I'm not particularly fond of seeing myself in the lower left corner of my computer screen as I talk to him.

Tonight is the second time we've tried it. The first time had mixed results. Halfway through the conversation I noticed that my eyebrows bounce up and down when I get excited and that there's some strange sniffle flare that happens with my nostrils while I'm in deep listening mode. When I tried to correct these things, I overcompensated, and by the end of the conversation I felt like I was having some sort of bizarre face spasms. It was like the time I tried to examine everything I do when I surf and it made me pearl over the front of my board. I've solved the issue by taping a small piece of paper over the image. Now all I see is Ben.

"Hi," I say. "How ya doing?"

"I'm okay, I guess," he says. "Better now that I see you."

Tonight is especially tricky. I'm still walking on air because of the incredibly romantic gesture Ben made with the surfboard design, but he spent half the day in a courtroom talking to a judge about his parents' divorce. My goal is to keep things positive and be as low maintenance a girlfriend as possible.

"I love my surfboard! The design is . . . perfect."

"I can't wait to see it," he says.

"You don't have to wait. I brought it for show and tell."

I pick up the surfboard and try to hold it in front of the computer so he can get a look. The problem is, because I've taped over the part that lets me see what he's seeing, I have trouble telling if it's in the right spot or not.

"I'm going to try it out first thing in the morning," I say. "I want to break it in before the King of the Beach."

"Speaking of which," he replies, "have you read through the rules like I suggested?"

"Yes," I answer. "We all have."

"And?"

"And . . . the truth is . . . none of us can figure out what you're talking about."

Ever since the trip to the airport, Sophie, Nicole, and I have read and reread the rules of the King of the Beach. Ben seems to think there's some great secret hidden in them, but we've given up finding it.

"It all seems pretty cut and dry," I continue. "We enter a team. Every surfer earns points based on how well he or she finishes in the individual competition. The team with the most points wins the title."

"Yes, but . . ."

There's a pause on the other side, and I try to read the expression on his face. I can't tell if he's angry, frustrated, or something else.

"I'll just tell you," he says, with a distant tone to his voice. "If there's one thing I've learned this week, it's that my ideas of fairness and cheating are outdated."

The divorce proceedings must be going even worse than I thought. He's never said it outright, but I've gotten a strong indication that his father cheated on his mother. I don't want to get lumped in with that vibe.

"Stop right there," I say. "Your ideas of fairness are no different from mine. I don't want you to help us by cheating. Never in a million years would I ask you to do that."

"I know, I'm sorry," he says. "It's just been . . . bad up here. It's kind of shaken my confidence."

"Well, in two days you'll be back down here," I say, trying to boost his spirits. "And we are going to have an amazing time. You can be confident about that."

There's a brief pause, and I wonder if he's about to deliver some bad news. I've secretly been worried that because it's so late in the summer, his parents might just have him stay up there and not come back at all. Instead he says, "I've missed you even more than I thought I would. And that's saying something, because I thought I'd miss you a lot."

I let this sink in for a moment and smile.

"I miss you . . . so much," I say. "And, I would never want you to go against your sense of right and wrong. I promise you, if there's something to be found in the rules, I will find it."

We talk for a little bit more, but I can tell he's worn out, so I wish him sweet dreams and blow him about a thousand kisses. When we end the call, there's a brief moment when the image on the screen freezes and the look on his face kind of breaks my heart. He seems so troubled, and I want to be able to ease that pain but have no idea how. Then it disappears, and I'm left staring at my computer screen.

I begin to obsess over the call the instant it's over. I'm not sure why, but I feel uneasy about it. Everything he said was positive. Not only does he miss me, but he misses me a lot. And he can't wait to see me again. Still, there's a knot of uncertainty in my stomach. I give myself a little mental pep talk and pull up the Parks and Recreation Web site and go to the link for the King of the Beach. It's just past midnight and I am determined to find whatever he thinks is important in the rules.

There are more rules than you'd expect. The King of the Beach is part of what's known as the Summer Series. There are contests held all over Florida, and surfers earn points by competing in those contests, which count toward the series championship as well. Because of that, there are twenty-three pages of rules I have to scour through. They address everything from eligibility to how each surfer is judged to guidelines set by the series sponsor and ones specific to the contest in Pearl Beach. I read them as closely and carefully as I can, but nothing strikes me as important.

At 12:45, I decide to print them out, and I then arrange them across the floor of my room. By 1:15, I'm convinced that because Ben doesn't know much about surfing, he thinks something is more important than it is. I'm going to call it a night and go to bed, but then I see my new surfboard.

The Eye of the Storm. It's pretty awesome and inspires me to dig some more.

At exactly 1:47 I see three words that catch my attention. I check the page numbers to make sure I have them in the right order. Then I reread the rule a few times. I go back to the Parks and Rec Web site and make sure the rules I printed are the most up to date. By 2:03, I am convinced. Those three words aren't just significant.

They change everything.

What's so important that we had to meet before the shop opens?" Sophie asks. "On my day off, I might add."

"Three words," I say.

"If those three words are 'I love you,' do not expect a hug."

I have called an emergency team meeting, and despite Sophie's attitude, I can tell that I have at least caught the attention of the others.

"What three words?" asks Mo.

I hold up a copy of the King of the Beach rules, all twenty-three pages, and wave it in the air for emphasis. "'From . . . all . . . divisions.'"

"Now you really shouldn't expect a hug," says Sophie.

"There are four divisions in the contest," I continue. "The most important one is the Main Event. Whoever wins the Main Event is named the King of the Beach. But there are three other age group contests: Menehunes for kids twelve and under, Teens for thirteen- to nineteen-year-olds, and Legends for anyone over forty-five."

"Yeah," says Nicole. "Why is that important?"

"Because every year the people on the Surf City team, and all the other teams for that matter, only enter the Main Event. They all want to compete for the individual title."

"I still don't see your point," says Sophie.

"Listen to the rules for the team competition." I read from the rule book. "'Competitors will be awarded points based on their finish in their individual competitions. The team championship will be awarded to the team whose members accumulate the most total points . . .' And here's the tricky part, because the sentence starts on this page but continues on this one," I say as I flip to the next page. "'. . . from all divisions.'"

I let this sink in for a moment.

"I still don't get it," Nicole says.

"You can earn points for your team in any age group," I say. "But none of the other teams ever do it. If we enter surfers in Menehunes, Teens, and Legends, we could earn a lot of points. We could build a really big lead before the Main Event even starts. We might even be able to win this thing."

Now I see the expressions I was hoping for.

"Are you sure?" asks Mo.

"Look for yourself," I say as I hand her the rules.

"Most teams are just made up of young guys at the peak of their skills. So of course they all enter the Main Event. It never occurred to anybody to make up a team that spanned different age groups."

Mickey flashes a big smile. "At least not until now."

"I think I've changed my mind," says Sophie. "I deem this hug worthy." She wraps her arms around me and squeezes so much that it lifts me off the ground.

"Sophie, you and me in the Teens," says Nicole, thinking aloud. "Mickey and Mo in Legends. That leaves us with three spots. Who else can we get? We need some Menehunes."

"I've been thinking about that," I say as I break free from Sophie's hug. "Rebecca and Tyler are the two best surfers in summer camp. I bet they'd do it."

"Those two make seven," says Sophie. "We can add one more."

"I know who would be perfect!" says Mickey with a Cheshire grin.

"Who?" I ask.

"Your dad," she says. "Is he over forty-five?"

"By six months," I say excitedly.

"He'd be great," Sophie says. "He's really good."

"Oh my God. He'll pass out when I tell him."

"That gives us three Legends, three Teens, and two Menehunes," Nicole says. "If everyone does well—"

"It still won't be enough," Mo says, interrupting.

We look over to where she has the rules spread out on a surfboard. She's writing numbers on the back of one of the pages.

"Why not?" I ask.

She scratches out some more math and looks up at us. "The points count from all the divisions, but the point values are bigger in the Main Event. There's a very real chance that Surf City will sweep that, and if they do, it doesn't matter how well we do in the others. We'll still fall a few points short."

She holds up her paper to show us the math.

We all think about this for a minute and try to figure out a solution.

"We have to have someone in the Main Event who finishes high enough to score points," Mickey says. "Those will count double because not only will we be adding them to our score, but we'll also be subtracting points from their total points. That could put us over the top."

"Considering we've got two past champions on our squad, I still like our chances," I say. "One of you can surf in the Main Event and the other in Legends with my dad."

Mickey shakes her head. "I'm afraid it will have to be one of you three."

"Why?" I ask. "You've both won it before. You've got the skills."

"Our skills have faded," says Mickey. "We can do some damage in the Legends, but it would be a miracle if either one of us made it out of the first round in the Main Event."

"She's right," says Mo. "It needs to be one of you."

"And if we're going to be honest," says Nicole, "I'm not in the same league as Izzy and Sophie. So it shouldn't be me."

I feel my pulse pick up pace as Sophie and I lock eyes on each other.

"That means it's got to be you," I say to her. "You're much better at cutbacks and tricks than I am. You can earn a big score. You can do this."

Sophie laughs. "You know that's not true. You know that I am nowhere near the surfer you are. This is your time to be bold. This is your moment."

"Well, it's got to be one of you," Mo says.

"How do we decide?" I ask.

Mickey smiles at me. "That's easy. The same way we always decide disputes at Surf Sisters. We're going to go to the register."

"But we're not open yet," says Sophie. "No one is working the register."

Mo nods. "I know that. But since Izzy is the one who first came up with the idea of competing, and since she's the one who found this wrinkle in the rules, we'll say that she's officially on register. We'll let her decide."

I breathe a sigh of relief. Bullet dodged.

"That's not fair," says Sophie. "You know I'm right and you just gave her a way out."

Mo looks at me with an intensity that's unnerving. "I don't know about that. There's a lot of responsibility that goes with being on the register. If you take the tradition seriously, you don't just make the easy choice. You make the right choice. I think Izzy takes things seriously. I think she'll make the right choice."

That last bit gets to me. I do take tradition seriously. I look at them one by one, and each one stares right back at me. I think about the contest. I think about the summer.

Back in June the idea of me competing in the King of the

Beach would have been laughable. But so much has happened. I'm definitely not the same girl I was then. I'm not even the same girl I was on the Fourth of July. Then I start to think about the girl I want to become. No one rushes me. No one says a thing. They just wait for me to respond.

"Okay," I say. "I'll make the decision."

"Who's it going to be?" asks Mickey.

There is no hesitation in my voice. "Me."

*B*en's first day back in Pearl Beach doesn't follow any of the romantic comedy movie plots that have played out in my imagination. There is no indie pop love song playing as we rush into each other's arms at the airport. (I have to work so his uncle picks him up without me.) I don't walk out of the shop after my shift and find him waiting for me across the street as he sits on the hood of a sports car. (His flight's delayed two hours, so he's still not back when my shift ends.) And we don't go on a picnic and have it ruined by a sudden rainstorm only to kiss passionately after we take cover beneath an abandoned gazebo. (Okay, so I was pretty certain this one wouldn't happen but, man, how cool would that be?)

In fact, Ben's first day back in Pearl Beach doesn't even include me until it's almost over. I still haven't heard from him by ten o'clock, so I try to call and it goes straight to voice mail. I figure (at least I hope) that it's because his battery is dead and not because he hit ignore when my picture popped up on his phone. Without really thinking it through, I ride my bike over to his uncle's house and knock on the door. I regret this decision the moment I see his face.

"Hi," I say as he opens the door.

He smiles, but it feels forced. "Hey." I can tell that he's exhausted both physically and emotionally.

"How was your flight?" I ask.

"Long . . . like the week."

There's an awkward silence, and I'm not getting any encouraging signs, so I decide to cut my losses.

"Well, I was just riding home from Nicole's and wanted to make sure you got back okay. I'll see you tomorrow."

I turn around and try to speed walk over to my bike, but he runs up behind me and takes me by the shoulder.

"Wait a second," he says. "Why are you in such a hurry?"

I turn around and try to read his face, but it's hard in the darkness.

"I don't know. I figured you'd be happy to see me. But you don't seem happy. So I thought I should leave."

"I *am* happy. It's just that I'm tired and I have to get up early for work."

("You gave two excuses. Which one's the real one?" I think as I remember what Nicole said to me just a couple of nights ago.)

"I completely understand. Let's just act like this never happened. We'll see each other tomorrow and run into each other's arms."

I really could use a laugh right here, but he looks serious.

"Why don't we go for a walk?" he says. "So we can talk."

All these signs are worrisome. I start to breathe heavily, but I try to hide it as Ben tells his uncle that he'll be right back.

189

I'm not sure how to describe the vibe as we walk down to the beach. Our chemistry feels completely different. The problem is that I don't know if this is because things have changed between us or if it's because he's tired and I made a mistake by coming over this late. I'm also a bit concerned by the fact that he said he wanted to talk, but he's keeping awfully quiet.

I decide to take charge of the conversation.

"If you want to talk about what went down with your parents and the judge, you know that I'm more than happy to listen," I tell him. "But if you just want to forget about that stuff, that's fine too."

He thinks for a moment. "Maybe another time, but right now I'm just happy to be away from it."

It's night, but it's still too hot and humid to snuggle as we walk down the beach together. We hold hands, but there's a formality to it.

"I hope you got to have at least some fun while you were up there."

"There was a big party at the lake, and I saw a lot of my friends from school," he says with a faint smile, "so that was fun."

I can't help it, but the first thing I do when I hear this is wonder whether or not his ex-girlfriend, Beth, was at the party. Amazingly, I resist the urge to ask him and instead let my crazy worrying stay in my head.

"What did you want to talk about?" I ask, not sure I really want to hear the answer.

"I really missed you," he says.

"I really missed you, too."

"But in a couple weeks I'll be going back for good and . . . I wonder if we should—"

I put my finger up against his lips to quiet him.

"Why don't you stop right there," I say. "We both know that September's coming. But I don't think we should talk about it. I think we should just enjoy the moment."

He takes a deep breath and considers this. "It's just—"

"I don't even want to talk about surfing," I say, cutting him off again. "I just want to hold your hand and walk along the beach."

"Okay," he says reluctantly. "We can do that."

We don't say much after that. We just walk, and as we do I hold on as tightly as I can.

The next few days aren't much better. Ben and I both smile and say all the right things, but there's a definite distance between us. He even cancels on me twice. Yesterday he backed out of lunch because there was a problem at work, and today I was supposed to give him another surf lesson, but he bailed at the last moment. He said that he had to go listen to a couple bands he was considering for the Sand Castle Dance. I offered to go along with him, but he said that since it was work, he really shouldn't bring anyone along.

I'm pretty sure he was about to break up with me on the beach, and now I wonder if I should have just let him do it. Rather than sit in my room so I could stress and obsess, I call Sophie and ask her to meet me at the pier for some intensive training.

"What's wrong?" Sophie asks when she sees the expression on my face.

"I don't really want to talk about it," I say. "I just want to work."

She nods. "Okay. Let's work."

I haven't mentioned it yet, but my new surfboard doesn't just look amazing. It is amazing. Mo told me that because our styles are so similar, she knew just how to shape it. (We'll call that the understatement of the year.) It's perfect in every way and feels like an extension of my body whenever I'm in the water. At first I was worried that it had too much curve to it, but that curve has opened up my ability to attack my cutbacks. That's what I'm working on today and the reason I called Sophie. She's great at them.

The cutback is probably the most important surfing maneuver of all. As the energy of the wave pushes you forward, you can get too far in front of it. When that happens you have to turn, or cutback, into the wave and go against it until you're closer to the power source. It lets you ride the wave longer and gives you the power to do bigger and better turns and maneuvers.

If you do a cutback right, you look like you belong in the Bolshoi Ballet. If you do it wrong, you look like my Uncle Barry doing the chicken dance at a wedding reception. After thirty minutes I'm looking more like Barry than Baryshnikov. I think this is partly due to the fact that I'm trying to add some flair to the maneuver in order to look good for the judges, but also because of my Ben funk.

"So tell me," I ask Sophie as we sit on our boards in the lineup, waiting for the next set of waves. "What am I doing wrong?"

She gives me that Sophie smirk and asks, "Are we talking about surfing or Ben?"

I think about it for a moment before answering. "Surfing."

"I think you're trying too hard. The thing that's so great about your technique is how smooth it is. But today you look uncomfortable, like you're fighting the waves."

I nod as I make mental notes.

"When you drop down into that turn, try leaning back more, right up to the point where you feel like you're going to fall into the wave. And then picture big round circles in your mind as you start to whip around. It will make the move more fluid and help you pick up speed. No wasted energy."

I think about this for a moment. "Okay," I say. "That all makes sense. I think I can do that."

"I know you can do it," she says, with just the right amount of enthusiasm in her voice.

We look back at the ocean and all we see are pancakes. There are no real waves coming our way, so we just bob quietly for a few moments until I break the silence.

"All right," I say with a smile. "What am I doing wrong with Ben?"

She thinks about it for a moment. "The same thing. I think you're trying too hard. You look uncomfortable."

"It's not just a look," I say. "I *am* uncomfortable. It used to be that when we walked on the beach our hands fit together like pieces of a puzzle. It was just perfect. But ever since he came back from Wisconsin, there's been a distance between us. Physical and emotional. I keep hoping it will go away, but it doesn't."

"Do you think it's because of what happened when he went home?" she asks. "Is he freaked out because of his parents' divorce?"

"Maybe." I shrug. "I have no way of knowing. He doesn't talk about it, and I'm too scared to ask."

"I understand him not volunteering it," she says. "But you can't be scared to ask him something. If you're a couple, you should be able to ask him anything you want. Don't be shy. You know what happens to timid surfers?"

"They wipe out."

"You bet they do. It's the same with boys. If you're timid, you wipe out. Now show me that cutback."

I see a set of waves coming right at us and pick out the one that's just for me. I catch it, and as I ride along the shoulder just ahead of where it's breaking, I think about the advice that Sophie gave me. I lean back farther and farther. At first it feels like I'm going to fall off the surfboard, but instead of falling I start picking up an amazing amount of speed. I shoot out in front of the break and do a wide sweeping turn known as a roundhouse. I can hear Sophie squealing with delight and cheering in the distance. After another hour of practice it's almost second nature.

By the time we're done, I'm exhausted. The practice has taken my mind off Ben, and the fact that my cutback has improved so much at least gives me something positive for the day.

"You own that move," Sophie says as we carry our boards back toward the shop. "You need to be that bold with Ben."

"I'll try," I say honestly. "But that's easier said than done."

"All the great things are."

Throughout the week I try my best to be bold with Ben. It's not my default setting, but I'm determined to do whatever I can to make things right. It works best one morning when I convince him to come out for another lesson. At first he's reluctant, but I'm able to fill the lulls in conversation with surf talk. Then the instruction starts to pay off, and he catches a few waves in a row. This is without a doubt the happiest I've seen him since he's come back from Wisconsin. And best of all, he doesn't pearl and end up with a bloody face this time.

I try to extend this emotion when we finish, so I tell him that I'm taking him out for lunch to celebrate his success. When he says that he really should get to work, I say, "I won't take no for an answer."

This is me being bold. This is also me being stupid, because he really does have a lot of work to do. We're only a few bites into our pizza when he gets an angry phone call from his uncle, wondering why he's late for work. Lunch ends abruptly and this blah vibe carries over into everything we do for the next few days. I pick a movie for us to see and it's terrible. I arrange a picnic on his lunch break and we get rained out. And unlike the movies, there's no romantic gazebo to hide under. Karma is doing everything it can to keep us apart.

On Tuesday we hit rock bottom.

Ben arrives at Surf Sisters with the summer campers, but we can't let any of them in the water because there's a rip current. It's hard because everything looks fine on the surface of the water and the kids don't understand. This makes them cranky, and when I try to convert the lesson so that it works on the beach, it all falls flat. Their bad mood boils over into mine, and I wrap up the lesson a half hour early.

"We're done?" Ben asks.

"Yeah," I say. "I've stretched it out as much as I can without going in the water."

"What am I supposed to do with them?" he asks. "The van won't be here to pick them up for another thirty minutes."

I'm sure that I will look back on this moment as a lost opportunity. But my funk keeps me from coming up with any creative solution to the problem. So, instead of saying, "We can go shell hunting," or something like that, I say, "I'm sure you'll figure out something."

He shakes his head and asks, "Why are you being this way?"

"Because I can't change the ocean current," I snap. "And I can't magically put kids in a good mood. And I sure can't seem to make you happy about anything."

It is totally irrational, and I can't believe it as I hear the words come out of my mouth. But that's what I say. I can't really read Ben's reaction. I'm not sure if he's angry or just confused, but I am totally off the rails. Luckily, Sophie has come down to help with the lesson, and she distracts the kids before they get to watch me break down.

"Who do you think can build a better sand castle?" she says. "The boys? Or the girls?"

The kids all shout, and within thirty seconds Sophie has them split into two groups who are happily building away. Fearful that I might start crying in front of everybody, I say a quick good-bye and head up to the shop. This is strategic on my part because I know that Ben can't leave the kids, so he won't be able to follow me.

I hide out in the shop's storeroom for about twenty minutes and make it back down just as they're finishing. The sand castles look great, and the kids are having a wonderful time. I'm really disappointed that I acted the way I did. I feel like I let them down. Ben walks up to me, and I still can't read his face.

"I'm really sorry," I say, convinced that it's too little too late.

"Me too," he replies.

There's an awkward silence.

"Do you want to do something tonight?" I ask, half prepared to hear him say that he doesn't ever want to do something with me.

"Sure," he says. "Whatever you want."

I am so not good at this. Considering my current track record of bad ideas, I decide to stop with the boldness.

"I want you to pick," I say. "None of my ideas seem to be working out too well lately."

He gives me a little smile. "The picnic almost worked out."

"You mean except for the thunderstorm."

"Yeah, but the sub sandwich tasted good. Wet . . . but good."

It feels nice to joke, even a little bit. "Still, I'll let you pick. Surprise me."

He nods. "I'll pick you up at eight."

*T*he ultimate surf maneuver is to ride inside the barrel or tube of a wave. It's super difficult, especially here in Florida where there aren't usually waves big enough, but when you do it, you are surrounded by water collapsing on you from all sides. Your only hope is to keep aiming for the light at the end of the barrel where you come back out again. That's how I'm feeling about things with Ben. Everything is collapsing around me, but I'm still aiming for that light, still hoping to ride this wave all the way in to the shore.

Since I don't know what he's got planned for us, I'm not sure what I should wear. I decide to turn a negative into a positive. Rather than worry about what's appropriate, I just pick out the cutest outfit I can find: a navy skater skirt with a white tank and a sleeveless plaid shirt. I like how it looks, but just to play it safe I text a quick picture to Nicole, and she responds with a row of smiley faces. The most important smiley face, though, is the one Ben shows me when I greet him at the door.

"You look great," he says.

"Thanks," I reply. "Is this appropriate for where we're going?"

"That all depends. Can you dance in it?"

Dancing. I like it already. I should always let him decide what we're doing.

"I can dance in anything," I say with some surprising confidence. "Where are we going dancing?"

"There's a party down the beach."

Suddenly my mood drops.

"Whose party?"

"I'm not exactly sure," he says. "Kayla promised that it was going to be huge and fun."

"Kayla?" I say, trying to control my anger. "Seriously?"

He looks utterly confused by my reaction. "Is that a problem? She invited us to a party, and I thought it would be fun."

"Kayla didn't invite *us* to a party. She invited *you* to a party because she likes you. She saw me have a breakdown today at camp and probably figures she's in the perfect position to swoop right in."

"No," he says, completely oblivious. "She knows you're coming with me. I thought you would like this."

"Why on earth would I like this?"

Is it possible that he doesn't know that Kayla and I are mortal enemies?

"You said you never get invited to these parties. I thought you might like to go to one and meet some new people."

I'm trying to keep my voice down so my parents don't hear, and as I take a deep breath, I realize why he went for this.

"Is that what this is about? You want me to *meet* people?"

"I don't see why that's a bad thing."

"I don't want your charity," I reply. "I don't need you to find people for me to hang out with once you're gone."

"It's not charity."

"Did it ever occur to you that I have in fact met all of these people? It's not that big an island. I've grown up with them, and they never became my friends. That's not going to magically change because they see me arrive at a party with you. They might be nice to me while you're around, but they'll be making fun of me the second we leave."

None of this has occurred to him, and I see him trying to make sense of what I'm saying.

"It's just a party," he says. "You said you wanted me to surprise you."

"Well, you certainly did that."

"We can just drop by and then do something else."

"You still want to drop by?" I reply, incredulous.

"I don't want to be rude. I told Kayla I'd go."

"Oh, yes. Let's make sure we look out for her feelings and not mine."

"Fine," he says. "We won't drop by. We can do something else."

"No," I say. "I don't feel like doing anything. You go to the party. You have fun. Meet all the people you want. I just want to stay home. Alone."

It's at this point that I think we might be breaking up. It is excruciating and painful and more than I can bear.

"Okay," he says. "I really am sorry."

There is a hesitation, and for an instant I think he can save the moment. I don't know what he could do, but I know I don't want it to continue this way. I look at him with sad eyes and wait for him to say something. Anything. But he doesn't. He bites his lower lip for a second, and then he turns and walks away.

I don't start to cry until I'm back in the house with the door shut. I don't know how I made it this far, but once I'm clear of the outside world, the tears start to fall. My mom comes down the hall toward me, and from her expression I can tell I failed miserably at making it so my parents didn't hear me. I bury my face into her shoulder. She doesn't say a word. She just puts her arm around me and hugs me tightly as I sob uncontrollably.

*I*zzy."

A hand grabs me by the shoulder and tries to wake me.

"Izzy, get up."

I am completely disoriented as I wake up from the deepest sleep. My eyes are still sore from last night's extended crying jag, and they're also bleary due to the early hour. I squint and look out the window and my fears are confirmed. It's still pitch-black outside.

"Dad? What time is it?"

"Five oh seven," he says.

My head slumps back onto the pillow. "Leave me alone. I need to sleep."

He yanks the pillow out from under me, and my head plonks down on the bed.

"Oww!"

"We'll take the pillow with us," he says. "You can sleep in the truck."

Now I am completely confused. "Where are we going?"

I'm finally able to focus on him as he flashes a huge grin.

"Sebastian!" he says. "It's going to be epic."

Now I'm starting to wake up. Sebastian Inlet is the best surf spot for over a hundred miles.

"How epic?" I ask.

"There are two hurricanes in the Caribbean, and according to the surf report the waves might be as big as we've seen in years."

I let this sink in. "We better get going."

Dad has an orange and blue Ford Bronco that was old when he got it back in college. It's not much to look at, but it's weathered decades of salt air and sand, and is the ultimate surf vehicle. We load our boards into the back and minutes later pull out onto A1A, the highway that runs right along the Florida coast. It's going to take us about an hour and a half to reach Sebastian, so I tuck my pillow against the window and fade off to sleep.

At the halfway point we pull off for a pit stop at a hole in the wall diner that serves amazing breakfast burritos. They have egg, peppers, chorizo sausage, and salsa all rolled up in a homemade tortilla. Dad and I stop here whenever we get the chance.

"That is so good," he says as he savors his first bite.

I'm still too tired to talk much, so I just nod my sleepy agreement and smile before taking another bite. We sit there silently eating for a moment until Dad catches me off guard with a comment.

"Despite what you may be thinking," he says, "Ben really cares about you."

I continue to eat in silence, but I flash him the expression that says I'm not interested in having this conversation.

He totally ignores it.

"He's probably not great at expressing it, but he's heart-broken about his parents. It makes him doubt everything."

I swallow another bite of my burrito and look right at him. "I don't want to talk about it, okay?"

He nods. "Okay. I just know you're hurting."

"I'm serious, Dad. I don't want to talk about it."

"All right, my mistake. Let's finish these in the Bronco and get back on the road."

We climb back up into the truck, and after silently finishing my burrito, I resume my sleeping position. I'm not actually sleeping this time, but I figure it's the best way to keep him from trying to talk about Ben.

When you drive along A1A, you can see the ocean in between gaps in the sand dunes, and with the sun rising over it, it all seems kind of magical. I think about what Dad was saying in the diner, and after about twenty minutes of mulling it over, I ask him, "How do you even know?"

"Know what?"

"That Ben cares about me? Parents just say that stuff to make their kids feel better. You can't know that."

"You're wrong about that," he says. "I can know it. I see it in the way he looks at you and in the way he talks to you. But I also know it because he's told me so."

Now I sit up and look right at him. "When?"

"We run together three times a week," he reminds me. "What do you think we talk about?"

"Sports?"

"No," he says. "Well, sometimes we do. But mostly we talk about life and things. He talks about you a lot."

"What does he say?" I demand. "I want specifics."

Dad shakes his head. "I can't tell you that. It wouldn't be fair. Just like I wouldn't tell him things you told me in confidence. But I can tell you that he cares about you more than he's cared about anyone in his life. You mean the world to him, Iz."

"It sure doesn't seem like it," I reply.

He smiles the same smile that he's smiled at me my whole life. "I know, baby. Being a teenager can be really confusing, can't it?"

"You're not kidding."

"Just remember that sometimes it can be amazing."

"Like when?"

"Like right now," he says as we pull in to the parking lot

and look out at the surf. The sun has just broken over the horizon, and there's enough light to see that the waves are amazing.

"You weren't kidding," I say, referring to his prediction. "Epic."

We spend hours surfing the inlet. It's crowded, so you have to wait your turn, but the wait is more than worth it. These are the biggest waves I've ever surfed, and the fact that I'm sharing them with my dad makes them even more special.

We're both working on specific skills to help at the King of the Beach. I'm still trying to be more aggressive, and Dad is practicing his carving. Carving is what you do when you make turns and dig the rail—the side of the surfboard—into the wave and send water spraying.

"You've gotten so much better," he says while we wait in the lineup. "It's unbelievable."

"Really?"

"Really," he says. "I bet you're ready to try an aerial."

"Come on. There's no way."

An aerial is when you ride up the face of the wave, launch into the air, and then come back down and land on the same wave. It's an incredible move, and not only have I never done it, I've never even tried it.

"The waves are big enough," he says with a wink. "You can get the speed."

I shake my head as though it's a ridiculous idea, but in my mind just a little part of me considers it. Completing an aerial would be awesome. I remember the first time I saw one. My dad and I were watching a DVD of surf highlights, and seemingly out of nowhere Kelly Slater just rocketed right off the wave. I couldn't believe it. I made Dad pause it and go through it frame by frame. Last year Bailey Kossoff did one during the King of the Beach, and that's the moment I knew he had it won.

"Just try it once," Dad says. "For me."

I give him another skeptical look, but I don't completely reject the idea. Am I good enough to land an aerial? I guess there's only one way to find out.

The next wave I catch is my biggest one of the day. I am flying across the face, and I pass up some prime turning opportunities to look for just the right spot. I see it on the lip and shoot right up into the air.

For an instant I feel like I'm flying. It's breathtaking.

I reach down and grab the rail with my right hand to keep the board from separating, and then I land back on the wave. Or rather, I try to land. I come in awkward and fall off the back, slamming hard into the ocean. It takes my breath away, figuratively and literally. That doesn't take away from the experience one bit. I try it a few more times, and each time I come close but struggle with the landing and wind up eating a face full of ocean. By the time we climb back into the Bronco, I am battered, bruised, and exhausted. I'm also inspired.

"So, what do you think?" asks Dad as he pulls out of the parking lot and back onto A1A.

I know he's asking me what I think about the day in general, but my answer is much more specific.

"What do I think?" I reply with a big grin on my face. "I think I can land it."

Dad cackles as we start to glide down the highway. "That's my girl."

As I blend in with the tourists near the bandshell, I watch the summer campers get picked up by their parents outside the Parks and Rec office. None can leave without sharing a high five or a supersecret handshake with Ben. Kayla's there too, which complicates things, but luckily she heads off in the opposite direction and doesn't see me. Once Ben is alone I walk over to him.

"Hey," I say quietly as we make eye contact.

"I tried to call you yesterday, but you never answered."

"Sorry about that. My dad and I went on a day trip that was kind of sudden."

There is an awkward pause before I ask the question that has been eating away at me for the last forty hours. It's one that I have to ask in person.

"Did we break up? The other night on my porch, was that what happened?"

He shrugs. "I don't know."

"Neither do I," I reply honestly.

We stand there for a moment, and I can tell that he's in real turmoil. I certainly don't want to be the cause of that.

"Can we maybe grab a bite at Mama Tacos and try to figure it out?" I suggest. "I promise there will be no drama. No raised voices. No tears."

"Sure," he says. "That sounds good."

Mama Tacos is at the other end of the boardwalk, so we hop into his truck and drive down Ocean Ave. I don't know what to say, so I just fiddle with the radio.

"Where'd you go?" he asks. "With your dad?"

"Sebastian Inlet. It's a great surf spot, and the waves were really good because of a couple storms out in the Caribbean. It's kind of our special place. We go there every once in a while but never with anyone else. It's always just the two of us."

"That's nice."

We arrive at Mama Tacos between the lunch and dinner rushes, so we're able to get a quiet booth in the back. Once we place our order, there's no one around to hear us talking.

"First of all, I want to apologize for how I acted the other day," I say. "In fact, for how I've acted a bunch lately."

"You didn't do anything wrong," he says. "I've been a mess. I'm trying to figure things out, and you keep getting caught in the cross fire."

"What are you trying to figure out?" I ask. "I'm not sure if I can help, but I'd like to try."

He picks up a tortilla chip and studies it for moment as he tries to think of what to say to me.

"We were a happy family when I was growing up," he says. "At least I thought we were. We took trips together. We had fun together. Everything seemed perfect. Well, the last few years weren't perfect. I knew my parents were arguing, but I still thought they loved each other. But the people I saw when I went home—I can't believe they ever loved each other. Not the way they acted."

"I'm so sorry," I say.

"You and your dad have . . . What's the name of the place where you went surfing?"

"Sebastian Inlet."

"Right. Sebastian Inlet. It's your special place. I bet just seeing it on a map makes you think of him and smile, right?"

"Yeah."

"My parents had that. There's a place in Michigan called Mackinac Island. It's beautiful, with old Victorian buildings. Very romantic. They went there when they were dating and liked it so much they had their wedding there. They even went back a few times for their anniversary. It was their special place."

"It sounds really nice," I say.

He looks up at me, and I see tears welling up in his eyes. "When we were going through everything with the judge, I found out that Dad already took his new girlfriend there. They even stayed in the same bed and breakfast where he and Mom got married. Why would he do that? I mean seriously, how messed up is that? Isn't it enough that he broke her heart? Isn't it enough that he has totally ruined everything? He has to go back and ruin the past, too?"

I reach across the table and take his hand, gently rubbing my thumb across his fingers.

"I wonder if she wishes that she never saw Mackinac Island in the first place," he says. "At least then it wouldn't hurt so much."

The conversation stops when the waiter brings our food, and I feel terrible for Ben and how he's feeling. Once we're alone again, I ask him a question.

"Do you wish you hadn't come into the shop that day to give us the poster?"

He doesn't hesitate at all. "Of course not."

"Neither do I," I tell him. "Even though I know it's going to hurt when you go home, I would not trade this summer for anything in the world."

He looks deep into my eyes. "Really?"

"Not one second of it . . . Well, maybe the meltdown on the beach the other day . . . and the fight on the porch . . . but other than that, not one second."

For a moment I think he's going to cry, but he holds it off and smiles.

"Neither would I."

"We don't have to put a label on this. We don't have to say that we're girlfriend and boyfriend. But I still want to spend as much time as I can with you before you go home. I've been a better version of me ever since I met you."

Now he reaches across and takes both of my hands.

"Me too."

On Saturday I have him over to the house, and for the first time since he returned from Wisconsin, he seems like the old Ben.

"Are you ready for a surprise?" I ask as I greet him at the door.

"I guess so," he answers cautiously.

I get behind him and cover his eyes, which is not easy considering how tall he is. I guide him down the hallway and through the kitchen, and we only run into two chairs along the way.

"Happy Birthday!" I yell as I pull back my hands and reveal my miniature surprise party. There's a cake, a pizza, and three presents.

"This is surprising," he says with a crooked smile. "Especially because . . . it's not my birthday."

"I know that," I answer. "But tomorrow is the King of the Beach and we're both going to be really busy, so I thought we'd celebrate a day early. Besides, Mom and Dad are out, so I get you all to myself. No charades. No parents liking you more than they like me."

"You got me presents?" he says.

"And I baked a cake. There are a couple cracks on the top layer, but where other people might see that as a negative, I see it as a place to hide bonus frosting."

He leans over to give me a kiss, but it's just a peck. Our relationship is undefined, and at this point I'm determined not to push it any.

"Everything has a special meaning," I say as we sit down. "The pizza's a Big Lu from Luigi's Car Wash. . . ."

"In honor of our first meal together."

"Exactly."

"And the presents . . . They have special meaning too?"

"Why don't you open them and find out?"

First I hand him a flat, rectangular box. I have a slight panic attack as he starts to unwrap it, because I've never bought anything for a guy who isn't named Dad. I'm not sure if I found the right mix.

"Saltwater taffy!" he announces. "That means you—"

"Yes. That means I went into the wilderness that is the board-walk."

"With all those tourists?" he says, as though they were dangerous animals.

"What can I say? I'm dedicated. The taffy is to remind you of the differences between the tourist beach and the locals' beach. It was also my sweets backup in case the cake didn't turn out."

He unwraps a piece of candy and pops it in his mouth. "I know you say it's a scam, but I still stay it's delicious."

"I'm a little nervous about this next one," I tell him. "If you don't like it, you can return it. I promise it won't hurt my feelings. But if you like it, it's the final stage in your wardrobe makeover."

"I can hardly wait," he says as he opens the package.

It's a wool beanie with a Surf Sisters logo on it.

"I love it!" he says, much to my relief.

"I hear there's snow up in Wisconsin. So I wanted to make sure you can stay warm and have a little beach with you at the same time."

He tries it on and turns his head from side to side to model it for me. "How's it look?"

"Very nice," I say, in the understatement of the night. "Now, this last gift was hard to get. Consider it a birthday-slash-graduation present."

"Graduation from what?"

"Summer school," I say as I hand it to him. "You asked me to help you blend in, and after months of hard work, well . . . you'll see."

Even in the wrapping paper you can tell that it's obviously a

T-shirt, but he plays it up, holding it next to his ear and shaking it as though he were trying to figure out what it is.

"I have no idea what it is," he says. "It could be anything, but I hope it has Surf City written on it."

I slug him in the arm. "Another joke like that and you're going to have that cake all over your face."

He opens it, and when he sees what it is, he has the exact expression I was hoping for.

"I thought these were only for the locals," he says as he holds up an Islander T-shirt from the Islander Ice Cream Shop.

"I had a long talk with the owner," I explain. "Sophie and Nicole were there too, and we convinced him that you were a legit local. It helps that you were born here."

"I love it so much," he says as he holds it up to look at it closely. "I promise to wear it only on special occasions."

He turns to look at me, and for the moment at least, most of the distance that has been between us lately is gone. And it's not because of presents or anything superficial like that. It's because we've reconnected with the special moments from the summer. It's like the cutback; I turned and went back to the power source of our relationship.

Now, if only I could figure out exactly what that relationship was.

I take it as a good sign when we walk down to the beach to check on the sea turtle nest. We hold hands, and once again it feels natural and easy. There's no sign of activity around the nest, but the ocean seems more turbulent than usual. There's another tropical storm in the Caribbean, and it's sending bigger waves our way.

"I hope those keep up for the King of the Beach," I say.

"Are you nervous about it?" he asks.

"What? Nervous about competing against the best surfers in the state? Just a little."

"You can't let them intimidate you."

"It's pretty hard not to," I answer.

He thinks for a moment. "You should do that thing they tell you to do in order to relax before you give a speech. You know, you're supposed to imagine that everyone's in their underwear."

"They're already going to be in bathing suits," I point out. "Underwear's not that different."

"Good point," he says as he tries to think of a different tactic. "Then you should imagine they're in grass skirts and coconut bras."

This makes me laugh. "Well, that might do the trick."

"I like it when you laugh," he says. "I get to see that wrinkle in your chin. I've missed it."

I hold my chin up in the moonlight for him to see it.

"I'm sorry about everything," he says.

As he says this, he gives my shoulder an extra squeeze. I think back to what Sophie said, about telling him that I love him and giving him a chance to say it to me. Instead, I decide to fight that urge as we continue walking on the beach. It's taken a while, but I'm beginning to learn that sometimes it's best not to say anything at all.

*B*rrrrrrrrppppppppp!

The blast of an air horn rattles through the house, waking me from a very enjoyable sleep. Either I've traveled in a time machine back to World War II and we're under attack, or my dad is being totally dadlike.

Brrrrrrrppppppppp!

Yeah, it's Dad.

"Good morning, sunshine," he says as he pokes his head in my door. "It's King of the Beach Day!"

"I thought Mom confiscated all of your air horns," I say as I wipe the sleep from my eyes.

"I had this one hidden for special occasions!"

He sticks his hand with the horn through the door, and I cover my ears just in time before he sounds another alarm.

Brrrrrrrppppppppppp!

"Can't I get a few more minutes of sleep?" I ask.

"Sure," he says. "But your bacon pancakes will get cold."

That wakes me right up. "You made bacon pancakes? You should have led with that and not the stupid air horn."

My dad makes amazing pancakes that have pieces of bacon mixed in with the batter. This lets you get the full spectrum of breakfast tastes in every bite. He makes them for me every year on my birthday. He's obviously stoked about the contest.

"Steady Eddie taught me how to surf," he says between bites. "I can't believe I get to compete on his team. This is a huge day for me."

We discuss strategy about picking the right waves and what we think the judges will be looking for. Then, after breakfast, we load the boards into the back of the Bronco and drive over to the pier.

All of the competitors are required to attend a meeting before the contest begins. It's held in a giant tent, where we have to sign in and pick up an information packet. Ben's working and I'm competing, so to make sure no one thinks there's any favoritism we keep the contact professional.

"Isabel Lucas," I say when I reach the front of the line.

"Which division are you competing in?" he asks. I can see that he's anxious to hear my answer.

"Main Event."

He flashes a broad smile.

"Excellent," he says as he checks my name off a sheet. "You are competitor number twenty-seven. Please sign here and pick up an information packet."

We both smile at our little charade. When I'm done signing, he adds, "Good luck today."

"Thank you."

I look down at the sign-up sheet and see that there are more than seventy competitors in the tournament. Over half of them are in the Main Event. Only the top eight finishers earn points, and that suddenly seems a whole lot more difficult.

Ben's uncle Bob, who is the Parks and Recreation director, addresses everybody at the meeting. He introduces the five judges and explains the basics of the competition. He goes into detail about how the surfers will be scored. Basically, each round lasts twenty-five minutes, and while you can ride up to six waves, only your top two scores will be counted. This was part of my strategy discussion with Dad. The important thing is to get two solid scoring rides in early. That way you have a chance to take some bigger risks on the final waves.

Once he's gone over all of the basics, Bob announces, "I need at least one representative from every team to stay, but everyone else can leave."

Even though I'm not the captain, I hang around to keep an eye on what happens next. The next five minutes could be the most important part of the day. There are a total of five teams in the team competition. In addition to Surf City and us, there is a team sponsored by a surf shop in Cocoa Beach, and two made up of friends who have joined forces.

Mickey is our captain, and she's the one representing us in the meeting. She stands away from the others and I don't know if this is her way of trying to protect our strategy or her way of avoiding Morgan Bullard. He's the manager and captain of the Surf City team and—surprise, surprise—he's a total jerk.

"I need everybody to turn in your final team rosters to the young man behind the table," Uncle Bob says, pointing to Ben.

Once again Mickey lags behind the others, trying not to show our hand.

"Why don't you save yourself some trouble, son, and start engraving these names on the trophy," Bullard says with a cocky wave as he slaps the Surf City roster on the table in front of Ben. "Everyone else is competing for second place."

Ben looks over the roster as Bullard starts to walk away.

"Excuse me, sir," he says, calling him back and making me cringe. "You have eight people registered for the Main Event."

"That's right," he says. "And I guarantee you that one of those eight is going to win."

"I want to make sure that you've read the rules," Ben says. "All of them."

I don't know where this is going, but I'm a little nervous. Mickey shoots me a raised eyebrow look.

"Surf City has won this trophy twelve years in a row," Bullard scoffs. "I'm pretty sure we've got the rules down."

"Then why did you forget to sign here?" he says, turning the roster back to him. "It needs your signature for the roster to be finalized."

Bullard is beyond annoyed as he scratches his name across the bottom of the paper. "I wrote nice and big to make sure you could read it," he says. "Are you happy now?"

Ben looks up to him and smiles broadly. "Extremely, sir."

Mickey is the last one to turn in a roster, and when she does, Ben looks it over carefully. He is obviously delighted, and I can tell that we've done what he was hoping we'd do. I linger around after the others leave and talk to Ben for a moment.

"Did any of the other teams enter surfers in all the different divisions?"

"No," he says. "Everyone on the other teams is entered in the Main Event. Surf Sisters was the only team to figure out the advantage of entering all the divisions."

I smile. "Let's hope it pays off."

A horn sounds, and I worry that it's my dad bringing his special brand of crazy to the beach, but Ben tells me that it's the ten-minute warning for the first competition.

"That's Menehunes," I say. "I'm going to go give Rebecca and Tyler a pep talk."

"See you later!" he says as I go in search of my junior surfers. "Remember to picture them in grass skirts and coconut bras!"

"I will," I call back to him.

Surf Sisters has staked out a chunk of beach for the staff and our families to cheer us on. Even though there would be big sales, Mickey and Mo decided to close the shop for the day so that everyone could come down and turn the event into a party atmosphere.

"Thank you for making this happen," Mo says as I walk up.

"What do you mean?"

"Competing in the King of the Beach was all your idea," she says, pointing to our cheering section. "You gave us something positive to think about. You saved the summer."

She gives me a huge hug.

"Well, here's hoping that we bring back a trophy to put up in the store."

She shakes her head. "I don't care if we finish last. This is a win. A huge win."

I know what she means, but I can't think that way. "Maybe so. But I have no intention of finishing last."

I walk down to the water with Rebecca and Tyler.

"Are you guys nervous?"

"Nope," says Tyler.

"No way," says Rebecca.

Their confidence takes me by surprise. "Not even a little?"

"Why should we be nervous?" Rebecca says. "We've practiced and we're ready. We're going to go out and do our best. If we win, we win. If someone beats us, then they probably deserve it. There's no shame in that."

Just like back in the Fourth of July parade, I think I just got schooled by the nine-year-old version of me.

"I like that."

"Besides," she continues with a confident gleam in her eye, "no one's going to beat us."

"Come on, Bec," Tyler says as they head out into the water. "Let's show 'em how it's done."

They wade into the ocean, and I am blown away. Sophie's been coaching them, and more than a little of her confidence has worn off on them. They back it up with their actions. Tyler rips off a couple of long rides to finish second, and Rebecca shows off the skills of someone at least four of five years older and wins the Menehune title going away.

They are swarmed by our cheering section when they come back up to the beach. After I give each of them a hug, I head over to the scoreboard and wait for the fireworks. Our secret is about to get out, and I want to be there for any reaction.

When Rebecca's and Tyler's scores are posted by our team name, we're moved up into first place in the standings. It takes about a minute or so before we see Morgan Bullard hotfooting it through the sand straight toward the scoring tent.

"How is it possible that Surf Sisters already has points on the scoreboard when the competition hasn't even started yet?" he bellows at Ben's uncle.

"The competition *has* started," Uncle Bob replies calmly. "We just completed the Menehune event, and the competitors from Surf Sisters took the top two places."

"Menehune?" he asks. "What do a bunch of little kids have to do with the King of the Beach?"

"According to the rules, a team can earn points in *any* division," Bob says.

"That's ridiculous," Bullard says.

"No," says Bob. "That's the rules."

Bullard thinks for a moment and realizes his vulnerability. "Does Surf Sisters have anyone in the other divisions?"

Bob turns to Ben, who hands him the roster. Bob looks it over and then turns back to Bullard. "The Surf Sisters team has competitors in each of the divisions."

I look up at Mickey and Mo and both of them are smiling.

"This is not right," Bullard replies. "I want to move some of my boys into the Teens division then."

"You can't."

I look over and see that Ben has entered the conversation.

"Your roster was finalized the moment you signed it," he says. "You can't change divisions."

Now Bullard is really putting things together, and he's not happy about it. He points an angry finger at Ben. "This boy is trying to rig this," he says to Bob. "He did not tell us about this rule!"

"Actually," Uncle Bob says, coming to the rescue, "this morning when he tried to make sure you knew the rules, you mocked him and treated him with disdain."

There's really nothing that Bullard can say in response to that, so he storms off. As he does, he passes right next to us and stops in front of Mickey and Mo. "Think you're clever, huh? It won't matter. My boys are still going to win this contest, and you are still going to be out of business once the summer's over."

The sisters don't even reply to him. Instead, they just bust out laughing, which only makes him angrier. He walks away, and they turn to me.

"Well," Mo says. "I think this is going to get pretty interesting."

There are more than twenty competitors entered in the Teens division, and even though none of them are on the Surf City team, the group is loaded with talented surfers. Sophie and Nicole stand out because there aren't many girls, and Nic even more so because of her height. To keep the waves from getting too crowded they only go out in groups of six surfers at a time. Sophie's in the first group, so I stand with Nicole to watch.

"Look at Sophie," I say, pointing at her as she takes off on a wave.

The judges are looking for maneuvers that demonstrate speed, power, and flow. Sophie rips off a ride that demonstrates each as she attacks her wave with a series of cutbacks that show off her athleticism. It's a ten-point scoring system, and she gets sevens and eights across the board. She tops that a few minutes later, and by the time the buzzer sounds ending the session, she has the second highest score in her group. She's almost certain to make it into the finals.

Nicole doesn't go out until the last group, which is a shame. The waiting around has made her stiff, and seeing surfer after surfer post good scores has made her nervous. I try to calm her nerves before she goes out.

"Don't worry about the score," I say. "Just dominate the wave and the score will take care of itself."

Sophie and I join the rest of the group to cheer her on. She has twenty-five minutes, and despite some promising swells, she lets the first dozen waves go by without catching any.

"What's she doing?" Sophie asks. "Why does she keep letting them pass?"

"You know Nic," I say. "She's waiting for the perfect wave."

"She better not wait too long," she says. "She's only got fifteen minutes more."

Just then Nicole pops up on a beautiful wave. Normally, her height works against her, but she has such a smooth ride it just makes her look that much more elegant. She does a beautiful roundabout cutback, and as she rides it up the face of the wave and attacks the lip, a cheer erupts from our group.

Moments later the judges flash a series of eights and nines, one of the highest scores of the day.

"Okay," Sophie says, a bit relieved. "That was awesome."

Unfortunately, when Nic paddles back out there's a lull, and we start to worry that she'll run out of time.

"She needs two scores," Dad says. "She knows that, right?"

"She knows," I answer, without taking my eyes off her.

Even from this far away I can tell she's keeping calm. She knows the situation and she's not going to panic. Another wave comes, and even though it's not big, she paddles along and catches it. There's not much to work with, but she gets the most out of it, and we all feel relieved that she's going to post a second score.

And then the horn sounds, marking the end of the session.

Sophie's still riding her wave, which means she didn't complete it in time and that the judges don't give it a score. Despite the big number on her first wave, she's disqualified.

She stands up in waist deep water and hangs her head, waiting for a few moments before she slowly begins to wade in. Sophie and I rush down to console her.

"I'm so sorry," she says, as tears stream down her face. "That's incredibly stupid. I can't believe I did that."

"It's okay," says Sophie. "Thirty seconds more and you would have had it."

"We're still doing great," I say, trying to boost her spirits. "We are going to win this thing."

The good news is that Sophie did qualify for the finals, which means she's guaranteed to earn some points for the team. As the eight finalists stand side by side to pose for a picture, Sophie's size and gender are impossible to ignore. Not only is she the only girl, but the guys on both sides of her are nearly a foot taller.

You can tell they think they can intimidate her, which is funny if you know Sophie. A few minutes later, they're all out on the water and one of the tall guys tries to drop in on a wave that she's already riding. It's a total breach on his part, but rather than pull out, she keeps her line without flinching. To avoid a collision he has to bail, and Sophie ducks under his flying board and pops back up to ride the wave to its finish.

The Surf Sisters crowd goes wild, and the judges reward her with straight nines. She finishes in third place, a great showing in such a strong division. The team is definitely in the running.

*T*he Menehunes and Teens were both exciting, but I get goose bumps when the horn sounds to start the Legends. Mickey and Mo had both retired from competition before I was even born, so I've never gotten a chance to see them in this type of environment. With my dad thrown in, it's almost more than I can handle.

Right as they're about to start, I make eye contact with Ben. We're keeping our distance during the competition. Still, he smiles at me, and I can tell he's excited for this too.

"What am I looking for?" my mother asks me as we watch Dad paddle out to the lineup. She is the one member of the family who knows nothing about surfing. "How do I know if he's doing well?"

"It's all about showmanship," I say. "If he makes a long ride and manages to show off a little, we should be good."

Mom smiles. "Showing off is his specialty."

The girls and I laugh in agreement. "It sure is."

The first one of our Legends to catch a wave is Mo. She cuts a long, elegant line across the face and looks like she was born to surf. You'd never guess she was in her fifties, especially toward the end of her ride when she does something that no one else has done all day. She gets air.

It's not particularly high, but she rides up the face of the wave and launches. She doesn't even reach down and grab the rail. The board stays with her like it's glued onto her feet, and when she lands it, we are all in stunned silence.

"Did that just happen?" Sophie exclaims. "Did that really just happen?"

"Fifty-three years old and she pulls off an aerial," I say in amazement.

"Your dad's not going to do that, is he?" Mom asks, with more than a hint of worry in her voice.

"I don't think so, Mom. But up until a few seconds ago I didn't think Mo could do it either."

Mickey comes right behind her and floats along the top of the crest before pulling a fins-free snap, a sharp turn where the fins slide off the top of the wave.

As I watch her, I wonder what's going through her mind. I imagine she's channeling all of her emotions about the shop into this ride. Steady Eddie would be proud if he saw his girls today. They are something special.

"Here he comes," Mom squeals as Dad catches his first wave. "Don't fall, honey!"

We all laugh again, but Mom couldn't care less.

When we went to Sebastian, Dad practiced carving, and now it's really paying off. He is, to use the eighties lingo he loves so much, totally shredding the wave. Mom's squeals continue all the way until the judges post their scores of sixes and sevens.

"Is that good?" she asks me, uncertain.

"You bet," I say. "That's definitely going to put him in the top eight."

When the horn sounds ending the round, I'm happy because of how well they did, but a little sad that it's ending. It was great watching the three of them out there. They wade in together with big smiles on their faces. Mom wraps my dad in a huge hug that leaves her dripping wet. She couldn't care less.

"Not too shabby for a bunch of senior citizens," Mickey says as we all greet them. "Not too shabby at all."

It's no surprise that Mo and Mickey take first and second, and Dad is more than pleased with his fifth-place finish.

"My first . . . and last . . . surf contest," he says. "Fifth is more than I could have hoped for."

With the exception of Nicole's misstep in the Teens division, our plan has worked perfectly. We've picked up points in each division and have a big lead. That's the good part. The bad part is that Surf City is ready to dominate the Main Event and I'm the only one we've got left.

With so many people entered in the Main Event, there will be six different preliminary groups. The top sixteen will make the semifinals, and then the top eight will compete in the finals. I won't go out until the fourth group, so I try to relax while I wait my turn.

I watch the other competitors to get an idea of what types of moves and tricks they're doing, but mostly I try to visualize the waves and think about what I'm going to do. In the middle of this, Ben comes out of the scoring tent and walks over to me. Nicole and Sophie come over too, so they can hear what he has to say.

"How does it look?" I ask.

"You're still in it," he says. "But just making the final eight isn't going to do it. You won't have enough points."

I see the disappointment on Nicole's face and love it seconds later when Sophie puts a reassuring arm around her shoulder.

"How high do I have to finish?" I ask.

"It depends on how many from Surf City make the final, but I think you're going to have to finish in the top five for the team to win."

Gulp.

When it's time for my group, I paddle out just like I have every morning for more than a month. The pier feels like my surfing home now, except for the fact that it's filled with spectators. I try to block them all out and focus on the waves. I wash all doubt out of my mind.

When the first one comes along, I am amped and ready. The strategy is to get a solid score out of the way. I'm not going to do anything showy. I'm just going to surf smart.

I start to paddle along, and I can feel the wave grab hold of my board. I pop up and feel a surge of confidence as I race across the face of it. There's a moment of hesitation when I'm trying to decide if I want to carve or do a cutback, and it's in the middle of that hesitation when I pearl like a grommet, which is what we call a new and inexperienced surfer. The tip of my board digs into the water and sends me flying over the front. I slam face forward into the water.

Everything's in slow motion as I rag-doll underwater. I cannot believe it. This was supposed to be my safe ride and I don't even put up a score. I'm already behind. I instantly panic about time. I can't let it run out on me like it did on Nicole. I get back on my board and paddle back to the lineup.

The other surfers smirk when they see me. It's obvious to them that I have no business in the Main Event. As I wait my turn I feel like I have let everybody down, and I start to hyperventilate. Then one of the guys says something to me.

"What's up with him?" he asks as he points toward the pier.

Sophie warned me about getting distracted, so I ignore him. I'm straddling my board and looking for swells. But then I hear a laugh. And then another. The other surfers are all looking at the pier, so finally I look over too.

It's Ben.

He's standing at the end of the pier wearing a grass skirt and a coconut bra. It's just like he described to me and it makes me laugh. Sophie and Nicole are with him, and the three of them are all doing the hula.

This cures my panic attack. My friends know me well.

I take a slow breath. I see a wave coming, and now I am confident that I am dialed in. On the next wave I combine a floater, where you ride along the top, with a snap, when you shoot down off the wave, and then a roundabout cutback that is as pretty as any I've ever done. I finish by pumping across the wave, which is a showy form of carving, and finally end it by smacking the lip.

When I go back out to the lineup, the smirks are all gone. I can tell they wonder why they've never seen me before.

"What's your name?" one of the guys asks me.

"Izzy Lucas," I say as I straddle the board and catch my breath.

"Sweet ride, Izzy," he replies.

"Thanks."

*M*y tenth-place finish in the first prelim easily puts me in the semifinal, but it's going to take more than that to make it to the finals. We go out in two groups of eight, and I am in the second group. This is good because it lets me rest a little and work up a strategy.

"What are you thinking?" Dad asks as he comes up to me.

"You know what I'm thinking," I tell him.

I can tell by his expression that he does. I thought I'd try the aerial in the final, but now I think I'm going to have to do it just to make it into the final eight.

"Don't forget that you have to post two scores," he says.

"Don't worry. I know what I'm doing."

I love the expression he gives me. It is one of total pride and confidence.

I let that confidence build inside me when I paddle out for the semifinals. Bailey Kossoff, the defending champion, is in this group. He's quiet and focused, and I study him to see what he's doing. He's the first one in the group to catch a wave, and he sets the bar high with an aggressive run that flows as easy as water.

"Damn," one of the other surfers says. "We're just playing for second."

I take off on the next wave, and even though I'm looking for a chance to get air, the wave doesn't really play out that way. Instead, I execute a flawless floater along the top, then I drop down and do what's called a vertical backhand snap. You build up as much speed as you can and then stick the board up off the top of the wave and whack it back down.

I feel good about it, but I still think it's going to take something bigger to get me into the finals. I'm determined that it be an aerial. I try to get air on each of the next two waves I catch, and even though I'm close to landing it, I fall off each time.

I paddle back out and am concerned about the amount of time I've got left. I've only posted one score, and if I try the aerial again and fail, I might not get another chance.

I can't think that way. I know I can do it, so I'm going to give it everything.

I catch the next wave and keep things basic with some carving while I look for the perfect spot to launch. It comes to me like a vision, and the wave unfolds perfectly. I take off into the air, and this time I don't reach down and grab the rail. I trust the board and fly. And fly. It feels like I'm up forever. My legs buckle a bit when I land it, but I stay on the board and feel a rush of adrenaline charge through my body. I do another cutback and finish my ride.

I'm too exhausted to go back, and even though there's a little bit of time left, I decide to call it for the round. If I have not posted high enough scores with those rides, it's just not going to happen. I wade up to the waterline and plop down on the sand.

"When did you learn to do that?" Sophie asks as she sits down next to me. "When did you learn to catch air?"

"Just now," I say with a laugh. "That's the first time I landed it."

"Well, you picked a pretty good first time," Nicole adds. "You really got up there."

Once I catch my breath, I get up and head over to the Surf Sisters crowd. My dad is beaming.

"I told you you could land it!"

I smile at him, but I'm still a nervous wreck.

We have to wait a few minutes for the scores to be tabulated, and when they are, I am in the final. I've climbed all the way up to sixth place, but that doesn't matter now, because all the scores are reset at zero for the finals.

Before we go out, all the finalists pose together for a picture beneath the King of the Beach sign. Not only am I the only girl in the group, but I'm also the only one who's not competing for Surf City.

I start walking over to Mickey and Mo to get some last second pointers when Morgan Bullard suddenly cuts me off.

"Morgan Bullard," he says, extending his hand to me. "Surf City."

"I know," I say. "I was there earlier when you were yelling at everybody."

He doesn't let this faze him one bit. He just chuckles and says, "What can I tell you? I'm passionate about surfing."

"Is that what you call it? Passion?"

"You were . . . impressive out there. Izzy, is it?"

I nod my head yes, my eyes wandering for Mo, wondering if she had anything to do with Morgan Bullard taking time out of his precious life to talk with me.

"I just wanted to introduce myself and say that there might be a spot on our team for you in the future. It's a sad thing that Surf Sisters is going to close, but I hope you'd consider joining up with us next season."

"That's very nice of you to offer," I say, mustering all the politeness I can.

"Well, it's not an official offer, not yet," he says. "I just want you to know it's a possibility."

"Of course," I say.

Bullard leans in to me, his lips mere inches from my ear. Considering that sharing an entire miles-long beach with this overly tanned "my surfboard don't stink" sellout is borderline unbearable, it takes each and every drop of my Zenlike calm to bare his intrusive stance.

"Think about it," Bullard whispers, turning to leave as Ben comes to my rescue, ready to give me the latest on scoring.

"You're amazing," Ben says. "When you flew up in the air, I had chills. I am so proud of you."

"Thanks," I say, trying to shake my run-in with Bullard and keep my focus on what's still to come. "What's the magic number? How high do I have to finish?"

"Third," he says, and I feel the air race out of my lungs.

"Really? Third? I thought you said top five."

"That was before Surf City took all of the seven other spots in the Main Event final. Fourth would tie it, but Surf City would win the tiebreaker. You're going to need third to get the trophy."

At this point my strategy is simple. I have to surf better than I ever have in my life to get to third place. I need to post two monster scores. There's no value in getting a couple of safe scores out of the way like in the earlier rounds. I've got to go for as much as I can get.

I come out swinging and nail an aerial on my first ride. I don't know how far I get into the air, but Bailey Kossoff high-fives me when I get back to the lineup. I have another great run during which I pull several moves in quick succession, each one flowing directly into the next. In a weird way they all play like music in my head, as if I'm riding from note to note.

I feel good about my rides, but it doesn't feel like third. I need one more and I need it to be epic. As the clock winds down, the only two people left in the lineup are Bailey and me.

"It's all yours," he calls out as a wave comes. I start to paddle, but then I pull off. I don't think it's going to be any good. He smiles and takes it instead. A part of me worries that I just blew it.

I know I'm short on time, but there's something I've learned coming out here every day. The pier is an odd break, and a lot of times after there is a set of good waves, there will be one stray wave that comes along even better. I look down at the board for a moment and see the Eye of the Storm design. It gives me focus. Then I look back at the water and see the stray wave I was hoping for.

"There it is!" I say, even though no one is around to hear me.

I lie flat on my stomach and paddle with all I've got. I try to flush everything out of my mind, but I can't. Except, instead of thinking about the wave and surfing, I think about everything else. All these images shoot through my mind: meeting Ben, teaching the campers, the kiss on the end of the pier, waving good-bye to him at the airport, the look on Nicole's face when we got our surfboards. It's like I'm watching ten televisions at once.

A wave is a cosmic event, and this one is more than just the gravitational pull of the moon and the force of the ocean. This wave is the result of a summer like none I've ever had before. My ride is almost dreamlike. And before I know it I am surrounded by water on all sides. I am in the barrel of the wave, and everything is collapsing around me as I shoot for the light at the end of the tunnel.

I can imagine how nuts they're going up in our little cheering section, and when I burst back out of the tube and ride up the face of the wave, I feel invincible. I snap back and turn and ride until the last bit of it dies off. That's when I step off into the shallow water. It's like I'm asleep, and then the horn sounds and wakes me up. Time's up. I finished with only seconds to spare, but I finished in time.

The first two to greet me are Nicole and Sophie, who wrap me in a hug so violent that we end up crashing into the water.

"That was awesome!" Sophie screams. "Awesome!"

It's strange because, other than when I rode through the tube, I'm not really sure how it went. I just kind of did it all by instinct.

"Oh my God, Izzy!" Nicole says as she kicks water on me. "Oh my God!"

I pick up the board and we walk up onto the beach, where I take off my leash and sit on the sand to catch my breath. I can see a lot of activity in the scoring tent as they add up the final scores, and I get up and walk over there.

"Sweet ride, Surf Sister," Bailey says as I walk by him. "Very sweet."

"Oh, and Bailey!" I shout after him. He turns around, swiping away the wet hair sticking to his forehead. "Tell your fearless leader thanks, but no thanks." With a deep breath, I try to take it all in. The beach, the sound of the ocean, the amazing feeling rushing through me. "I can't surf for him. I won't."

Bailey smiles. "I'd hope not. Till next time, Surf Sister," he says, joining his team, already congratulating him.

Mo breaks free from the clutch of people in the scoring tent and walks over to me. Her eyes are red, and I think she's about to cry. My heart sinks.

"Did I make it?" I ask. "Did I finish third?"

She quietly shakes her head. "No, sweetie. You didn't."

Heartbroken, I lower my head forward onto her shoulder. She puts her arm around me and pats my back. And then she whispers something into my ear that I never imagined I could possibly hear.

"You won."

*T*he Surf Sisters victory celebration starts on the beach and migrates to the shop, where it turns into a full-fledged party with music and food. There are more celebratory hugs and kisses than I can count, and at one point I even cry when Mickey and Mo have me pose for a picture with the King of the Beach trophy in front of the original STEADY EDDIE'S SURF SCHOOL sign.

Hours later it still hasn't sunk in. I cannot believe that I won. I don't know how I did it. I've heard various descriptions of the final wave, but I still don't remember most of it. But that's more than okay right now as I slow dance with Ben on the roof of the shop. It seems an appropriate location considering this was the place where I challenged everyone to try to win back the trophy from Surf City. But never in my wildest dreams did I see us actually doing it.

"If you're the King of the Beach, what does that make me?" asks Ben. "The First Dude? The Royal Boyfriend?"

"Boyfriend?" I ask with a raised eyebrow. "Is that a label we're using?"

He hems and haws for a moment.

"I win King of the Beach and suddenly we're boyfriend and girlfriend again?"

Now he looks horrified, and I bust out laughing.

"I'm just kidding," I say. "You pretty much sealed the deal as my boyfriend the moment you put on the coconut bra and danced the hula. That saved me. I was panicked and flustered, but when I saw you out there on the pier, I realized that everything was going to work out. And not just in the contest. Everything."

"The end of the pier's been pretty good for us," he says.

"It most definitely has."

He leans over and gives me a quick kiss.

"You know, at some point, we're going to have to have the talk."

I look up at him as we sway to the Hawaiian music wafting from the sound system below. We have not talked about how all of this comes to an end. There haven't been any discussions of attempts to make something work long distance. It's so complicated. But I'm still not ready to say it all out loud.

"I've got ten days left in the most amazing summer of my life. I know it's going to end, but there's nothing that I can do about that. So I'm going to make the most out of every one of those days."

"You certainly did that today."

I allow myself a moment of pride as I flash a big grin. "I did, didn't I?"

"Okay," he says. "We'll wait and have the talk the night before I leave."

"At the end of the pier," I say. "But for now we just dance."

He gives me a little look. "I didn't realize you were in charge."

"You didn't? We're on the beach and I am the king. I've got a trophy over there to prove it."

He laughs some more and holds me tighter. I press my ear against his chest, and we continue to move to the mellow music. I feel completely different than I have ever felt in my entire life.

*E*arlier in the summer I had expected that these last days would be the worst. I thought I'd be filled with dread as the clock kept counting down toward August twenty-fifth. Oddly, that's not the case. I don't know if it's because I'm living in some sort of denial and will be a total cry factory on the twenty-fourth, or if I've somehow come to accept that I can't control the things I can't control. This is not to say there aren't moments when I get in a funk or wallow in a momentary flurry of self-pity. But for the most part these are just quick and they pass.

The last day of summer camp is memorable because all of the kids celebrate our victory in the King of the Beach. As members of the Surf Sisters team, Rebecca, Tyler, and I are presented with cardboard crowns that we wear for most of the class. Normally I wouldn't, but the kids really want me to, and I can tell that it drives Kayla crazy. Ben has a special little waterproof camera that he uses to shoot video of all the kids surfing. Then he pulls out a surprise and shows them how good he's gotten at surfing too. At the end of the class, we have a graduation ceremony where Mickey and Mo present them with their official surf-plomas and we all pose for a group picture.

Every night Ben and I walk on the beach and check on the turtle's nest. Sometimes we just sit there in the sand for over an hour looking at the nest and talking about anything and every-thing, except for the future. Then one night we're about to get up when I notice the sand above the nest shift ever so slightly.

"Check it out," I whisper. "I think it's time."

The sand begins to drain down and we see a tiny loggerhead, less than two inches long, pop his head up from underground.

"He's so tiny," says Ben. "How does he grow to be so big?"

There's a flurry of activity, and one by one little turtle heads start popping up from the sand as the hatchlings use their tiny flippers to crawl out onto the beach. Within thirty seconds, there are nearly a hundred of them.

"Look at them all!" he says in total amazement.

"They're going to follow the moonlight," I remind him. "The reflection of the moon on the ocean is their guide."

"This is the most amazing thing I've ever seen." Ben looks over at me in the moonlight and adds, "Well, maybe the second most amazing thing."

"Is that so?" I ask. "What's first?"

He gives me a coy shrug, then gets up onto his feet and fol-lows behind the hatchlings as they scamper to the sea.

I follow too, and once the last turtle reaches the water, I hug Ben from behind and press my cheek up against his back.

"What's the most amazing thing you ever saw?"

"There was this girl," he says. "And she had a wrinkle in her chin."

"And eyes that seemed to change colors?" I joke.

"That's right," he says. "And a big old guacamole stain on her shirt."

He turns around to face me, but I still keep my arms around him.

"You're never going to let me live that down, are you?"

"Well, I'm certainly never going to forget it."

"You also better not forget that I have pictures of you . . . on the beach . . . in shoes and socks, coach's shorts, a belt, and a tucked-in shirt. I'm talking photographic evidence that can be enlarged and printed."

He pulls me even closer. "I only dressed that way to get your attention. I knew that you'd have to rescue me."

I stand up on my tiptoes and give him a kiss. I close my eyes when I do and let my lips linger on his for a moment.

"You know, I haven't officially asked you to the Sand Castle Dance," he says.

"I was wondering when you'd get around to that," I say. "And I think it was a big oversight on your part."

"Is that so?"

"Earlier in the summer I'm sure I would have jumped at the chance to go with you. But now that I'm King of the Beach, I've got other offers to consider."

He looks down at me, and I can see the moonlight in his eyes.

"Don't even joke like that," he says.

I give him an apology kiss. "I'm sorry."

"Isabel Lucas, would you like to go to the Sand Castle Dance with me?"

"More than you can possibly know."

He kisses me again, and then we walk back down the beach. There are three days left of summer.

*F*or more than fifty years the Sand Castle Dance has signaled the end of the summer season as the locals come out to the bandshell to dance the night away. Nicole and I have been many times, but this year is significant because it's the first time we'll be going with dates. We're at my house and I'm putting on the finishing touches.

"You look amazing," Nic says when she sees me in my dress.

"Really?"

"Absolutely."

"So do you," I say.

I'm wearing a white summer dress with floral lace over a soft interior layer. I'm hoping to strike a balance between cute and comfortable that will still look good after hours of dancing outside on a hot and humid night. A tall order indeed.

Officially Ben and I are doubling with Nicole and Cody. Sophie's boyfriend, from Florida State, is coming, but they're going to meet us there.

"Can you believe this summer?" I ask her. "I mean seriously."

"It's been a whirlwind," she says. "Starting with Sophie's first day back at the shop."

"That's the day I met Ben."

"And the day you sentenced me to talk to Cody."

I smile. "That turned out to be a good day for us."

She looks at me, and I can tell that she's concerned. "Are you going to be okay?"

I nod. "I'm going to have to be."

"Have you told him?"

I shake my head. "No."

She goes to say something else, but there's a knock on the door.

"They're here!" I say as I get up and start to walk down the hall to the front door.

Nicole comes right behind me, and before I answer it, she takes me by the shoulder. "Tell him how you feel. You owe it to him and you owe it to yourself."

I nod.

Both of us take a breath and we open the door. Ben and Cody are standing together on the porch. In keeping with tradition, each one is wearing board shorts, a short sleeve button-down shirt, and a tie.

"Okay . . . wow!" Ben says. "You look sensational."

"You look pretty good yourself," I say, trying not to blush too much.

The dance is great. The band, which Ben picked out, is fun and plays covers of music from all different eras. This is important because the dance is for all ages. There are couples who have been married for more than fifty years dancing right next to teenagers like us.

"I know our big talk isn't until tomorrow night," I say while we're slow dancing. "But there is something that I kind of need to tell you tonight."

"Sure," he says. "What is it?"

"I lied to you."

He looks down at me with deep concern in his eyes. "When?"

"The first time we climbed up into the lifeguard stand. I asked you about Beth and why you broke up."

"That was a fun conversation."

"Anyway, you told me that you broke up with her because she loved you and you didn't feel that way toward her. Then I said—"

"'Lucky for us we don't have to worry about that,'" he says, quoting me from that night. "'We both know that this is just for the summer.'"

"So, you really do remember," I say, surprised.

"I really do," he says.

"It was a lie," I say.

"I know."

This catches me off guard. "What do you mean, you know?"

"I knew it was a lie that night. You were worried that if you told me that you loved me, then I might break up with you, too."

I stop dancing and look right at him. "You knew that I loved you?"

He nods.

"But you didn't break up with me."

He shakes his head.

"Does that mean . . ."

"That I love you too?" he says. "Yes, it does. I've loved you from the beginning, Izzy. I am hopelessly, helplessly in love with you. Don't you know that?"

Tears stream down my face. "Well, I do now."

Luckily there are a couple more slow dances in a row, which gives me a chance to compose myself.

"Very nice, Ben," Sophie says as we go back to a table and meet with the others. "You have organized a very nice Sand Castle Dance."

"Why, thank you," he says.

The boys head over to the snack bar to get us some sodas, and Nicole sees the tears in my eyes.

"You told him, didn't you?"

I nod.

"And?" asks Sophie.

"And," I say, "he loves me too."

This is the moment it hits me. This is the moment I realize what's really been bothering me. I haven't been worried that he didn't love me. I've been worried that he did. Because that makes what's about to happen all that much worse.

"He's loves me and he's leaving."

"You're going to be okay," Nicole says. "You really are."

I nod. "I know. It's just hard to imagine."

I try to compose myself again as I see the boys come our way. Then the most unexpected thing happens.

"'The Rockafeller Skank'!" I shout as the music blares from the speakers.

The band has taken a break and a DJ has taken over.

"Did you do this?" I ask Sophie.

"No, I didn't," she says, laughing.

The boys reach the table and I turn to Ben. "Did you pick this song?"

He nods. "I picked all the music. You like it?"

I smile. "You could say that."

I look at each of the girls, and we know exactly what we have to do.

"All right, boys," Sophie says. "Try to keep up."

The three boys have no idea what's about to happen, but Sophie, Nicole, and I all head out to the dance floor, turn to face them, and do the once unthinkable. We unleash the Albatross in full public view.

The shy girl that was once me is no longer.

*A*ugust twenty-fourth is Ben's last full day in Pearl Beach. Unfortunately, I'm not the only one in his life, and I have to share this day with others. He has a shift at Parks and Recreation, and they take him out to lunch. He also has to eat dinner with his aunt and uncle. That means I get a little bit of time with him in the afternoon, and then we're meeting on the pier after dinner.

Judging by the tears that started falling at the dance, I'm beginning to worry about how emotional that conversation will get, but I'm determined to keep things light and happy in the afternoon when he comes to say his good-byes at Surf Sisters. That is, *if* he comes by. At the moment, he's forty-five minutes late.

"Stop looking out the window," Sophie says. "He'll get here when he gets here."

"I know. You're right."

The phone rings and I see that it's him.

"Hey," I say. "Where are you?"

"I'm sorry," he replies. "I got held up at work. Is either Mickey or Mo there?"

"Mo's off today, but Mickey's here. Why?"

"I need to talk to her," he says cryptically. "It's important."

This all strikes me as odd, but I take the phone to Mickey and they have a brief conversation.

"What's all this about?" I ask when I get back on the call.

"I'll explain it when I get there."

And just like that he hangs up.

Twenty minutes later, Mo arrives with a man I don't know, and the two of them meet with Mickey in the garage.

"What's going on?" Nicole asks.

"I have no idea," I reply.

Finally Ben walks into the shop. He smiles when he sees me and gives me a huge hug and a kiss.

"Sorry I'm late," he says. "Where are Mickey and Mo?"

"In the garage," I answer. "Why?"

He smiles again. "Come on. I'll tell you when I tell them."

Luckily there aren't many customers, so Sophie, Nicole, and I are all able to follow Ben into the garage.

"I'm sorry I've been so cryptic," Ben says, addressing us. "But I've been trying to come up with a really great good-bye present for Izzy, and I think I've done it."

We're all confused.

"What's your present?" asks Mo.

"I think I've figured out how to save the shop."

Mickey and Mo both gasp. The three of us girls are equally breathless.

"What are you talking about?" asks Mo.

"It's the best present I could think of," says Ben. "Izzy loves this place, so I thought that I should try to save it. You see, my dad's a pretty awful husband, but he's an amazing attorney. We'd always talk about the cases he was working on, and he taught me how to look for loopholes."

"Like the team loophole in the King of the Beach?" I say.

"Exactly."

"And you found a loophole that helps us?" asks Mo, trying to contain her excitement.

"I hope so," he says. "Is this the attorney you told me about?" He motions to the man with them.

"Yes," the man says.

Mickey and Mo are practically glowing with excitement.

"What's the loophole?" asks Mickey.

"Luigi's Car Wash," says Ben.

It takes a moment to set in, but everyone in the room, except for Ben, deflates. He doesn't realize that they've already pursued this option.

"Luigi's Car Wash is protected because of the laws that were in effect when it first opened," Ben says, continuing. "Luigi can't be forced to sell his property and neither can you."

"Actually, we can," says Mo, her hopes dashed. "Surf Sisters opened four months after the new law was passed. We're not protected."

"No," Ben says. "Surf Sisters isn't protected." He unzips his backpack and pulls out a large file. "But Steady Eddie's Surf School is."

He hands the file to the attorney and continues. "Part of my job this summer was turning old paper files into digital ones. I had to scan thousands of documents that the Parks and Recreation Department has accumulated. Among those files were contracts for Steady Eddie's Surf School to teach surfing and water safety to the summer campers. These contracts go back more than twenty years before Mickey and Mo founded Surf Sisters. The address on all of those contracts is his house, which I believe is the building we are standing in right now."

I look over and see Mickey and Mo are on the verge of tears.

"Even to this day, Steady Eddie's Surf School is listed in the contracts. That means that the same business has been operating out of the same building for more than fifty years, which more than meets the standards of the law."

Mo is the first one to reach him. She wraps her arms around him and gives him a huge hug. Mickey is right behind.

"How did you do this?" Mo asks.

Ben shrugs his shoulder. "What do you mean?"

"I mean, what made you come up with all of this?"

"That's easy," he says. "Izzy loves you . . . and I love Izzy."

*T*he full moon hangs over the ocean and floods its light across the waves. I walk down the pier and try to think of what I can possibly say to Ben. He has just given me the most amazing summer of my life, and tonight I'm going to have to say good-bye to him. Technically, I'll say good-bye tomorrow at the airport. But there will be people there and a plane to catch. This will be the real good-bye. Just the two of us on *our pier*.

I look ahead and see that he is already waiting. His back is turned to me as he sits on the end of the pier, and even though he is only a silhouette in the moonlight, I know every inch of him.

Wordlessly, I sit down next to him and take his hand.

He turns to me and starts to talk, but I press my finger against his lips so I can speak first.

"I've thought about it, and even though people say that long distance doesn't work, I'm not about to let you walk away forever. We can video chat and call and write. Certainly you'll come down and visit your uncle, and I'm already saving up money to fly to Wisconsin. You can show me Madison just like I showed you Pearl Beach. And we're only a couple years away from college. For all we know, we might end up at the same school."

He shakes his head ever so slightly, and I feel my heart sink.

"I don't think that will work."

"Why not?"

He reaches over and touches my cheek with his hand. "It turns out that my mother wasn't exactly honest with me."

"How do you mean?"

"When she told me that she wanted me to spend the summer down here to protect me from all the arguments, that wasn't the only reason she wanted me to come here."

"What was the other reason?"

"She wanted me to see if I liked it here," he says. "She's planning on moving back to Pearl Beach to start a new life after the divorce is final. The only question is whether she's going to do it now or after I graduate from high school."

"When did you find out?"

"Tonight at dinner. She flew down to surprise me and talk to me about it. If we decide to stay, she's going to start looking for a new job."

My heart races.

"How will she decide?"

"She told me that it's my decision," he says. "She knows it's hard to move in the middle of high school. And all of my life is up there. . . . Well, almost all of it."

"Don't move here because of me," I say.

"What?"

"It's not fair to you and it's not fair to me," I say. "I would love for you to live here. But if you move here because of me, then anytime that something goes wrong, it will be my fault. You'll end up resenting me. If you really love me like I love you, then we'll figure out a way to make the distance work. But if you move here, it has to be because you think that this is home."

"I know," he says. "I came to the same conclusion. Which is hard because you're a big part of everything that's here. I've spent the last hour debating back and forth, trying to figure out the right thing to do."

"Good," I say.

He stands up and looks out over the water. I stand up next to him.

"Actually," he says, "I spent fifty minutes of it trying to figure out the right thing to do . . . and ten trying to figure out how to tell you."

That sounds ominous, but oddly I feel strong enough to hear it, even if it means he's heading home. He turns so that he's looking right at me and his back is toward the ocean.

"Okay," I say. "I'm ready. Whatever it is."

He has a strange look on his face, and it takes me a moment to realize that he's slowly falling backward. By the time I do, I reach out to grab him, but it's too late. He plummets toward the water fifteen feet below and lands with a big splash.

I let out a surprised squeal as I look down at him. "What on earth are you doing?"

"First of all, it's not on earth, it's in the sea," he calls up. "And it's just what all good loggerheads do. I'm following the moonlight into the ocean."

I look down and see that smile, that amazing smile, as he looks up at me from the dark water.

"What's your decision?"

"You're going to have to come down here to find out."

"How's the water?"

"How do you think it is? It's awfslome!"

I empty my pockets, take off my sandals, and without so much as a second thought, I jump. I feel a charge rush through my body, and I close my eyes to brace for the impact, ready to splash into the water and see where the current takes me.

STEADY EDDIE'S
SURF SCHOOL GLOSSARY

aerial: when a surfer rides up the face of a wave, launches into the air, and comes back down, landing on the same wave

barrel: a breaking, hollow wave, also called a tube

boogie board: also known as a body board; used in order to ride waves lying flat on the belly

carving: turning on top of a wave

cutback: turning back into the wave, closer to the wave's power source

duck dive: paddling under a wave that is coming straight at a surfer

fin: the curved piece underneath the surfboard

fins-fee snap: a sharp turn where the fins slide off the top of the wave

fish: a short and thick surfboard used to ride smaller waves

floater: when a surfer rides along the top of a wave

grommet: a new and inexperienced surfer

hang ten: riding a surfboard with the toes of both feet hugging the front edge

Kelly Slater: born and raised in Florida; considered to be the greatest surfer of all time

leash: the cord that attaches a surfer's ankle to the surfboard

pearl: when the nose of the surfboard digs under the water and propels the surfer over the front of the board

rail: the side edge of a surfboard

rash guard: a swim shirt worn to protect one's skin from the wax and sand on the surfboard

rip current: a strong current flowing from the shore out toward the sea

roundhouse: turning one hundred and eighty degrees

snap: when a surfer shoots down the top of a wave

soft board: a beginner's surfboard with a soft, foam top

stringer: a thin strip of wood that runs down the center of a surfboard, making it stronger

shred: term used to describe a person surfing well

vertical backhand snap: when a surfer builds up as much speed as possible before sticking the board up off the top of the wave and whacking it back down

Her future first love lives in the past.
Lose yourself in this totally awesome sneak peek of

summer of yesterday

by Gaby Triana.

M iss? Miss, are you okay?"

I cough water. My tongue hurts.

"I think she's waking up."

"Don't crowd her. Give her room."

All around me I hear water rushing, kids screeching, and people talking in hushed tones. Except for this one guy who sounds like he's in charge. "She's coming to."

My eyes hurt. My head hurts. I'm outdoors. I know the sun is out because I see orangey red behind my eyelids. I'm lying on sand, I think.

"Miss, can you hear me? Are your parents here?"

I can hear you. My parents wouldn't be here together.

"Just give her a minute."

A different voice, a woman's. "Did she slide with you? How come you didn't see her, Becky, for goodness' sake!"

"Mommy, she was already there when I slid down the slide," a little girl cries. "I fell right on top of her!"

"Ma'am"—the guy in charge is talking again—"she couldn't have slid with her. The lifeguard up there makes each person wait until the person ahead of them passes the orange flag. Then they can slide." I crack my eyelids open to peek at him. "My guess is she fainted when she entered the water." He's crouched on his knees hovering over me, but he's talking to people around him. He has black hair and a white tank top. And a mustache. Like, an actual mustache.

"It might've been a seizure." Another guy's voice, somewhere behind my head.

"But she wasn't on the slide, I'm telling you!" the little girl continues to argue with her mother. Her blond pigtails are dripping wet, and she has a pink one-piece on. "She wasn't ahead of me in line!"

"Ow. My tongue hurts." I bit it.

The people around me—I see them now, there're like ten or more of them—are all watching me, though it's hard to see their faces with the sun shining directly above them. "She's opening her eyes. She's talking."

"Told you it was a seizure," that guy says again. This makes the tank top guy in charge come closer, taking up my whole view. He looks like a lifeguard.

"Miss, don't move. You passed out in the water. Now you're on the beach. Just tell me your name so I can find your folks."

"I found you in the water," the blond girl says, crouching close to my face, "or else you might've *died*."

Thank you, I say, or think I say. I don't even know where I am. What is this place? Where's Mom? Or am I with Dad today? Is this camp? I can't even think of my name. I can't talk. I have to get up. "Ow."

"You sure you want to do that?" A whistle around his neck dangles above my face. He turns his attention back to the people standing around us. "It's common following a seizure for the victim to be confused." He turns to me. "Are you confused?"

Right now, I'm more irritated by his questions than anything. I want a place to lie down that's not in front of a bunch of people in weird bathing suits. I sit up, trying to get onto my feet. The crowd makes room for me. The upside-down lifeguard offers his hand. "Here, let me help you."

I look at this tanned hand a moment, then take it. He pulls me easily to my feet. He's wearing shorts that are a little on the short side. The lifeguard steadies me, then lifts a walkie-talkie to his mouth. "This is Jake at RC. We need a medic unit, pronto. Over." He attaches it to his waistband and holds my arms as a reply crackles through the speakers. Jake says, "You need me to carry you?"

"Uh, I'm fine. This happens all the time. Thanks," I say. Actually, I don't remember this happening ever. I think. Or has it? Yes, once before. In school, right before my exams.

The mustached lifeguard, Jake, taps the younger guy, the one who said I told you so, on the shoulder. "Jason, walk her to a picnic table. See if you can find her folks, and keep an eye out for the medics. I gotta get back to my post, man."

"Sure thing. Come on." Jason nods, placing his hand softly against my back. He's tall, tanned, and wearing a thin gold chain around his neck, and the hairs on his arm shine yellow in the blazing sunlight. Why I notice this above everything else, I do not know. "What's your name?"

"Haley," I say, but for a second I'm not sure. Is it? Yeah, that sounds right. Haley . . . Haley . . . "Petersen." I start heading across the sand. It's a weird beach. There's no ocean. Just a lagoon-type thing. Not sure where I'm going. And why don't I see anyone I know? I look at my guide again. "I take it you're Jason."

"Yup, but this isn't Camp Crystal Lake, so you don't need to worry." He laughs softly. I have no idea what he means by that. He must see my blank expression. "Uh, never mind. That was stupid, what I just said. Not everybody's seen that movie." He shakes his head, chastising himself.

"It wasn't stupid. I just . . . I'm not . . . ," I mumble. Is he talking about *Friday the 13th*? That's kind of a random thing to tell someone.

"Like I said, never mind."

I shield my eyes from the sun to scan the beach. Are my parents here? Which one am I with today? Where the hell am I, and why are so many people wearing the same tacky shorts? They're like running shorts with a white border along the hem and side.

"It's all right. You're disoriented. That's why I shouldn't be joking with you. So, Haley, any idea where your folks are?"

Folks. They really like that word around here.

I stop dead on the beach and really search for someone I know. Anyone. I don't remember coming here, but I couldn't have come alone, could I? I see green sun umbrellas, tan beach chairs, the old kinds, with plastic straps across the frames, and a lot of kids of all ages standing on a wooden bridge over the water, but no one I recognize. "That water's really green," I say.

"It's from the lake. It's got bromine in it. You haven't the faintest idea where your parents are, do you?" He puts his hands on his hips and peers at me, his eyes squinching in the sun so that I can't tell what color they are. Even *he's* wearing the same weird shorts. High on the waist. It doesn't stop him from being cute, though, in a blond, retro-fresh, all-American way.

"Where'd you get those shorts?" I'm sure they must be a uniform. He's probably embarrassed to be wearing them. I force a smile to show him I'm just teasing.

He looks down at them. "JByrons, I think. What's wrong with them?"

"J-what?"

His eyebrows crunch together. He examines me from head to toe. "Well, I suppose a girl who dresses like a shipwreck castaway wouldn't shop there, huh?"

Shipwreck? I look down. I'm wearing the most normal tight white tank and jean shorts ever, artfully ripped at the hem, a little drippy at the moment, maybe, but he talks like he's never seen clothes before. It would be good if I could find someone a little less clueless to help me.

"Let's go wait for the medics over there," he says.

"No. Listen, Jason, I appreciate your help, but I got it all under control. Seriously, this happens all the time." It doesn't, but the last thing I need is medical attention when I don't even know where I am, and I feel fine now. I'll just call my mom; everything will be fine. Instinctively, I feel my pocket for my phone.

"I insist, Haley. Come on. They'll just check you out a minute, and you'll be on your way."

There it is. I pull out a plastic bag, and—*why* is my phone in a plastic bag? "Sorry, I'm just going to call my—" I freeze, staring at my baggied phone. Now I remember. Dina—a girl named Dina told me to put it in a bag so it wouldn't get wet. We were going to swim. We were doing a scavenger—

Jason comes up to me and stares at my phone. "What in the world?"

"I know, I don't usually keep it in a Ziploc, but it's just that . . ."

He picks up the bag by the corner and examines it like it's dog poo. "What *is* this?"

"What does it look like?" Okay, now this is just silly. It's like I've landed on a different planet. He's never seen an iPhone? Oh, wait, he means he's never seen this model. "I know, it's old. I was going to trade it in for the new one, but my dad's about to switch contracts, and, anyway, I want the new iPad for my birthday."

Jason hands me back the plastic bag. "Sure, whatever you say." He stares at me like I just fell out of the sky, like I'm the strange one, even though that girl standing there staring at me is wearing a headband and a rainbow one-piece bathing suit when she obviously has the body to be rocking a bikini.

God, I have *got* to find my way out of here.

"Hey, are you all right?" Jason asks.

"Yeah." *No.*

I've seen that bridge before. In fact, I've seen those waterslides, except they weren't so clean. They didn't have water gushing out, and they didn't have people on them. I have to sit down, gather my bearings, and call someone. I march all the way across the sand toward the tree-lined shore where there're fewer people. This place is really packed.

Bah. I have no signal here.

I plop down and try to think, even though Jason, following me, has made it difficult. He sits next to me and draws in his knees. "You sure? Because you still seem a bit off-kilter. I don't feel right leaving you alone. I'm sorry. I know that's the chauvinist pig in me talkin', but I don't."

"A what pig?" I ask, but then a familiar sight out across the water, behind a spattering of little blue and red boats, distracts me. I'd know that A-shape building anywhere. "The Contemporary," I mutter, my eyes fixed on the famous hotel. Wait, I'm in Disney! I came here with my dad and Erica. I have a little brother and sister. We're staying in Fort Wilderness!

I look down at my phone again. There's an unread message— *r u inside river country? i'm here looking for u.*

"River Country . . . yes," I mumble.

I turn and take another good look around.

White sandy beach, people in old-looking bathing suits, Bay Lake, inner tubes, and those wooden beams and wire? Kids sliding down a zipline, holding on to a metal handle. They hit the other end of a wood pole and fall into the water. Behind that are the waterslides, and these people on the bridge? They're in line for the slides. The line starts at those big rocks over there. I remember those big rocks, but it wasn't like this when I last saw it.

"Yup. River Country," Jason says, scooping up a handful of sand and letting it out slowly. "The ol' swimmin' hole."

I press the center button on my phone to return to the main screen, but I hold it a tad too long and Siri's bloop sound pops up.

"Did that thing just make a noise?" He leans in to study my phone. "It looks like a personal video game machine. Can I see?"

"But . . ." I tear my eyes away from all the people and really look at Jason for the first time. Blue. His smiling eyes are blue. How is this possible? "But River Country is closed," I say cautiously. Of course it is. I saw it empty and abandoned. That lake area was overgrown swamp, and that pool and kiddie area were drained and full of grass. I saw it!

"Closed?" Jason glances at his black plastic watch. He presses a silver button until it beeps. "Nah, it's Thursday." He smiles at me. "Today we're open till seven."

Jason seems wholesome and pure. And a little clueless, apparently. Not the kind of guy who would play a joke on anyone, especially a girl he just met, a girl who just awoke from a seizure. "Please tell me you're kidding."

"Why would I be? We really do close later on Saturdays." He shakes his head. He didn't understand that I meant closed *permanently*. "Do you have somewhere you need to be? You lost track of time or something?"

I take my wet hair and twist it nervously. "Are you sure this place isn't closed to the public? Like, open only for private parties? Because I was told . . ." I pause, then let out a heavy sigh. What I was told makes no sense right now.

His mouth is slightly parted, and he seems to be trying to

understand this strange language called English that I'm speaking. "Miss, I don't know what you're talking about. First, let me find your parents or where you're supposed to be staying." He stands up and brushes the sand off his legs. "What loop are you in?"

"Twenty-one hundred." I remember that from when my dad was driving around, trying to find our cabin.

Again, he shakes his head, then looks at me, disappointed. "Our loops aren't numbered. Little Bear Path, Bobcat Bend . . . any of those sound familiar?"

"No. Not at all."

"Why don't you come with me, and I'll let you use the courtesy phone to call your trailer. You just press star nine then your trailer number."

"I'm not staying in a trailer. I'm staying in a cabin. It's twenty-one hundred loop. I remember it clearly."

"Miss . . ." He stands there with his hands on his hips. "I don't know what it is, but it's like you just got left behind along with E.T. We don't have cabins in Fort Wilderness. I think you got your campgrounds crossed. Let me guess, you don't know what *E.T.* is either."

"Of course I know what *E.T.* is!" I place my hands at my hips to appear more sure of myself. "My dad only made me watch the twentieth-anniversary edition like fifty times when I was little."

He smirks. "The movie *I'm* talking about just came out last month. Steven Spielberg?" He shrugs, walking away from me in a hurry.

I scramble to my feet and start following him. He may be cute, but he can't tell me that *E.T.* came out last month. I know when *E.T.* came out, and it wasn't June, wasn't this year, and definitely wasn't while I've been alive. It was a long-ass time ago, so he'd just better lose the attitude, or else I'm going to have to . . .

Wait a minute. He's really leaving. "Jason, hold up!"

There's a family just arriving and settling into the picnic table that was next to us a moment ago. The father's hair is layered, and he wears a beige suit that looks like it's made from terry cloth. The older boy has white socks all the way to his knees. Hot! And the younger boy has on these big headphones wired to a small yellow box in his hand. Is that . . . ?

"Hey, man, neat Walkman. Is that waterproof?" Jason asks, passing him by.

"Thanks. Yeah, it is. I just got it today!" The boy smiles at him, then at his dad, and then the whole family looks at me funny as I try to keep up with Jason.

"Jason, hold on. Wait. Can you wait, please?"

He stops, puts his hands on his hips, and sighs. "What is it? Look, first you make fun of my dolphin shorts when yours look like a shipwreck. Then you try telling me that there're cabins when I've known this place for eleven years, and what we have are *trailers*. You won't tell me what that device is you got there, and now you're questioning my knowledge of new movies?" He huffs. "I just used up my entire break trying to help you. You're free to use the courtesy phone. The medics should be here any moment. But I need to get back to work."

"Just . . . Can you just answer one question for me, please? One question, and then I'll leave you alone. I promise." He keeps walking, and I have to run ahead of him, then turn around to get him to stop. My feet start burning on the hot sidewalk. "Where do you work?"

"Towel rental booth. Your one question is up."

"No. No, no, no, that wasn't it. Okay, look, please don't think I'm crazy—"

"Too late." He crosses his arms. I'm trying really, really hard not to notice his tanned biceps when he does that. I don't remember any Disney cast members being this friggin' cute any other time I've stayed here.

I point at him. "That's . . . that's very funny. And entirely understandable." I take a step closer to him. I honestly don't want anyone overhearing what I'm about to ask. He seems taken aback by my closing in on him. "Okay, here goes. Ready?" I let the words float out of my mouth as sensibly as possible. "What . . . year is it?"

He gets that look again, where he's trying to understand my language, read my face, my thoughts, analyzing everything. He's killing me here with this nonresponse thing of his. Then what does he do? He laughs. "Whoa, that is just radical, man. I can't believe I fell for that." He brushes past me.

"What? I'm serious. That's my question for real, Jason. *What year is it?*"

He turns around, and it's as if he suddenly remembers his Disney cast member manners. "Miss, it's July first, 1982." He smiles a big Disney smile. "Is there anything else I can do for you today?"

A lightning bolt shoots out of the sky and splits me in two as I stand there looking at him. At least it feels that way. Nineteen eighty-two? As in 19 . . . 82?

As in my mom and dad were . . . fifteen and sixteen?

Slowly, a smile spreads across my face. I laugh. This is great. This is just friggin' fantastic! I'm just going to enjoy this until I wake up, and then I'm going to write it all down as the awesomest, most vivid, wacky-packy dream I have ever had in my entire life. "No, that's all, thank you."

"You're very welcome. Have a magical stay here in Walt Disney World!" Jason smiles politely, then proceeds to make his way behind the help counter at the rental shop.

"Thank you!" I call out, watching him assist the next customer, a mom with a striped shirt tucked into white, elastic-banded shorts, and her little girl with pleated barrettes in her hair, carrying a Strawberry Shortcake doll. The girl has on light blue shoes that look like they're made of jelly, and I *so* want a pair!

I love this dream!

But there's only one way to know if it really is or not. I turn back around, open up my camera app, and start snapping off picture after picture of the famous River Country. The green lagoon ahead of me; the quiet beach area to my right, next to all the cypresses I swam through; and the blue pool to my left, where people are plunging down two slides that drop them about six feet above the water level. Those had vines all over them just yesterday, or whenever it was that I last saw them. If it's all still on my phone when I wake up, then I wasn't dreaming.

I smile and take in the sights and sounds. Even the smells of suntan lotion and BBQ cooking from somewhere nearby. I can't send these photos until I have a signal, but at least I have them. And just to ensure that Dina, Rudy, and Marcus don't think I stole these off the Internet, I turn around and snap off a few selfies with the water park in the background as well.

Say River Country!

"I see you're feeling better," someone says. Shielding my eyes, I find the source of the voice lying on a long towel on a lounge chair in a really cute red bikini. "I was over there when they pulled you out of the water. It was a bit scary, I gotta say. Glad you're okay, though."

She sort of looks like Dina in that sandy-blond-hair way, but a tad older and with feathered hair. She opens a little door in her music player, flips a cassette tape around, closes it, and presses down the play button. Then she puts big foamy headphones over her ears and closes her eyes against the sun. I take a quick pic of her, too.

I sit in the grass bordering the sandy tanning area. *Think, Haley. What do you do?* A good plan would be to Google symptoms of seizures again. Back when I had my first one in March, I read somewhere that people sometimes experience time-travel hallucinations during one. This could be one. Yet it's all so real. These chairs, that loglike garbage can right over there, that water tower that says RIVER COUNTRY, the people having a good time. How can any of this be a dream? But I can't research anything, because according to Jason, it's 1982, so there're no computers, that I know of, much less Google.

Next plan . . .

I watch Jason inside the rental booth. Look at him. He's already forgotten about me as he hands out tickets and towels. Given a different haircut and a better pair of shorts, that dude would make the perfect summer fling in real time. He's sweet, even though I exasperated the heck out of him. But there's no point in flinging with him, because I have to find my way out of this hallucinogenic episode of *Doctor Who*.

But how do I do that? Find my way back home?

Jason catches me staring at him. Embarrassed, I look away. A moment later my gaze finds its way to him again. He's writing something on a clipboard. He turns it around, and I'm a little surprised when I see that it's for me. In permanent marker, he wrote: "Medics on their way. Wait there." Is that how they did it before texting? How cute!

I nod, but the thing is, I can't wait for the medics. How will I explain where I came from?

"He's a bit the loner type, but cute," Red Bikini Girl says. She taps her feet to the music. "I'm partial to Jake, his older brother, but Jason's nineteen. Perfect for you."

"Oh, I don't really . . ." *Whoa. Nineteen? Nice.*

"Honey, girls have been swooning left and right since he

started working here last month, yet he hasn't dated a single one of them. You've gotten the most attention out of any girl here. That makes you the pick of the litter."

What makes her think he'd want to date me? He can hardly stand me!

A second later a guy appears next to us, oiled and shiny, brandishing two big cups of soda—one for her, one for himself. He looks a little young for her, judging from his skinny body type, if I could only get a look at his face.

She looks up, surprised, and takes the drinks. "Oh, thanks, Oscar. You didn't have to do that."

Oscar? Funny, that's my dad's name.

"This is my friend, uh . . ." Bikini Girl waits for me to give her my name.

"Haley."

"Oscar, this is Haley."

The guy sits on the lounge chair next to her, and . . . no . . . way. I see the familiar, sunny-eyed smile I've known all my life, minus thirty pounds, the gray hair, and, apparently, the ability to recognize me. You have *got* to be kidding me!

Deep breaths, Haley.

Dad? Paternal parental? *No way! No friggin' way!*

Immediately, I feel like he's going to yell at me for not answering his texts. My instinct is to turn around and run. But then I remember—1982. My dad has never even seen me before! He can't possibly know who I am.

"Hey, Haley. Nice to meet you." As soon as I hear his voice, his identity is confirmed. *Oh my God, Dad!* He smiles a smile I adore, have always adored, and does a little *what's up* nod.

Someone taps my shoulder lightly. "Miss, are you the one needing medical attention?" Which is great, because staring at my dad as a teen right here in front of me, I just about have another seizure.

First crush · First love · First kiss

fLiRT

SimonTEEN

Simon & Schuster's **Simon Teen**
e-newsletter delivers current updates on
the hottest titles, exciting sweepstakes, and
exclusive content from your favorite authors.

Visit **TEEN.SimonandSchuster.com** to
sign up, post your thoughts, and find out what
every avid reader is talking about!

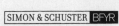